Five Studies on
Khun Chang Khun Phaen

The Many Faces of a Thai Literary Classic

EDITED BY

Chris Baker and Pasuk Phongpaichit

 Silkworm Books

ISBN: 978-616-215-131-6
© 2017 Silkworm Books
All rights reserved

First published in 2017 by
Silkworm Books
104/5 M. 7, Chiang Mai–Hot Road, T. Suthep
Chiang Mai 50200 Thailand
P.O. Box 296, Phra Singh Post Office, Chiang Mai 50205
info@silkwormbooks.com
http://www.silkwormbooks.com

Cover art shows detail from a mural painting of the Khun Chang Khun Phaen tale at Wat Palelai, Suphanburi, by Muangsing Janchai

Typeset in Minion Pro 11 pt. by Silk Type
Printed and bound in Thailand by O. S. Printing House, Bangkok

5 4 3 2 1

CONTENTS

INTRODUCTION

This book presents five essays on the Thai folk epic, *The Tale of Khun Chang Khun Phaen*. Someone reading these essays with the tale's title disguised might find it hard to believe that all five are about the same single work. One measure of a literary classic is that it reflects the complexity of real life and can be read in many different ways. In the case of *Khun Chang Khun Phaen*, two other factors add to this complexity. First, the tale is not the product of a single author composed at a specific time, but instead evolved over several centuries within both oral and literary traditions. The work has many layers reflecting different historical periods, different authors, and different intentions. Second, the tale has had a unique role in the evolution of Thai literary criticism. Three of the essays, each here translated from Thai for the first time, were intended as contributions to the discipline of criticism in the Thai context. The remaining two share this pioneering spirit. In this introduction, we present some brief background to the five essays, beginning with the history of the tale's gestation.

The tale and its history

Khun Chang Khun Phaen is a long folk epic that developed in an oral tradition of storytelling for local audiences. The plot, set in the provincial urban society of central Siam, is a love triangle ending

1

in tragedy. Khun Phaen is handsome and dashing, but his family is ruined after his father is executed by the king for an error on royal service. Khun Chang is the richest man in the local town, but is fat, ugly, and crass. The two compete for the lovely Wanthong. Khun Phaen woos and weds her, but Khun Chang uses his wealth and court connections to take her away. Khun Phaen abducts Wanthong from Khun Chang's house, flees with her into the forest, and kills two senior nobles sent in pursuit; he is accused of revolt and becomes an outlaw. The rivalry continues through pitched battles, court cases, trial by ordeal, imprisonment, treachery, and other mayhem. Tiring of this disorder, the king summons the three and commands that Wanthong be executed for failing to choose between the two men.

Stories cross borders easily, and there are versions of *Khun Chang Khun Phaen* in Lao, Mon, and Khmer, but the Thai-language version is the most developed and probably the original. It is unique in being the only literary work from its era that is set in the present day, that is located in the real geography, and that sets out to present a realistic picture of the society. Nobody knows for sure when the tale began. Working from clues in the text, we suggest that it originated around 1600 CE, possibly based on true events that were taken up by storytellers. The fact that it was elaborated to such length suggests it was very popular, inducing poet-performers to add new episodes and greater detail in response to demand. Parts of the poem were probably written down in the eighteenth century, but none seem to have survived the fall of the Siamese capital of Ayutthaya in 1767. The written work as known today was developed over the nineteenth century. Evidence within the text suggests episodes were transcribed from oral performers who survived from the Ayutthaya era. Parts were rewritten in the literary salon of King Rama II (r. 1809–24), and a few episodes were added or embellished later, especially by a famous performer known as Khru Jaeng. The first printed edition appeared in 1872, but the work is known today through an edition published in 1917–18 by Prince Damrong Rajanubhab, half-brother of King

Chulalongkorn.[1] Our English translation, published in 2010, was based on Damrong's edition, while adding several passages which Damrong had omitted, and providing alternative versions of some episodes.[2]

As a result of this long and varied history, the tale is complex. At some point during its history, probably in the late Ayutthaya era, a sequel was added about Khun Phaen's first son, Phlai Ngam. The plot of this sequel closely tracks Khun Phaen's own story and may have been adapted from an alternative version of the tale. This sequel was not placed at the end but inserted into the body of the tale, probably to preserve Wanthong's death as the dramatic ending. The insertion is easily seen because the scars of the surgery are visible in the text.

The five studies

The five essays in this book originate from two eras roughly forty years apart. The first two appeared in the early 1970s, and were intimately connected with the momentous events of those years, and the special role of literary criticism in those events.

From the outset, the study of Thai literature was bound up with the construction of a nation. The term *wannakhadi* was coined by King Rama VI in the early 1910s to replace a phonetic rendering as *literachoe*. In 1914 the king founded the Royal Literary Society

---

1. Samuel Smith published the first printed edition in 1872. We have seen only a partial copy, but this is virtually identical to the edition published by the Wat Ko press in 1889: *Khun chang khun phaen*, forty vols., (Rattanakosin: Wat Ko, 1889), an original copy of which is in the William Gedney Collection at the University of Michigan library, from which we have published *Khun chang khun phaen chabap wat ko* [The Wat Ko edition of *Khun Chang Khun Phaen*] (Chiang Mai: Silkworm Books, 2013). Prince Damrong's edition is reprinted in several forms, including a three-volume edition, *Sepha rueang khun chang khun phaen* (Bangkok: Khurusapha, third printing, 2003).

2. For more information on the development of the poem, see the afterword in Baker and Pasuk, *The Tale of Khun Chang Khun Phaen* (Chiang Mai: Silkworm Books, 2010), 881–913, and the Wikipedia page on *Khun Chang Khun Phaen*.

(*wannakhadi samoson*) whose primary function was to define a Thai literary canon.[3] *Khun Chang Khun Phaen* was inducted in 1916 as an example of *sepha*, a ballad in verse for recitation. After King Rama VI's death, the Society was superseded by the Royal Institute of Thailand. The effort to construct a "national literature" continued through the transition from absolute to constitutional monarchy in 1932 with only slight changes of emphasis.[4] The work of the early generations of literary scholars concentrated on preserving a text, and discussing issues of dating, authorship, classification into genre, and use of meter and other literary devices. Perhaps the exemplary work of this era is the monumental *Prawat wannakhadi thai samrap nak sueksa* (History of Thai literature for students) by Plueang na Nakhon, first published in 1952 and still in print.[5] Works of this era had little that could be called "criticism" and had a strong streak of national glorification. Somrot Sawatdikun, a prominent poet and literary scholar in the 1940s, claimed that "Thai artistic creation was one of the best in the world, so good that it was beyond any comparison."[6]

The first two essays here were pioneering ventures to advance the study of Thai literature by drawing on Western models.

The 1970s

The first essay is by M.L. Boonlua Debyasuvarn, who was born in 1911, the thirty-second child of a senior noble from a core royal lineage (Kunchon). Her father was keeper of the royal elephants and manager

3. Thanapol Limapichart, "The Royal Society of Literature, or, the Birth of Modern Cultural Authority in Thailand," in *Disturbing Conventions: Decentering Thai Literary Cultures*, ed. Rachel V. Harrison (London and New York: Rowman and Littlefield, 2014), 37–62, especially 44–50.

4. Manas Chitakasem, "Nation Building and Thai Literary Discourse: The Legacy of Phibun and Luang Wichit," in *Thai Literary Traditions*, ed. Manas Chitakasem (Bangkok: Chulalongkorn University Press 1995), 29–55.

5. The first edition was published by Thai Wattanaphanit (Bangkok, 1952) and the most recent edition by the same publisher in 2002 (dropping "for students" from the title).

6. As summarized by Manas, "Nation Building and Thai Literary Discourse," 45.

of the royal drama troupe for King Chulalongkorn. While the Fifth Reign court ardently pursued modernization, he remained totally traditional—innocent of English, scarcely literate in Thai, devoted to traditional arts, and determinedly polygamous. Two events took Boonlua out of this environment and shaped her extraordinary life.[7] First, because both her parents died by the time she was eleven, she was sent to Catholic convents, first in Bangkok and then in Penang, where she became fluent in Western languages and schooled in open thinking. Second, after the absolute monarchy was overthrown in 1932, she studied in the first class of Chulalongkorn University to admit women and found her calling as a teacher of literature, and more unsteadily as an educational administrator. After retiring in 1960 at age forty-nine, she married for the first time, wrote five novels, and turned her teaching experience into a stream of essays on literary criticism.

The chapter by Boonlua here is extracted from a textbook for university students of literature.[8] Although this textbook was published in 1974 after she had retired, it probably represents her teaching in earlier years. Within the academic context of its time, her teaching was considered rather liberal and forward-looking. Compared to most of her colleagues in this discipline, Boonlua had more international exposure through her overseas convent schooling and her spell in the US. In the textbook, she introduces her students to Western approaches to literary criticism, particularly the approach of I. A. Richards (1893–1979). She teaches her students how to analyze plot, characterization, and social setting using *Khun Chang Khun Phaen* as one of her examples.

In her analysis, the plot is driven by the character of the two major figures. Khun Phaen is a loyal servant of the king, but utterly

---

7. Superbly documented in Susan Fulop Kepner, *A Civilized Woman: M.L. Boonlua Debyasuvarn and the Thai Twentieth Century* (Chiang Mai: Silkworm Books, 2013).

8. Boonlua Debyasuvarn, *Wikhro rot wannakhadi thai* [Analyzing and savoring Thai literature] (Bangkok: Social Science and Humanities Textbook Project, Social Science Association of Thailand, 1974).

irresponsible. Wanthong is "strong-willed, strong in both words and actions, prone to anger and heated emotions, and deeply affected by love." The tragedy is a result of Khun Phaen's irresponsibility and Wanthong's strong will. Boonlua's analysis becomes more surprising when she advances beyond the characters to her overall assessment of the work: "In my judgment, the message of *Khun Chang Khun Phaen* is that Thai society is a society without principle." People do not follow the precepts. The authorities are incompetent. Wrongdoing goes unpunished. Boonlua makes explicit that her judgment applies to the past as well as the present: "If Thai society had progressed significantly we would not find the society still governed as shown in *Khun Chang Khun Phaen*, but the essence of current events can be found in the tale. In sum, Thai society is a society that lacks principle."

Susan Kepner's outstanding biography, *A Civilized Woman: M.L. Boonlua Debyasuvarn and the Thai Twentieth Century*,[9] depicts Boonlua as an aristocrat who responded positively to the transition from absolute monarchy to fragile and fractious democracy during her lifetime. Still, in age and social background she was far removed from the generation that flowered in the 1970s. In October 1973, a student-led uprising overthrew the military government that had taken power sixteen years earlier. This event was part of a much larger change brought about by accelerating economic growth, expansion of higher education, and the crumbling of the Cold War.[10] As Prajak Kongkirati has shown, the students who flocked onto the streets in October 1973 were often the first from their families to enter higher education, and were entranced by many new ways of thinking ranging from American liberalism, through New Left ideology from Europe, to Japanese youth culture.[11]

---

9.   Susan Fulop Kepner, *A Civilized Woman* (Chiang Mai: Silkworm Books, 2013).

10.   See Ben Anderson's essays on this era, especially his introduction to *In the Mirror*, collected in Benedict R. O'G Anderson, *Exploration and Irony in Studies of Siam over Forty Years* (Ithaca: Cornell SEAP, 2014).

11.   Prajak Kongkirati, *Lae laeo khwam khloen wai ko prakot: Kan mueang watthanatham khong nak sueksa lae panyachon kon 14 tula* [And then the movement

Cholthira Satyawadhna was a star student at a prestigious demonstration school in Bangkok and then at the Faculty of Arts at Chulalongkorn University. Her MA thesis on "The application of Western methods of modern literary criticism to Thai literature" was submitted there in 1969 and approved in June 1970.[12] The abstract explained, "The research is an attempt to explore some new interesting approaches to Thai literature by applying Western methods of modern literary criticism to Thai literary work" in the "hope that this work may provide deeper insights into and a better appreciation of the meaning and value of Thai literature." The thesis discusses three Western approaches to literary criticism and applies each to some Thai works. The first is the Freudian psychological approach, applied to *Khun Chang Khun Phaen*; the second is the archetypal approach, mostly associated with Robert Heilman (1906–2004), which is applied to several works by the nineteenth-century poet Sunthon Phu; and the third is the aesthetic approach, principally associated with I. A. Richards, which is applied to some classical poems and several works by *Angkarn Kalayanapong (1926–2012)*. By far the most controversial—and memorable—part of the thesis was the section on *Khun Chang Khun Phaen,* here reproduced in full in translation.

In her introduction to the thesis, Cholthira reviews the development of literary criticism in the west, noting the up swell of left-wing approaches in the early twentieth century, followed by attempts to mount mainstream criticism on a better theoretical base, including the three approaches above. She then turns to Thailand. Most students, she notes, do not enjoy studying literature, and the subject is not flourishing. She blames this on "the current system of studying literature" which focuses on the historical background, dating, authorship, and language to the exclusion of plot, characterization, and structure.

---

emerged: Cultural politics of students and intellectuals before October 14] (Bangkok: Thammasat University Press, 2005).

12. Cholthira Satyawadhna, "Kan nam wannakhadi wijan phaen mai baep tawan tok ma chai kap wannakhadi thai" [Application of Western methods of modern literary criticism to Thai literature] (MA thesis, Chulalongkorn University, 1970).

There is little interest in criticism and assessment of literary works, and what there is follows ancient models in which judgment is based on sentiment without any clear underlying principles. . . . Some institutions now have courses on literary criticism in their curriculum but the content is rather outdated in comparison to the West, China, or Japan.[13]

Cholthira's chapter on psychological approaches to literature begins with a general discussion of Freudian analyses of human aggression, focusing on the consequences of people's experience in childhood. After a survey of the poem, Cholthira concludes, "virtually every character in *Khun Chang Khun Phaen* of any age and gender displays aggressive behavior." She then focuses more closely on the two principal characters, Khun Phaen and Wanthong, drawing on Freudian analysis of the conflicting roles of the "death wish" and "life wish" in sexual relations, and concluding that Khun Phaen shows sadistic tendencies and Wanthong masochistic tendencies. Throughout she makes extensive use of quotations from the poem to underline her points. In the conclusion, she anticipates the accusation that her analysis "destroys the literary value of a work," claiming that it rather "highlights a truth that many may not grasp . . . that aggression, bloodthirstiness, and the desire for death are buried in the psyche of every human being of any race or language without limitation of age or gender."

The novelty of what Cholthira was attempting at the time is evident from the reaction to her thesis, which focused on the segment about *Khun Chang Khun Phaen*. This segment became famous among students challenging the old order, and infamous among those defending it, even though it never appeared in published form. Most of this reaction was oral and ephemeral, but one important instance by Suphon Bunnag is preserved in print.

13.   Cholthira, "Kan nam wannakhadi wijan phaen mai baep tawan tok ma chai kap wannakhadi thai," 6.

Suphon Bunnag (1921–74) was primarily a writer. She studied in the Faculty of Arts, Chulalongkorn University, produced her first short story in 1951, and wrote ten novels and several short stories over the next two decades. In 1960, she produced three studies of Thai classical works under an umbrella title of "Poetic treasures." By far the largest of these was on *Khun Chang Khun Phaen*, filling almost seven hundred pages in two volumes.[14] The work is an act of love, summarizing and explicating the story. She explained at the outset, "In truth every work of Thai literature has its distinctive value. In my opinion, the most outstanding quality of *Khun Chang Khun Phaen* lies in the fact it is about the ordinary life of the Thai."[15]

In 1973, Suphon published an article entitled "Stuffing sexual complexes into Thai literature" in the journal of the Thai Writers' Association.[16] The article does not mention Cholthira by name or cite her thesis, but there is no doubt what the subject of the article is. Her argument may be summarized as follows.

Psychology has appeared in the West to fill the gap left by the loss of faith in religion. Using psychological theory to analyze works of modern Western literature is legitimate because these works have been written precisely to illustrate the theories of Freud and others. Ernest Hemingway and D. H. Lawrence are good examples. However, even in the West this process has gone too far as psychological interpretations are being foisted on historical characters, such as King Henry II and Thomas Beckett, who cannot "stand up to admit or deny it."[17]

---

14. Suphon Bunnag, *Sombat kawi chut khun chang khun phaen* [Poetic treasure of *Khun Chang Khun Phaen*], printed on the occasion of the royally sponsored cremation of the author, March 15, 1975 (original two-volume edition, 1960).

15. Suphon, *Sombat kawi*, 61.

16. Suphon Bunnag, "Kan yatyiat pom wiparit rueang phet nai kae wannakhadi thai" [Stuffing sexual complexes into Thai literature], *Phasa lae nangsue* [Language and literature] 8 (August 1973): 9–39.

17. Suphon, "Kan yatyiat," 34. Suphon alludes to the 1964 film adaptation of Jean Anouilh's play *Becket,* which strongly hinted at a gay relationship between the two men.

Thai literature, however, is different because it is based upon real life. In that real life there is no sexual deviance or sexual complexes, and hence there cannot be any such thing in the literature either. Nothing like *Lady Chatterley's Lover* could happen in Thai society. "The Thai do not believe that men and woman are sexually equal, because women are the gender that own the womb, the origin of new human life . . . Thus the womb must be kept pure and free of promiscuity." There is nothing hidden about Thai sexual conduct. Thais "never do anything sexually dirty, and authors will not portray anything titillating because they don't titillate themselves." Thai writers "have not put any sexual deviance in their works because we don't like it."[18]

Hence any deviance or sexual abnormality found by a literary critic must have been "stuffed" into the Thai literary work so that the critic can make a name by seeming to say something new. This trend has already spread from *Khun Chang Khun Phaen* to other literary works like *Lilit Phra Lo*, and before long will be applied to the heroes of Thai history such as King Naresuan's relationship with his brother. This is dangerous because

> a treasure of the national culture is being misrepresented, and if there is nobody who values this treasure, who wants to preserve it, this literature will disappear, and the language on which it is based will disappear too, and nothing will be left of the national identity.[19]

Suchat Murray, a supervisor on Cholthira's thesis, wrote a rejoinder in a later issue of the same journal. She wondered whether Suphon had read the full thesis, and pointed out that "Thais are ordinary people like other nations," and subject to the same psychological analysis. Most tellingly, she suggested that Suphon allowed her dismay over the sexual behavior of American GIs on R&R (rest and recreation) to interfere

18. Suphon, "Kan yatyiat," quotes from 37, 39, 40.
19. Ibid., 20.

with her judgment and hence "use emotion more than reason, and attack with nationalism more than knowledge and analysis."[20]

But in truth, the most interesting aspect of Suphon's outburst is its emotionalism. As Manit Chitakasem has shown, since the late nineteenth century the literary establishment had constructed Thai literature as a pillar of the national identity. Some major contributors to this project had simply claimed that Thai literature was among the best in the world, without any need for comparative analysis.[21] The establishment now had to defend what they had constructed. Cholthira's 1970 thesis was an early challenge. At the time Suphon's article appeared, the student movement was on the point of overthrowing the military government on October 14, 1973, and many other challenges had appeared. The emotional pitch of Suphon's article shows what the participants thought was at stake in this clash.

On August 31, 1974, a year after Suphon's article, Boonlua appeared alongside Cholthira and Suchart Sawatsri on one of the many public panels of this era. Cholthira was by now (in)famous for the thesis and other more obviously left-wing essays, especially a critique of the Buddhist cosmology of the Three Worlds as a weapon of the powerful. Suchart was a prominent writer, editor, and activist. In contrast to these two, Boonlua represented the old guard, but with a very different standpoint from Suphon. In her essays, she punctured the mainstream view of old Thai literature as something sacred by insisting that classical and modern works be subjected to the same discipline of criticism, and by celebrating the earthier and more realistic aspects of the classical corpus. The panel was charged to discuss whether classical Thai literature (in her words) "was composed in order to drug the masses." Her comments on the *Ramakian* and *Khun Chang Khun Phaen* probably surprised the audience:

---

20. Suchat Murray, "Jitwithaya kap wannakhadi thai" [Psychology and Thai literature], *Phasa lae nangsue* [Language and literature] 10, 1 (January 1974): 16–24; quotes on 13 and 24.

21. Manat, "Nation Building and Thai Literary Discourse," 44–46.

As for Prince Rama, oh dear, he can't seem to get anything right, can he? I am quite amazed at Khun Suchart's contention that the *Ramakian* extols the ruling class. In fact, the ruling class is good for nothing at all in the *Ramakian*. . . . Prince Rama himself is consumed with jealousy and has a shocking inferiority complex. . . . As for the ruling class as portrayed in *Khun Chang Khun Phaen,* can anyone who reads it say that it shows *good* rule? I say we're awfully lucky not to have such a king ourselves.[22]

On this occasion, she made no comment on Cholthira's work (and Cholthira's contribution to the panel is not preserved). At another seminar three years later on August 2, 1977, Boonlua gave her judgment on Cholthira's work, again without citing her name.

If we try to use a psychological approach without knowing it well, the result may be unrealistic and may invite many questions. Using the psychological approach of Freud is very difficult. One foreign critic said that literary critics should not set themselves up as mental analysts; any practitioner of Freudian analysis has to study and practice for two to three years before analyzing anyone. It takes time. Psychoanalyzing a literary character such as Khun Phaen as a sadist is very difficult if we don't really know what a sadist is.[23]

By this time, Suphon Bunnag had died at the age of fifty-three, and Cholthira had fled from Bangkok after the massacre of October 6, 1976, and joined the guerrilla forces in the jungles of Nan Province in the far north. She went on to gain a PhD in anthropology from the Australian National University with a thesis on the Lua people she had

---

22. Translated and quoted in Kepner, *A Civilized Woman*, 297, from Boonlua, *Waen wannakam* [A lens on literature] (Bangkok: An Thai, 1986), 299–300.
23. Boonlua, *Waen wannakam*, 324.

lived with in Nan, and returned to a career as an academic and activist, working on anthropology, literature, and history.

Post 2000

The three other essays in this book originate a generation later. In the political debates of the 1970s, *Khun Chang Khun Phaen* was identified as literature of the old ruling class in contrast to the socially committed and left-wing novels and short stories that had emerged since the 1930s. This judgment lingered. Cutting-edge critics ignored such old-fashioned works. The few studies of the tale over the following decades continued to concentrate on characterization, social background, and ethical values.[24]

Over the years 2010 to 2012, Warunee Osatharom published two related articles on *Khun Chang Khun Phaen*. Her essay here is translated and adapted from these two articles. Warunee examines the religious messages embedded into the tale in the early Bangkok era.

In reaction to the fall and destruction of Ayutthaya in 1767, there was a movement to draw on Theravada Buddhism to discipline and strengthen the society. This movement was reflected in a new version of the Buddhist cosmography of the Three Worlds, produced during the First Reign, which incorporated a Discourse on Humanity with

24. On characterization, two examples are: Saowalak Anantasan, *Wannakam ek khong thai (Khun chang khun phaen)* [Major Thai literature: *Khun Chang Khun Phaen*] (Bangkok: Ramkhamhaeng University, 1980), and Suvanna Kriengkraipetch, "Characters in Thai Literary Works: 'Us' and 'the Others,'" in *Thai Literary Traditions*, ed. Manas Chitakasem (Bangkok: Chulalongkorn University Press, 1995), 130–47. Studies of social background include Arada Kiranant, "Kan chai saiyasat nai sepha rueang *khun chang khun phaen*" [Use of supernaturalism in *Khun Chang Khun Phaen*], *Warasan phasa wannakhadi thai* 2, 2 (1985), and Woranan Aksonphong, "Kan sueksa sangkhom lae watthanatham thai nai samai Rattanakosin ton ton chak rueang *khun chang khun phaen*" [Study of society and culture of early Bangkok from *Khun Chang Khun Phaen*] (MA thesis, Chulalongkorn University, 1972). Studies of ethical values include Phramaha Suradech Surasakko (Intarasak), "Itthiphon khong phra phuttha sasana to wannakhadi thai: Sueksa chapho korani sepha rueang *khun chang khun phaen*" [Influence of Buddhism on Thai literature: A case study of *Khun Chang Khun Phaen*] (MA thesis, Mahachulalongkorn University, 1965).

extensive instructions on living a moral life. It was also reflected in new graphical representations of this cosmography in illustrated manuscripts that mapped the geography of Siam into the cosmic geography of the Buddhist world. This geography was represented in the design and symbolism of *wat* in the era, particularly in the redesign of Wat Pho during the First and Third Reigns. In the latter redesign, parts of the moral codes from the Discourse on Humanity were inscribed in the cloister around the ordination hall. These codes offered easy-to-follow lists of actions for specific human circumstances, such as the proper conduct of a true friend, the improper conduct of a false friend, the proper conduct of women in general, or the attributes of a good wife and good husband.

Warunee Osatharom argues that the same mix of geography and ethics found in the new versions of the Three Worlds and in the redesign of Wat Pho is found in *Khun Chang Khun Phaen*, probably as a result of rewriting in the early Bangkok era, especially in the salon of King Rama II. The action of the tale takes place within a geography comprising the capital city of Ayutthaya, the provincial towns such as Suphanburi, Kanchanaburi, and Phichit, and villages in the hills. This geography matches the Mahanakhon (great city), Upcountry Cities, and *pajanta prathet* (Outer Country) in the Three Worlds geography. In the tale's dialogue, the main characters are shown to be constantly aware of the karmic consequences of their actions—that good will be rewarded with good and bad with bad over a sequence of lifetimes. One character summarizes, "Nobody born as an ordinary human being can escape sorrow. It depends on karma made in the past. When a time for happiness is over, sorrow begins. When a time for sorrow passes, then happiness returns again. This has been the nature of things forever."

Warunee shows that the overall fate and fortune of each major character in the tale depends on how well they comply with or offend against the codes of conduct that are found in the revised Three Worlds of the First Reign, in the inscriptions at Wat Pho, and in several didactic manuals produced in the early Bangkok era. Some are "good" characters who show the result of compliance, and others are "bad."

For all his minor faults, Khun Phaen is generally a "good" character because he serves the king loyally and is a good husband within the conventions of his time. Khun Chang and Wanthong are both "bad" characters. Khun Chang consistently offends against the code of conduct of a good friend. Wanthong allows herself to be driven by strong emotions, and consistently offends against the codes of conduct for a good women and a good wife. Hence, by the logic of karma, Khun Chang loses Wanthong, and Wanthong loses her life.

Warunee concludes that, in early Bangkok, *Khun Chang Khun Phaen* was transformed from a simple folktale into "a means of propagating the ideology of the Buddhist state and society that the early Chakri court aimed to establish."

Warunee is a native of Suphanburi, the cradle of *Khun Chang Khun Phaen*, and had written earlier on the tale's local roots.[25] She has had a long-standing association with the Thai Khadi Research Institute at Thammasat University, the leading center of Thai studies. She has played a leading role in publication and debates on issues of human rights, the position of women, the importance of local history, and relations between state and society. The two Thai-language articles that are translated and adapted into her essay here were produced in parallel with her retirement. They bring together many of the themes that have marked her career at the epicenter of the practice of Thai studies over the past generation.

The fourth piece also dwells on geography and mentality in *Khun Chang Khun Phaen*, but from a perspective that is almost diametrically

---

25. "Rueang lao mueang suphan kap kan sang paplak tua ton thongthin" [Oral history of Suphan and the creation of local identity] in *Saithan haeng adit: Ruam botkhwam than prawatisat nueang nai wara krop rop 60 pi sastrajan dr. piyanat bunnag* [The flow of history: Essays for Professor Dr. Piyanat Bunnag on her sixtieth anniversary] (Bangkok: Faculty of Arts, Chulalongkorn University, 2007). See also Kanjani La-ongsi, ed., *Sing la un phan la noi 60 pi warunee osatharom* [One each, a few thousand: Sixty years of Warunee Osatharom] (Bangkok: Piriya Krairiksh Foundation, 2004).

opposed to that of Warunee. David Atherton was writing at the outset of his academic career. He was located, not at the heart of the tale, but on the other side of the world. His 2006 master's thesis,[26] which has been condensed into the essay appearing here, counts as the first academic thesis written on *Khun Chang Khun Phaen* both outside Thailand and in a non-Thai language—and hence is another landmark in the poem's career.

In a classic article from 1991, Philip Stott described an antithesis in Thai thinking between *mueang* and *pa*, city and forest, safety and danger, civilized space and wild space, the realm of the king and the region beyond his control.[27] Starting from this framework, Atherton subdivides the civilized or social space into three levels: *mueang* or city, *ban* or village, and *ruean* or household. He shows how the characters in *Khun Chang Khun Phaen*, especially Khun Phaen himself, are constrained to behave within the rules, conventions, and expectations of each of these spaces. Moreover, there is a hierarchy of diminishing selfhood across these subdivisions. Within the household, a person can be closest to himself or herself, but in the upper levels, that ability is diminished. The loss of selfhood at the level of the *mueang* is symbolized by Khun Phaen losing his natal name (Phlai Kaeo) in favor of an official title, and being utterly subject to royal command—sent off to war only three days after his marriage, and later plunged into jail for fourteen years.

This is the background, Atherton argues, to Khun Phaen's decision at the axial point of the plot to abandon civilization, seize Wanthong, and flee into the forest. At that point, Khun Phaen has lost both his wives, and lost his position at court (because of Khun Chang's

---

26.   David C. Atherton, "Space, Identity, and Self-definition: The Forest in *Khun Chang Khun Phaen*" (MA thesis, University of Wisconsin-Madison, 2006), with thanks to Thongchai Winichakul, who supervised the thesis and first alerted us to its existence.

27.   Philip Stott, "*Mu'ang* and *Pa*: Elite Views of Nature in a Changing Thailand," in *Thai Constructions of Knowledge*, ed. Manas Chitakasem and Andrew Turton (London: School of Oriental and African Studies, 1991), 142–54.

machinations). He decides that "to be completely destroyed is better than to go on living."

In Atherton's reading, Khun Phaen and Wanthong's flight into the forest is much more than a romantic episode that offered nineteenth-century poets the opportunity to show their skill with the poetic conventions of describing nature. Here the flight into the forest is a recovery of the self from the constraints of convention. As they travel from Suphanburi ever deeper into the western hills, Khun Phaen and Wanthong free themselves from bickering over past events and recover a natural humanity, symbolized by the scene of feeding each other on lotus roots in an idyllic stream. In the *bot atsajan* ("marvel stanzas" or "wondrous scene") of their lovemaking in the forest, the boundaries between human and nature, metaphor and reality are dissolved away.

The poetry reflects this transformation. In describing the plants and animals in the forest, the poets abandon the literal use of words, and deploy them instead to capture sound, movement, and (by extension) the liberated emotions of the characters. Instead of being exercises in virtuosity, these passages of *chom pa* (describing or celebrating the forest) become expressions of the mental states of the characters, and also a chance for the poets themselves to break free of convention. Atherton concludes, "we may conceive of the forest as a space of self-making not merely for the characters depicted as inhabiting it, but also for the very poets who brought it into being. . . . it is difficult, after examining the forest in the context of words, identity, and the subjective, not to see a parallel between that vast, unbounded, dark, wild, rich, and beautiful space, and the limitless inner world that exists in some unseen region deep within every human being."

In the last essay, we look at a political aspect of *Khun Chang Khun Phaen*, and offer a different way to interpret the meaning of the poem's terrible climax, the execution of Wanthong.

Khun Phaen is an ordinary man who finds himself pitted against wealth and power, first personified by Khun Chang with his wealth and court connections, and ultimately by the king. This is a popular theme in literature from around the world, notably in the old story of Robin Hood, with which *Khun Chang Khun Phaen* has many parallels. When Khun Phaen feels totally thwarted by these forces, he draws on his military training, especially his skill to manipulate supernatural power. He defeats the armies sent against him, and charms the king to drop the charges against him for murder and revolt. He uses his exceptional power not only to protect himself and those around him, but also to defend Ayutthaya against its enemies.

Khun Phaen is shown as an adept in a certain kind of power, which we label as "mastery." This power has roots in a Hindu-Buddhist belief in self-mastery as well as old beliefs in spirits and magic. The poem presents a contrast between this kind of power, which is passed down by parents and teachers, and the formal authority of the king and the *sakdina* order, which resides in the institutions of kingship, noble hierarchy, law and so on. At key points, the poem shows mastery can triumph over authority, but not without some ambiguity.

This approach offers a new way to interpret Wanthong's execution. Usually her crime is interpreted as an offense against the laws of marriage, but the penalties for adultery or bigamy in the Ayutthaya law codes were fines, whipping, or shaming, not death. In the court scene which precedes Wanthong's sentence, the king accuses the whole group—Chang, Wanthong, and Phaen's family—of revolt or causing disorder, which in the law of the time was virtually the same thing. In delivering the sentence on Wanthong, the king uses a form of words, which in the laws of Ayutthaya is found only in the law on revolt. She is executed for revolt, not a sexual misdemeanor.

This interpretation raises many issues that cannot be neatly answered. The accusation of revolt should really be visited on Khun Phaen, who has used his powers to defy the king. Perhaps the king needs Khun Phaen's skills as a soldier but he executes Wanthong to discipline him. Perhaps the poem raises the issue of the contrasting power of the king and a figure like Khun Phaen, but does not attempt to resolve it. Certainly the enigma of this ending has contributed to the work's popularity.

Why is this aspect of the tale rarely if ever addressed? This political theme is buried deep in the work, at the level of the core plot, which may date back to the tale's beginnings many centuries ago. Such popular tales evolve over time: across eight centuries, Robin Hood changed from a common criminal into a rebel against church and state and then changed again into a loyal nobleman fighting corruption. The history of *Khun Chang Khun Phaen* cannot be traced in as much depth and detail, but some indications are clear. As Warunee shows, the meaning of the poem was deliberately changed in the rewriting of the early nineteenth century. Three of the important figures in the transmission of the tale to the present day have been King Rama II, who oversaw the rewriting described by Warunee, Prince Damrong, who edited the standard printed edition, and the royalist author M.R. Kukrit Pramoj, who wrote an influential summary and exposition in the 1980s.[28]

Conclusion

As these five essays show, *Khun Chang Khun Phaen* can be read as a study of a society without principle, as an inquiry into human aggression, as a carrier of Buddhist ethics, as a metaphorical recovery of selfhood, or as a disquisition on forms of power. And of course, in many other ways too. We hope these essays will prompt further enjoyment, appreciation, and study of this outstanding work of Thai literature.

---

28. Kukrit Pramoj, *Khun chang khun phaen: Chabap an mai* [*Khun Chang Khun Phaen*, a new reading] (Bangkok: Dokya, 2000 [1989]), originally serialized in *Siam Rath* newspaper from August 20 to November 5, 1988.

NOTES AND ACKNOWLEDGMENTS

The translations of Boonlua, Cholthira, and Warunee are by Chris Baker and Pasuk Phongpaichit.

Cited quotations from *Khun Chang Khun Phaen* given in the text as parenthetical numbers, e.g., (68), refer to page numbers in Chris Baker and Pasuk Phongpaichit, *The Tale of Khun Chang Khun Phaen* (Chiang Mai: Silkworm Books, 2010).

We are grateful to the Foundation for the Promotion of Social Science and Humanities Textbooks Project for permission to translate from M.L. Boonlua Debyasuvarn, *Wikhro rot wannakhadi thai*; to the Thai Khadi Research Institute for permission to translate Warunee Osatharom's two articles; and to Cornell University Press, Southeast Asia Program Publications for permission to reproduce Chris Baker and Pasuk Phongpaichit, "The Revolt of Khun Phaen: Contesting Power in Early Modern Siam," which originally appeared in Maurizio Peleggi (ed.), *A Sarong for Clio: Essays on the Intellectual and Cultural History of Thailand—Inspired by Craig J. Reynolds* (2015).

We are grateful to Cholthira, Warunee, and David for participating in this project, and being helpful at every turn, and to Charnvit Kasetsiri, Sarah Grossman, and Parkpume Vanichaka.

A SOCIETY WHICH LACKS PRINCIPLE

M.L. Boonlua Debyasuvarn

This chapter is adapted from the book *Wikhro rot wannakhadi thai* (Bangkok: Social Science and Humanities Textbook Project, Social Science Association of Thailand, 1974), literally "Analyzing the Taste of Thai Literature," maybe best rendered as "Analyzing and Savoring Thai Literature." In the introduction, Boonlua explains that "I chose this title . . . to make it understood that this is not a weighty textbook but a book that lovers of literature may read for pleasure." The book has two short introductory chapters on the principles of literary criticism, which she then illustrates using *Khun Chang Khun Phaen, Lilit Phra Lo*, and *Rachathirat* from the classics; Surapha's *Khanglang Phap* (Behind the Painting) and the works of Dokmaisot (her elder sister) as examples of the modern novel; and the works of Angkarn Kalyanapong as an example of a modern poet. This translation includes most of chapter 3 on "Analyzing plot and character," about half of chapter 4 on "Analyzing literary technique," omitting the passages on poetic style, most of chapter 5 on "An example of critiquing a long literary work," and some short passages from the introduction and conclusion. The title for this chapter was not used by Boonlua as a title but comes from her text.

In *Principles of Literary Criticism*, I. A. Richards states that he is nervous writing this book because the discipline of literary criticism is almost a thousand years old. That is a Western worry. I'm even more nervous about writing this book because literary criticism is a new discipline in Thailand. Before any kind of knowledge acquires the status of a discipline and is summarized in textbooks, a great body of knowledge must have been accumulated in the brains and expertise of many people. For example, people have been breeding orchids for almost half a century so now people are writing books on the subject. Yet in Thailand the number of people that I know either in person, or from books, or from popular reputation, who have knowledge about literary criticism, is very few.

Those who love anything Thai cannot avoid taking pride in *Khun Chang Khun Phaen* because it has a uniquely Thai character. It is the work of several authors in the same fashion as the royal *Ramakian* and the *Vessantara Jataka for Recitation*. This sort of composition is not found in the West, or at least is not valued by literary scholars. Composition by several authors might result in a work of uneven quality, but it is very difficult to find a bad passage in *Khun Chang Khun Phaen*.

Thai literature tends to depict feelings, not ideas. Thai literary works rarely deal with ideas, preferring the artistry of using words to convey the emotions of people who have uncomplicated lives. These emotions include love between man and woman, love between parents and children, jealousy, and revenge. The emotions arise from similar causes: a woman parted from a man she loves, a man parted from a woman he loves, anger between enemies who clash over power or love, or the vengeful feelings of someone who has been wronged. Some have wondered whether a literary work such as the *Vessantara Jataka* is really about ideas. They ask themselves whether Phra Vessantara does right or wrong when he gives away his wife and children as alms. While a reader might perceive this as an issue, the author did not. He was intent on portraying the Buddhist teaching on giving through the example of Phra Vessantara, who gives away even his wife and children so he may gain the reward of attaining nirvana. The author is not discussing the issue of whether Phra Vessantara did right or wrong but offering readers a teaching about the attainment of nibbana. The presentation of ideas or issues in Thai writing started only a few years ago, within my lifetime, and there is no agreement yet on whether such writing should be considered literature. Because Thai readers are not accustomed to ideas in literature, nobody has critiqued literature from this angle.

Critique of the plot

Thai literature of the old generation favored a dramatic plot, not one that depicts everyday life. For example, *Khun Chang Khun Phaen* deals with war, supernaturalism, violent killing, and abducting a woman into the forest. It is virtually the only story in which the characters are commoners not royalty. The tale was composed in verse for recitation, meaning the verses must enable the reciter to arouse several emotions appropriate to each passage of the story.

A tale must have a plot and characters. Some of the characters must have an unusual personality. If all have a similar personality, the plot will not emerge naturally because similar people do not make anything happen. For example, if the children of a family are all easy-going, dispassionate, and unargumentative, then nothing will happen. But if a fierce elder brother does harm to his younger sibling, who runs away from home, and the elder follows after him, meeting good and helpful people along the way, and eventually they are reunited, then there is a story but it lacks complexity. But if there is some conflict which creates a "bump" in the story, an obstruction that is eventually overcome, then the story will be more complex. A tale emerges from conflict between the personalities of its characters.

The tale of *Khun Chang Khun Phaen* emerges from conflict between ordinary people, arising from ordinary human failings. Two men both desire the same beautiful woman, Phim Philalai. One of the men, Phlai Kaeo, is handsome and clever but poor, while the other, Khun Chang, is ugly but wealthy. The beautiful young woman quickly falls in love with the charms of the handsome man, but her mother is interested only in the wealth of the other suitor. To get what she wants, the beautiful woman gives the handsome man the money needed to ask for her hand, and they are married in the customary fashion.

This is the first stage of the plot. If the story ended here, the tale would not absorb listeners' attention. But it doesn't end here. The wealthy man does not abandon his desire for the woman, but seeks an opportunity to disrupt the wedded bliss of the handsome man and the beautiful woman. Khun Chang finds an opportunity to have the king send Phlai Kaeo off to war. In the era of this tale, war took time because communications were poor. Delivering messages was slow. Travel was full of dangers. Those who went to war did not return quickly. Hence Khun Chang can deceive Phim's mother into believing that Phlai Kaeo met defeat in the war, and that by law the wife and children of anyone defeated in war are seized to become palace servants. Phim's mother, Siprajan, tries desperately to marry Phim to Khun Chang so that her daughter can both escape this punishment and become a rich man's wife, killing two birds with one stone. However, Phim does not consent and resists her mother's pressure until Phlai Kaeo returns.

While Phim is wasting away from grief at home, Phlai Kaeo returns from war, reporting to the capital first, attending in royal audience and being handsomely rewarded for his victory, then arriving home at Suphanburi like a prodigal son.

However, Phlai Kaeo does not return alone but with Laothong, a Chiang Thong woman gained according to the custom of that time as spoils of war from the headman of a village where the army stayed. Phlai Kaeo was a good commanding officer who did not oppress the villagers so the village head felt indebted and repaid him by presenting his daughter. Laothong is the same age as Phim, who has changed her name to Wanthong on the advice of a monk after she became gravely ill.

Wanthong tells her husband what has happened with a mixture of happiness and hurt, hoping he will save her from the pressure of her mother and Khun Chang. On hearing her account, Phlai Kaeo wants to kill Khun Chang in revenge, but Laothong comes out to prevent him. When Wanthong sees he has a new wife, and when the new wife shows her distrust of Wanthong, Wanthong is furious. She turns on Laothong, and refuses to listen to Phlai Kaeo. When she realizes Phlai Kaeo is more inclined to believe his new wife than her, the argument turns violent. Wanthong severs the relationship with Phlai Kaeo, and goes back into the house. Phlai Kaeo sets off for his old home in Kanchanaburi.

This segment of the plot is about conflict, not only the conflict between Khun Chang and Phlai Kaeo over the same beautiful woman, but also about the emotional conflict in one human being. Wanthong is happy to see her husband, but this happiness is swamped by resentment. She wants her husband to know about her sadness and suffering. She is not prepared for the fact that the husband who had said farewell to her with such love should return home with a new wife and allow this new wife to disrupt her attempt to get revenge. Even though she overflows with love for her husband, she allows her anger to triumph and make her sever the relationship.

Similarly in the case of Phlai Kaeo, his love for his old wife has not diminished, but he also falls under the power of anger that spirals out of control. Young love can be passionate. Young anger can be passionate too.

While Phlai Kaeo is in Kanchanaburi, Wanthong's mother Siprajan continues her attempts to marry Wanthong to Khun Chang. Siprajan is motivated by greed and has no internal conflict. Khun Chang has no internal conflict but he intensifies the conflict between Phlai Kaeo and Wanthong beyond the point of possible reconciliation. When Phlai Kaeo (now with the title of Khun Phaen) gets over his anger, his love for his wife resurfaces and he returns to Suphanburi. But when he finds that she has slept with Khun Chang, he is enraged. He reports Siprajan to a local official and abandons Wanthong again. This is another instance of Khun Phaen's internal emotional conflict—arriving with love and departing with anger, because his love is not enough for him to understand the constraint on his loved one. He believes that a man's honor depends on having a wife who is faithful to him, and who cannot be shared with other men—a belief that leads to further conflict.

After a temporary lull, another matter intervenes. The king, called King Phanwasa, orders both Khun Phaen and Khun Chang to enter royal service as pages. Khun Phaen leaves Laothong with his mother in Kanchanaburi. One day he hears that she has fallen ill, entrusts his duty to Khun Chang, and rushes to Kanchanaburi. Khun Chang informs the king that Khun Phaen has neglected his duty, and compounds the accusation by saying Khun Phaen climbed over the palace wall.

King Phanwasa punishes Khun Phaen by taking Laothong into the palace, forbidding Khun Phaen to contact her, banishing him from court, and sending him off to serve on the frontier. Khun Phaen's thoughts now turn to Wanthong. His old love for her is mixed up with his desire for revenge on Khun Chang. He enchants his weaponry, equips himself with supernatural powers, goes to Khun Chang's house, and boldly climbs in. Entering the room to find Wanthong sleeping with Khun Chang, he uses a spell to put everyone in the house asleep and another to arouse Wanthong alone. He threatens her and reproaches her over their former love until she agrees to leave with him, although she knows she will face hardship in the forest and not enjoy the comforts of a home like ordinary people from then on.

When Khun Phaen takes her away into the forest, their old love revives. She conceives. When her pregnancy is advanced, Khun Phaen realizes that she should give birth somewhere safe and decides to go to the governor of Phichit to surrender following judicial procedure. The governor sends Khun Phaen and Wanthong down to the capital as prisoners along with a report.

At Ayutthaya, Khun Phaen undergoes trial and receives a royal pardon, but then angers the king and is jailed. Khun Chang drags Wanthong off to Suphanburi. At this point, there is conflict at many levels of complexity. There is a conflict between law and justice, resulting from the power of a rich man without scruples. Khun Chang's feelings towards Wanthong are a selfish kind of love without any thought for the feelings of the loved one. This is the love of a man who is bent on triumph. There is also a conflict in government based solely on the exercise of power with no means to protect those who cannot help themselves, such as a pregnant woman whose husband is undergoing royal punishment.

The plot does not end here. Phlai Ngam, the son of Khun Phaen, is born and raised in the house of Khun Chang but flees to live with his grandmother after Khun Chang tries to murder him. He studies supernaturalism from his father's library until his knowledge almost matches that of his father. When he comes of age, war breaks out with Chiang Mai and Phlai Ngam seizes the opportunity to volunteer for the army and petition for the king to release Khun Phaen. Phlai Ngam and Khun Phaen win victory and are rewarded with promotions to higher ranks, a house, and wealthier standing. One day, Phlai Ngam forces his mother to come and live with Khun Phaen again. Khun Chang petitions the king for redress. The king angrily summons Wanthong for questioning and demands she make a definite decision on whether she will live with one of her husbands or with her son. She cannot decide because she has lived with Khun Chang a long time while Khun Phaen was jailed. Khun Chang made her comfortable and was a faithful husband so there was no rivalry among wives. She appreciates the goodness of Khun Chang, but her heart still loves Khun Phaen. She does not know what is the right choice. King Phanwasa angrily says she is an inconstant woman who has caused him trouble on many occasion, and so condemns her to execution.

This tragic ending to the story of two men's rivalry over one woman is really the conclusion of the plot of *Khun Chang Khun Phaen*. The story continues about the problems of the next generation, which could be called a sequel or part 2 in a Western book. We will continue the analysis on part 1.

Character analysis

A tale needs characters. If they have no personality they cannot be characters. And if a tale is to be interesting, their personalities must give rise to conflict, as described above. The authors of *Khun Chang*

Khun Phaen are unknown. The tale is believed to have origins in a true story but has been rewritten and changed for sure. The personalities of the characters are the creation of the authors. Here we will analyze how the personalities of the main characters give rise to the plot that we read.

First, we should analyze the setting or environment because human behavior is largely shaped by the environment. Only rarely do humans break out of their environment. There are literary works that depict characters or small groups that try to defy their environment, but in *Khun Chang Khun Phaen* the characters act in keeping with their social situation, so we should study their society.

First of all, it is a rural society. People are farmers. Some are rich men who have slaves and servants in big households. Khun Chang, Phim, and Khun Phaen all belong to the upper class of rural society. Khun Phaen is educated in the fashion of the time, namely by monks. As he is a descendant of a military lineage, he studies skills to use as a soldier along with the ability to make women fall for him through mantras. Khun Phaen is ordained as a novice in the monkhood, but the purpose of ordination is not religious but worldly, and Khun Phaen's values are totally worldly. He wants love. He is proud of his ability to make several women fall in love with him. He is adept at worldly matters. He rewards older women with his attentions, pursuing Saithong just like he pursues Phim to show his love for her. But Khun Phaen is not fascinated by the love he can arouse in young women, but rather by the supernatural powers that he learns from teachers for his own worldly advancement in the future. He is charming, physically attractive, and well-spoken with a beautiful voice. He does anything well. His teacher has him recite the *Mahachat*, the Great Jataka, in his place. People like to listen to him. He is not slow to make himself desirable when the occasion arises. He is never daunted in his pursuit of Phim. He loves her unreservedly and returns her unreserved love.

When he is recruited for the army, he behaves in line with military conduct. He happily agrees to volunteer with no mention of any hope for rank and reward. On campaign, he is a good commander, who upholds military standards, does not oppress civilians, and is loved by the Chiang Thong villagers. When he gets Laothong, he behaves according to the gentlemanly conduct of the time, giving her his love and respect and not making her feel like a war prisoner. On returning home in victory, he shows respect to the senior nobles in the capital and is consequently received with goodwill. But he is also proud of his new status as a soldier who has won victory for his country and been praised by the king. When he finds that someone is bullying his wife, he is overcome with the natural anger of a young man. He speaks like someone who is used to carrying weapons and ready to use them, saying he will kill those who trampled all over himself and his wife while he was away at war. When he is checked, he is not so violent that he cannot control his anger, but is on a short fuse. When Wanthong uses harsh words with him for favoring his minor wife, he explodes with anger and she severs their relationship without giving him a chance to explain. This is a clash between an emotional woman and a hot-headed man. Khun Phaen and Wanthong are thus temporarily estranged.

But Khun Phaen still loves Wanthong. Before long, he thinks of her and hurries back to Suphanburi. Gaining entry by using lore, he sees a scene that he should not see while his emotions are still inflamed. He ties Wanthong and his rival together to make them ashamed. He has enough sense to make local officials understand that he has behaved correctly, and then returns home full of resentment against the woman he once loved.

While he is in service to the king, Khun Phaen shows weakness of character, lack of principle, and carelessness. When he learns that Laothong is sick, he entrusts his duties to Khun Chang, someone he should no longer have dealings with, and as a result is punished by being banished from court. At home he starts to resent Khun Chang again, and decides to take revenge by abducting Wanthong. He shows his immaturity by choosing a course of action that is not clear. He is a Don Juan, unable to restrain himself when meeting a woman. When he enters Khun Chang's house in search of Wanthong, he comes upon

Kaeo Kiriya and makes love to her. But the author of this passage makes it clear that Khun Phaen is in a situation that a youth finds difficult to resist. Though someone less amorous and more fainthearted might have avoided becoming involved with a strange woman, Khun Phaen cannot avoid sowing his wild oats. He also shows he is easily trustful by giving her a ring in payment.

When he enters the room of Khun Chang and Wanthong, he shows his anger by slashing curtains to shreds. On finding them in bed together, he puts Khun Chang to sleep with a mantra and then has fun tormenting him. Khun Phaen could be said to have a humorous side, but that of a rather immature person. Yet Khun Phaen does not take revenge on Khun Chang in a violent way to the point of taking his life.

Towards Wanthong, Khun Phaen shows a mixture of love and resentment, both provoking her anger and prompting her to recall their first love. Khun Phaen has more changeable feelings than most men. When he is with a woman he loves, his feelings change. The tale shows how his feelings change all the time.

While he and Wanthong are traveling in the forest, Khun Phaen shows his appreciation of beauty. He is not the kind of youth who is bound up with himself alone but drinks deeply in the taste of love, and is courteous to the woman who shares his love and hardship in a way that is very affecting.

> At dusk as the sunlight faded, Khun Phaen and Wanthong rode down beside a flowing stream until they reached a landing. He asked Wanthong to dismount, / unsaddled the horse, shed his own gear, and walked her down to the landing. They drank the cool water and washed their hair among the blooming flowers. / He plucked lotus pods, and pulled up a lotus root that popped out of the earth in naked coils. He stripped the skin, leaving it white and curly, and begged her, "Try this, my love." / "Oh, I've never eaten the root. I'm afraid it'll make my mouth itch and my tongue sting. I'll just eat the seeds." "Try it. Believe me, it's delicious. I just fear you'll be captivated once you know the taste." (421–22)

"Oh, my utmost love, don't have such thoughts about me. You are equal to my own heart. There are no doubts. Don't stab me like that. / I love you as much as when we were first in love. Because I now know you well, there's not a single reason for doubt or worry. I'll tell you the truth but don't be upset. / I'm crying with heartbreak for the difficulty we're in. I keep looking at your growing belly. You'll give birth before long, and there's no one to nurse you." (423)

When Khun Chang leads nobles from Ayutthaya to arrest Khun Phaen, at first Khun Phaen acts sensibly, does no harm to the king's soldiers, and is careful with his words. But the royal soldiers are not equally cool. One of them defames Khun Phaen by referring to the fact that his father was executed. In anger, Khun Phaen kills this officer, thus becomes a criminal and has to flee with Wanthong into the forest. When Wanthong is heavily pregnant, Khun Phaen becomes concerned over his wife and child and decides to return to Ayutthaya to face charges. In this passage, Khun Phaen takes a calculated risk that turns out well, as the king believes his testimony and absolves him of guilt.

After being pardoned, Khun Phaen again acts like a young man by asking pardon for Laothong, angering King Phanwasa, who has him jailed. Khun Phaen then behaves like a trustworthy servant of the king by not using his lore to escape from jail. The guards, who have seen his powers, leniently allow him to stay in reasonable comfort, and Khun Phaen tolerates staying in jail for fourteen years until Phlai Ngam volunteers to fight Chiang Mai and asks for Khun Phaen to be pardoned. From this point onwards, Khun Phaen behaves like someone who has long experience of life by not acting emotionally as he had earlier.

To save paper and the reader's time, Wanthong's character must be analyzed only briefly. She is not a reserved type of woman but strong-willed, strong in both words and actions, prone to anger and heated emotions, and deeply affected by love, as can be seen from the passage when Phlai Kaeo is leaving for war:

"Oh, Phlai, my heartstring, you're not used to being far from love. You came to lie with me in the bridal house twice a day. You talked with me / about this and that, chatting playfully, teasing, and not letting me stray from the pillow. You let me cushion on your left arm. When you saw I was hot, you fanned me. . . . / I've seen many other couples but none loving each other like you loving me. Now my love must be severed away from me. How to bring it back to enjoy again?" (181)

In this lament on separation, she shows that she loves her husband deeply, and that she believes he loves her equally. While Phlai Kaeo is away at war, Wanthong shows her strength of character and is not vindictive towards anyone except the hated Khun Chang. She resents her mother but not to the point of severing relations. In sum, Wanthong is a normal young woman yet of an independent bent. She never laments her bad luck, but adjusts to a situation from which there is no escape. But at the critical point when she must decide between Khun Chang and Khun Phaen, she cannot decide. She does not know how to help herself. She thinks of the goodness of Khun Chang because of the comforts she received even though he had tried to murder her son.

Khun Chang need not be analyzed at length. He is an unlucky person born without physical beauty but unusually wealthy. He must use his wealth to compensate for his lack of physical beauty. He is oblivious to shame, and will do anything to achieve his own desires in the confidence that his wealth can buy what he wants.

These are the three principal characters of *Khun Chang Khun Phaen*. The supporting characters have personalities that help the plot along. Siprajan is a greedy person who serves as a device for ensuring that Wanthong meets the worst possible fate. Thong Prasi, the mother of Phlai Kaeo, is not a fair person. When she rages at Siprajan she does not recognize that her daughter-in-law has been faithful to her son, but is angry at her too. When Wanthong is taken to bed by Khun Chang,

Thong Prasi judges that Wanthong is also at fault. Thong Prasi is thus another device for making Wanthong meet her fate.

Another important supporting character is King Phanwasa. He acts on emotion and does not stay within the letter of the law. He orders the execution of Khun Phaen's father, Khun Krai, even though he is a good soldier, and later has to call on Phlai Kaeo, a youth of only seventeen years, to suppress the revolt of Chiang Thong, because no one else will volunteer. He remembers that Khun Chang's father had come to present his son at court, and thus summons Khun Chang to serve in the palace. When Khun Chang accuses Khun Phaen, the king does not make a careful enquiry but hands down a punishment at will. At other times he is less credulous. For instance, when Khun Chang accuses Khun Phaen of revolt, the king does not believe him and sends Muen Si and Muen Wai to investigate. When Khun Phaen comes to confess, the king grants a pardon easily, but when Khun Phaen asks for Laothong, he is jailed and forgotten for fourteen years.

Storytelling

From *Khun Chang Khun Phaen* we gain one picture of people in the Thai countryside outside the capital and another picture of the court. The picture of the countryside is much clearer. There are passages describing the behavior of the people of Suphanburi and the Thai in general, showing occupations, the nature of society, traditions of merit-making, marriage, supernatural rituals, and even life in jail. The description of various situations and customs is not done as a primer on Thai tradition. The author is not trying to teach Thai studies. These passages fit in to the rhythm of the tale. Every narrative of events and description of reality involves the characters of the tale and is related to the plot. For example, the *Mahachat* recital in Suphanburi is an opportunity for Khun Chang to see Phim's beauty and an opportunity for Phlai Kaeo to launch his love affair with her. The marriage of Phim and Phlai Kaeo is witnessed by the people of Suphanburi, which is important in the later case between Khun Chang and Phlai Kaeo. The rituals of supernaturalism such as the creation of Goldchild show the gruesome side of ritual performed by hard-hearted people who believe in magic. They reveal the personality of Khun Phaen and the beliefs of people of that time, as does the description of the Chiang Mai soldier Tri Phetkla preparing for battle. The description of Khun Chang's house when Khun Phaen abducts Wanthong shows the residence of a rich man in the provinces but also fits within the framework of the story and helps us understand the life of Wanthong and the feelings of Khun Phaen. When he sees the wealth of his rival and the circumstances of his beloved first wife, Khun Phaen feels deeply hurt, resulting in her having to forsake these circumstances and experience a different love in the forest with Khun Phaen, leading eventually to the indecision at the end of her life. The descriptions of life and customs are an integral part of the story, not something that can be separated out or passed over during reading.

Critique or assessment

After studying the plot, characters, and storytelling technique, we have come to the point of assessing the literary work. For such a critique or assessment, we must first appreciate the nature of literature a little more. In the composition of a book or tale or novel, the author uses various artistic techniques, both consciously and unconsciously. In addition, there are certain *conventions* that the readers and writer accept in common. For example, the readers must accept that the author will not describe every character. They must use their own imagination to draw their own portrait. In this tale, we are told that Khun Chang has a bald head but we are not told whether he is tall or short. When Phim refers to the slimness of Khun Phaen, we readers understand that Khun Chang is podgier and less attractive. In the case of other characters, such as Khun Krai, nothing is said of their appearance, but the reader may guess that he is not bad-looking. We are not told whether Thong Prasi's house in Kanchanaburi is grand or ramshackle, but we can infer that it is an adequately comfortable house of a wealthy rural householder and quite spacious as there are many servants.

There are conventions for displaying emotions such as sorrow, as at the death of Khun Phet and Khun Ram. The laments by their wives continue for many lines. In reality, ordinary people do not lament in such a way. They would express their sorrow in snatches over a long period, perhaps over several days, rather than in a single long speech. But there is a convention of writing laments in this form, and readers must understand that the lament would not really be long and continuous in this way. In dramas, laments are drawn out to last as long as they are dramatically effective. In today's drama performances, they are cut short to avoid boring the audience.

Literature can depict some aspect of reality through symbols that are unreal or exaggerated yet serve to convey reality. For example, the author of *Ramakian* gives Thotsakan ten heads to convey that this character can be ten times more stupid, ten times more infatuated, ten times more enraged than an ordinary person. Having ten hands shows that the character can create ten times more trouble than an ordinary person. Siva's four arms can mean that he has twice the power of other gods.

An author may show some reality quite unintentionally, but a real poet whose thinking is deeper and higher than normal can use words to describe a single flower or a single drop of dew that make readers gain new insight into the beauty of that flower or dew and its meaning for life. The reader profits from the exceptional insight of the author.

The depiction of reality uses many kinds of literary devices, depending on the inclination and expertise of the author. Some like to give a picture as close as possible to real life. Some use symbolism. Some lead the reader to dream the author's own dream. Before assessing any literary work, we must first study the devices used by the author.

Khun Chang Khun Phaen is similar to other old works composed in an age when people believed in sacredness, supernaturalism, and the power of gods, spirits, and magic. In both East and West, literature from this era combines both realism and supernaturalism. Both humans and deities or other non-humans have the same failings that are observed in everyday human life, but their powers (*itthirit*) are not equal. Deities have the ability to behave like people with everyday powers. For example, Siva gives his blessing to this ogre (*yak*) because the ogre takes the trouble to worship Siva, and that ogre then uses the special power bestowed by Siva to create trouble for deities and humans, so Siva has to deal with this ogre. Here Siva is portrayed as a deity with great powers but no judgment. He fails to detect the ogre's intention just like the powerful often do, whether human or non-human.

In such literature, the special power that comes from divinity or from magic does not lessen characters' human failings. The special power or special ability tends to make the character get into difficulties because of carelessness or excess, and then experience severe suffering before the difficulties are overcome. We cannot classify such literature as either "reality" or "fantasy" using categories from a later time. When humans ceased to believe in supernaturalism, turned towards science, and demanded things that could be objectively proven, then the content of literature changed and the categorization of literature too. *Khun Chang Khun Phaen* dates from the era prior to the belief in science. The story contains events that are considered unrealistic according to present-day belief but were not considered unrealistic in its own time. The author and reader both believed that such events could happen. We must understand that this was a feature of a certain culture.

However, supernaturalism can be depicted in various ways. In *Inao*, a work that is contemporary with *Khun Chang Khun Phaen*, the protagonist is a skilled fighter with no command of magic but a deity from heaven comes down to cause various events to happen. In Shakespeare's *Macbeth*, the three witches cause Macbeth to commit murder by predicting that he will become king. In *Khun Chang Khun Phaen* there is no deity causing events, but Khun Phaen and other soldiers have not only skill in using weapons but also command of magic or lore. Khun Phaen is clever and eager to learn so his teachers love him and are ready to impart all their knowledge. He is also determined. Anyone who has supernatural power needs another important quality, namely mindfulness. If he loses his temper in a critical situation, such as a battle, he may forget the mantras he has learned and be defeated by the enemy. This happens to both Tri Phetkla when he fights with Phlai Ngam and Khun Phaen, and to Phlai Ngam when he fights his younger brother in the later part of the story.

What is the essence of *Khun Chang Khun Phaen*? What is the writer saying to the reader? In summary, he portrays the life of a common man who has supernatural ability but cannot escape hardship. Hardship arises from human failings such as carelessness, anger, or greed. The most important passage of the story—the big "bump" in the plot—is the passage where Phim severs the relationship with Khun Phaen because she is too hot-headed to tolerate the many levels of hardship created by her mother's greed and the power of Khun Chang's wealth. In addition, Thong Prasi, who should have sympathy for her daughter-in-law being faithful to her son, instead turns against her after confronting Siprajan's greed. Phim appeals to Thong Prasi for help, but she stupidly and unjustly fails to respond.

The events that take place involving Phim, Khun Phaen, and their two mothers are very similar to the behavior of rural Thais who lack education even in the present day. They have no principle for making decisions on how to behave and in the end just follow their instinct. In addition, *Khun Chang Khun Phaen* depicts the absence of principle in government. Everything is very loose—a feature that has scarcely changed in the present day, though people's thinking has. Life depends on short-term decisions. If Thai society had progressed significantly we would not find the society still governed as shown in *Khun Chang Khun Phaen*, but the essence of current events can be found in the tale. In sum, Thai society is a society that lacks principle.

We must appreciate that the critique of literature is subjective, the same as making value judgments, the final step of criticism. Each reader may interpret the meaning of a particular work differently. Take the *Ramakian*. We may conclude that its essential message is that right triumphs over wrong. Thotsakan, the abductor of Sida, loses to Phra Ram, her husband. Phra Ram gets help from the gods on many occasions because he is a good son who keeps his word to his father. But if we were to read only up to the passage where Ram orders Sida's death because he suspects she loves Thotsakan, we might conclude that the work's message is that any hope that powerful men will have common sense is futile. Even a man who is a reincarnation of Vishnu can forget that his wife underwent ordeal by fire to prove her purity. Phra Ram turns out to be a jealous and stupid man. He cannot recognize the heart of a deer even though he has spent a long time in the forest. We might conclude that a person with absolute power is impervious to common sense, even when proffered by Phra Lak, his loyal younger brother who sticks with him to death for fourteen years.

Social analysis

My judgment that the essence of *Khun Chang Khun Phaen* is that Thai society is a society without principle points us towards analysis from a social science perspective.

Studies by anthropologists who have investigated the way of life in Thai villages make it possible to see the portrayal of life in *Khun Chang Khun Phaen* in an interesting way, including aspects of ethics and morality. Anthropologists and social scientists have studied rural society[1] including occupations, health care, the way of life in the family, and the maintenance of ethics, by which is meant preserving the peace and contentment of the community (precept one), protecting property

---

1. William Klausner, *Reflections in a Log Pond: Collected Writings* (Bangkok: Suksit Siam: 1972).

(precept two), upholding the family (precept three), creating mutual trust (precept four), and government, namely reducing hardship and enhancing the happiness of the society and its emotional bonds. Social scientists and anthropologists note that literature collects together the higher feeling of humans in a community—which makes it rather believable.

To prevent misunderstanding by literature specialists, let me explain that I do not propose that *Khun Chang Khun Phaen* has value as a social science record of some sort. A poetic work which is not good poetry has no other value. However, the portrayal of life in *Khun Chang Khun Phaen* gives this work value beyond its poetry alone. The characters in *Khun Chang Khun Phaen* behave in various ways for social reasons. The society that we see in this work is a society of Thai people engaged in agriculture, located not far from the center of the country's government. Travel takes a single day. The descriptions of this journey always describe only its start and its end, showing that Suphanburi people had no difficulty in communicating with those of the capital. Any matter can be relayed to the capital within a single day. The journey from Ayutthaya or Suphanburi to the border outpost of Kanchanaburi takes only two days by cart, elephant, or horse. Yet, officials from the capital do not chase after criminals or wanted people. When officials come to seize her property in Suphanburi, Thong Prasi escapes to live in Kanchanaburi where she settles down and makes a good living, not wealthy but having slaves and servants. This passage supports the view that Thai society has no principle. The law or royal order to seize the property of a criminal is not very sacred. The officials, who find that the wife and son of Khun Krai have fled, content themselves with seizing whatever property they can lay their hands on. Although the distances involved are not great, travel through the forest was not easy and was avoided unless necessary. Hence the officials do not give chase even though the journey would not take long.

People can be easily deceived about matters in the capital. Khun Chang deceives Siprajan into believing that Phlai Kaeo has died in battle and that his wife and child must become royal property. Siprajan is inclined to believe this anyway, but other people also make no objection when Khun Chang pulls down Khun Phaen's bridal house. Even local officials show no interest until Thong Prasi comes from Kanchanaburi to visit her daughter-in-law and goes to inform the officials that Phlai Kaeo's bridal house has been dismantled. Even then, the officials do not act, do not explain whether the law truly prescribes seizure of property for the family of someone defeated in war, and do not send an enquiry to the capital to discover the truth. Hence the life of those in Suphanburi, only a day's travel from the capital, is completely divorced from the capital's governance as a result of the people's ignorance and the negligence of officialdom.

Government in that era depended on laws that were loose principles. Enforcement mostly depended on the king, who could distribute pardons or punishment, including the death penalty, for reasons great or small, on the basis of oral testimony. If the king was not in a good mood, he could take decisions at will, or entrust the trial to his nobles, as in the case where Khun Chang accuses Khun Phaen of abducting his wife. When Khun Phaen kills two of the king's soldiers, the king is not bothered and sympathetically grants a pardon.

The high officials of the realm have no more principles than the officials in the countryside. They are incapable of saying a criminal is a criminal. Muen Si and Muen Wai are ordered by the king to arrest Khun Phaen, who has been accused of gathering people to stage a revolt. When they find that Khun Phaen is alone and there is no hint of a revolt, they first try to conciliate Khun Phaen. Before their conversation has gone very far, however, Muen Si loses his temper and orders his men to arrest Khun Phaen by force. When they return to attend on King Phanwasa, they report truthfully that they found him alone even though they risk being rebuked for failing to arrest a solitary person. Yet the king does not punish them for this failure. He shows his anger but does not seem to care that his arrest order has not been fulfilled. The king seems to act on a combination of custom and emotion.

King Phanwasa has the good fortune to have the services of a soldier as loyal and reliable as Khun Phaen, as well as the convicts that Khun Phaen requests to be released from jail. Given that these convicts all have supernatural powers, we must imagine that they were somehow arrested by chance. Their own testimony shows that they are naturally wicked people. Their crimes are deliberate, not acts of passion.

For the war with Chiang Thong, a child of seventeen becomes an army commander. For the war with Chiang Mai, there seems to be no noble brave enough except Khun Phaen and his son Phlai Ngam. If *Khun Chang Khun Phaen* were a present-day work, the author would be thought to have concocted an irrational plot. However, the story of *Khun Chang Khun Phaen* was passed down by word of mouth for many generations. The storytellers and the listeners were not interested in whether the various passages of the story fitted together or not. Yet this in itself shows that the Thai society, which was the audience for the *Khun Chang Khun Phaen* story, was not interested in rationality. The story was told for entertainment. The listeners knew the plot— that Phlai Kaeo goes to war and that he wins victory in Chiang Mai. Nobody raises an eyebrow over the fact that Khun Phaen is jailed for fourteen years because of the king's forgetfulness and the disinterest of all the senior and junior officials. Probably that is because people had their own experience of the lack of any clear principle. In the tale, King Phanwasa states,

> "As he had no wealth, his case lay hidden, isn't that so? If he were rich rather than poor, all you fellows would be asking on his behalf every single day." (549)

Apart from being a superbly skilled soldier, Khun Phaen shows due respect to the senior nobles (including Muen Si, a lieutenant of the pages, and Phraya Yommarat, minister in charge of public order) and consequently becomes one of their favorites. This indicates another aspect of the society that was the audience for *Khun Chang Khun Phaen*, namely the respect for seniority. The authors do not make Khun

Phaen insubordinate to his seniors. Were Khun Phaen the hero of a literary work today, the author might make Khun Phaen obstreperous with persons of high position to portray him as an independent man. Literary works do not only portray the nature of society in the work itself but illustrate the nature of the society that consumes the work as well.

As for matters of occupation and living, which today we would call the "economy," the people in Ayutthaya and Chiang Mai enjoy abundance and every happiness with no shortage of food or goods. The wealth of the rich lies in land, elephants, and other transport animals. The rich are held in esteem. Wherever Khun Chang goes there are people telling children to get out of his way.

When Khun Chang was three and went off to play, other children took fright at the sight of him. "What's that over there, Mummy, opening its mouth and baring its teeth. Horrible!" / Their mothers told them not to be afraid. "That's Khun Chang, son of the rich man with servants from Big Wall Village. Don't get in his way. Let him through." (7)

Nobles of the level of Khun Krai have gold articles to adorn their sons. Phlai Kaeo is decked with

> beaded bracelets with *sema*;[2] splendid golden bangles; gilt wristlets on both arms; a jewel-inlaid necklace made with a whole bar of gold . . . (11)

Siprajan owns and operates a cotton field. As part of training to manage the property, Phim is placed in charge of the servants, who seem generally to be happy. Apart from the cotton field, the family probably has other fields since Phim has time to practice embroidery,

---

2. เสมาปะวะหล่ำ, *sema pawalam*. *Pawalam* is a bracelet with beads or other items strung on a cord. *Sema* or *sima* are stones that demarcate the sacred space of an ordination hall in a wat. This is a bracelet in which the links have the inverted-shield shape of such stones.—Eds.

an occupation of people who have time on their hands and need not worry about making a living.

These economic conditions are not described in words in the tale but can be inferred from the actions of the characters without any disruption to the plot or any boredom for the reader.

Health care follows old practices. Significantly, the descriptions of sickness are credible, as in the example of Kaen Kaeo, Khun Chang's first wife. A present-day doctor would probably diagnose her ailment as typhoid. This fever comes and goes, and when it recedes the patient craves rich food because the body is compensating for the loss of energy caused by the fever. Before the advent of antibiotic medicine, the fever would cause inflammation of the intestine for around twenty-one days and then recede, leaving the body in need of food. The ailment should be treated by giving easily digestible food in small amounts until the intestine can properly accept the food needed to compensate for the lack of energy. But in the case of Kaen Kaeo:

> She came to live in his house as bedmate, sharing pillows side by side for over a year. Then she fell sick with a fever that lasted a long time, and developed into dysentery and piles. / She grew thin, her face turned hard and scaly, and her eyes became sunken. She had a huge craving for duck, chicken, and unwholesome things. Khun Chang was lonely and miserable. (61)

The "dysentery and piles" mentioned occur when the intestine has been inflamed for a long time, cannot accept good food, and develops a bloody lesion. Before antibiotics, typhoid sufferers would then die. During World War II, I worked as a nurse for typhoid patients and became something of an expert. When I re-read *Khun Chang Khun Phaen* for close analysis, I remembered the symptoms. The author clearly had experience of this ailment in real life, and related it for a humorous touch. Such little touches make this work constantly interesting, always giving the reader something new to ponder. This is a feature of all good literature, unlike a book that is only averagely good and will not bear a repeat reading. Literature of national heritage must have this quality.

The tale portrays the family relationship between father, mother, and child that has not changed down to the present day, and only now shows signs of changing in the near future. Children understand that parents have the right to determine their way of life. Parents try to use this right for the benefit of their children. Some parents worry about their child's feelings. Some use their power to arrange matters to their own satisfaction. Other members of the society accept that parents have this right. But whether or not parents use this right in an acceptable way, people in society tend to estimate the value of the child by the value of the parents. For example when Thong Prasi gets angry at Siprajan, she is also sarcastic about Phim.

> "You're sure, are you, Siprajan? If I'm lying, may I not live to see the sunset. I love my son and I warned him but he wouldn't listen. / He was just a youth and he fell in love—so besotted he didn't look where he was going. He pleaded with me so sincerely I was forced to follow his wishes. / Now you're going to snatch Wanthong away from Phlai. Well, I'm not a bit disappointed because with her lineage, there's nothing to be sorry about. I'm saying that because you forced me to. Enough!" (245)

The right of parents to determine the life of their children works only with daughters. Siprajan does not allow Wanthong to follow after Thong Prasi, and exercises her power to thrash Wanthong when she refuses to enter the bridal house. In the case of sons, even though they respect their mothers, they do not listen to their advice. When Khun Phaen is going to abduct Wanthong, his mother forbids him but he does not listen.

Daughters are not so afraid of their parents that they will not argue with them. Family relationships among country folk, such as those in Suphanburi, have not advanced to the point where children are truly disciplined and defer to their parents as a matter of course. Phim argues back with heated words. These passages are lively and witty compositions. Wherever the author crafts quarrels or the back and forth of conversation, the content is interesting.

An essential part of social analysis concerns social values or tastes. In *Khun Chang Khun Phaen*, there is a noticeable conflict of values. From a superficial understanding, the religion of Thai society is Buddhism. But in the tale, Buddhism is practiced only as ritual. Phlai Kaeo is ordained not to study the teachings but to study the arts of war, to become invulnerable, and even to make love charms to captivate women. The monks who are his teachers do not oppose this, but merely beg him to be socially responsible:

> His master laughed. "Young Kaeo, I know you're interested in the stuff about being a lover. Don't do damage to people's wives but old maids and widows, take them!" (61)

In this society, keeping one's word is highly valued—even more highly than upholding the precepts. Virtually all five precepts of Buddhism are violated in the tale. Taking the life of either animals or humans is not a matter of great concern, but keeping one's word is of major importance. Khun Phaen is the perfect example of a person who keeps his word. Even though he has command of lore, he will not use his powers because he has drunk the water of allegiance. His father, Khun Krai, is the same.

> "I, Khun Krai, made a mistake and paid for it with my life, / yet died with integrity in the manner of one from a line of valiant and victorious warriors." (33)

The King of Chiang Mai also keeps his word, and once Khun Phaen and Phlai Ngam understand this, they treat their enemy with great respect.

The first precept is given little thought. When Phlai Kaeo goes to stay with Muen Han, he is not bothered by the fact that Muen Han kills people at will. When Muan Han invites him to hunt a gaur, Khun Phaen gives no thought to the precepts. When Khun Phaen wants a Goldchild with special power, he splits open Buakhli's belly to take the child. When he goes to abduct Wanthong, he thinks about killing Khun Chang and is prevented only because the Goldchild warns him:

> "Hold off! Cool down. Don't kill him, Father. Don't you fear the power of the Lord of Life?" Khun Phaen ground his teeth and growled back, "No! I don't fear his power. / The wrong Khun Chang did me deserves a response this dire. I'll split open his chest with my sword. Back off and don't interfere! This is not your business. If I kill him secretly who'll catch me?" / Goldchild replied, "Don't make him die, just so hurt and ashamed that blood flows from his eyes. If you slash him dead, the gods may ensure you're arrested, and the story will spread around." (345–46)

Khun Phaen also violates the second precept on theft when he abducts Wanthong. Meanwhile Khun Chang is the character that violates the third precept on sexual conduct. Because he is a rich man, the people of Suphanburi do not seem to be bothered by this and Khun Chang continues to live comfortably there. Thai society in *Khun Chang Khun Phaen* is a society that esteems those with wealth.

Another social value is that a woman should not have two husbands. However, it seems that the woman herself is more offended than the society. The people of Suphanburi do not shun Wanthong when she becomes the wife of Khun Chang. Wanthong alone is embarrassed about her situation. When Khun Phaen finds out that she has slept with Khun Chang, Siprajan tells him,

> "Wanthong complained every day and cried her eyes out—tears as big as cowry shells. / For fifteen days she refused to go into the bridal house. She only gave up and went in two days ago—not

time for her to be worn away *that* much. Don't hold it against her. Take her back." (292)

People might argue that this passage is humorous, but a society that accepts this kind of humor has the same values as those depicted in the tale.

Khun Phaen does not hate Wanthong for becoming the wife of Khun Chang. He is angry that she slept with him as he thinks she had no faith in him. If he truly felt hatred towards her, he would not have come to spirit her away to the forest. Later, when Phlai Ngam goes to fetch Wanthong, Khun Phaen has no problem about making love with her.

Conclusion

In my judgment, the message of *Khun Chang Khun Phaen* is that Thai society is a society without principle. These are my own words. Those who contributed to the composition of *Khun Chang Khun Phaen* would not have used such words. If we could ask authors such as Khru Jaeng, King Rama II, or Sunthon Phu to explain what they were trying to portray, I suspect they would reply that they wanted to portray that human life is uncertain, that human beings cannot put faith in anything, and that the desire for revenge is useless; where there are young men and young women, there will be turmoil by the nature of things; when they grow older, the turmoil diminishes but never totally disappears as there is still carelessness of various kinds. For example, Wanthong is condemned to execution because her son abducts her from Khun Chang.

The work says something about people in our time. For me that is: a lack of principle. But is that lack of principle a good thing or a bad thing? Would we prefer to live in such a society or in a society with principle? That question remains to be considered.

THE AGGRESSION OF CHARACTERS IN *KHUN CHANG KHUN PHAEN*

Cholthira Satyawadhna

This extract is taken from *Kan nam wannakhadi wijan phaen mai baep tawan tok ma chai kap wannakhadi thai* [Application of Western methods of modern literary criticism to Thai literature], MA thesis, Department of Thai Language, Chulalongkorn University, 1970, 76–123. The thesis discusses three Western approaches to literary criticism and applies each to some Thai works. The first is the psychological approach, applied to *Khun Chang Khun Phaen*; the second is the archetypal approach, mostly associated with Robert Heilman, which is applied to several works by Sunthon Phu; and the third is the aesthetic approach, principally associated with I. A. Richards, which is applied to some classical poems and several works by Angkarn Kalayanapong.

Today, the Thai are often appreciated as a friendly people, and the country is called the "Land of Smiles." These views come from foreigners who visit Thailand, receive a good welcome from Thai people, and speak well of them in this way. The Thai are happy to be well thought of and most sincerely believe that the Thai are truly of this nature. Yet the front-page news every day, which is all about conflict, fighting, and abuse, and often includes reports of murder by grisly and peculiar methods, should make us wonder whether the Thai are really any different from any other people. All peoples are human, have a similar mental structure, and show similar behavior patterns.

Some differences certainly exist, but any honest scrutiny shows that these are inventions. Deep in the psyche, human beings of whatever ethnicity are very alike. In literature, one psychic state that is found among all peoples is the bloodthirstiness which manifests itself in waging wars. Greek and Roman mythology mostly consists of records of wars, both between the gods and between humans. Classics such as the *Mahabharata, Ramayana, Iliad, Odyssey, Taleng phai (Defeat of the Mon),* and *Ramakian* are war literature that exalts the bravery of heroes who are chiefs and kings.

The bravery shown in warfare, which involves killing or harming other people, has been analyzed by psychologists as a psychic state that is found among all peoples and is called "aggression." This aggression is present even among children and is developed through a person's lifetime. Many have speculated on the origins of aggressive behavior. For example, Charles Darwin proposed that it arose from the physiology of the individual: individuals with strong bodies and high energy levels need to release their energy, giving them an aggressive character, while weaker individuals without strong bodies are less aggressive. Psychologists such as McDougall, Scott, Frederickson, and Dollard believe that aggression is a reaction to frustration, a means to release tension in the psyche. Sigmund Freud hypothesized that aggression arose from a death instinct. Though psychologists disagree on the cause, all agree that aggressive behavior is common to all peoples of whatever ethnicity, religion, age, or era.

Berkowitz,[1] a renowned psychologist, explained aggression as an emotion that is expressed from time to time as thought, speech, or behavior in the form of anger, violence, madness, or deviance. The main purpose of this expression is to harm or destroy something. This aggression may be directed towards the environment in general, both animate and inanimate, or towards the self. Sometimes the cause of this aggressive behavior is hard to explain. One father slaps his child just two or three times with his own hand, but another beats the child

---

1. Leonard Berkowitz, *Aggression* (New York: McGraw Hill, 1962).

violently with a stick or cane for the same offense. We might assume that aggressive behavior arises from anger or hatred, and that the level of violence depends on the circumstances, environment, social situation, and stimulus. The form of aggression seen most among people of any age or gender is the expression of anger, temper, or tantrum. Some people are intent on destroying something, particularly vandalizing something of beauty. Some express aggression through madness or wanton destruction. Some are intent on physical injury of another person. Some are violent enough to commit murder. And some resort to self-injury, even to the point of committing suicide.

In some Thai literary works that are not specifically on the subject of war, such as *Khun Chang Khun Phaen*, a close study reveals that both the major and minor characters display a great deal of aggressive behavior of all the kinds described above. One common form is temper and the display of power to harm or destroy others, which is displayed by King Phanwasa of Ayutthaya, the King of Chiang Mai, commanders of conscript units, and soldiers at war.

King Phanwasa is so aggressive that his courtiers are extremely fearful. Whether or not King Phanwasa was a real figure, he is depicted throughout the tale as someone who tends to show aggression as a matter of course through displays of temper and rage. For example:

> The king raged like the heavens on fire. Not yet knowing the details, he angrily stamped his foot in the audience hall. (435)

To emphasize the king's aggression, courtiers are described throughout the tale as being greatly in fear of him.

> Guards unbolted the door. Horns were blown. Gong, drum, *shenai*, Khaek drum, and Java flute played brightly. Nobles bustled about in alarm. / Chaophraya and phraya took up their positions. Lesser people sat hidden behind screens, hushing one another to silence. Some trembled, bowed their faces, and prayed. / The curtain was swept aside. Nobles prostrated, their hearts fluttering

as if singed by the Lord of Darkness. When the king spoke, they saw he was in good humor, and they relaxed somewhat. Those with important business addressed him. (503–4)

Curtain attendants pulled back the curtain. The crowd of nobles trembled. (509)

The king's aggressive behavior accords with psychological theory. When he experiences severe frustration, his aggression rises to a level of wanting to put people to death. He commands the execution of Khun Krai for depriving him of an opportunity to hunt buffaloes, even though Khun Krai was trying to protect the king.

The king was inflamed with rage, as if a black vapor had blown across his heart. He bellowed like a thunderclap. / "Hmm! What are you up to, Khun Krai, spearing so many buffaloes? Do you mean to offend me? I saw it with my own eyes! Because of your fooling around, the buffaloes have all fled into the forest. / Heigh! Heigh! Bring the executioners here immediately. I cannot keep him. Off with his head! Stick it up on a pole and raise it high! Seize his property and his servants at once!" (32)

When Wanthong cannot decide between two men, the king's aggression is expressed as an order for her execution:

Heigh! Phraya Yommarat, execute her immediately! Cleave open her chest with an axe without mercy. Don't let her blood touch my land. / Collect it on banana leaves for feeding to dogs. If it touches the earth, the evil will linger. Execute her for all men and women to see!" Having given the order, the king returned to the palace. (801)

The King of Chiang Mai is also rather aggressive and tends to lose his temper often: "At this news, the King of Chiang Mai was as angry as if seared by fire" (167) or "The King of Chiang Mai raged like the sky on fire" (515). Whenever his intentions are frustrated, he becomes aggressive and wants to destroy or harm whatever has been the cause of his frustration. For example, when he learns that the ruler of Chiang Thong has sided with Ayutthaya, he orders his troops "to crush them on the spot" (168). And when the King of Lanchang decides to present the princess Soithong to Ayutthaya, he announces "I'll attack the city of Lanchang and leave not even one blade of grass standing" (515).

Whenever an army is conscripted, the authors of *Khun Chang Khun Phaen* describe the scene of overseers or army officers showing aggression towards the conscripts by whipping and beating them violently: "Some ached and collapsed with exhaustion, but overseers beat them back to work. . . . Some were so tired they stopped work and fell asleep snoring, but woke with a loud thwack on the rear from a unit head. . . . Supervisors kept strict watch, handing each person a blow or two" (30), and "The lords and chiefs set about conscripting troops. They beat, bribed, and badgered people into the army" (168).

Such aggressive behavior appears whenever there is a war. The victors inflict violence on the vanquished, who are unable to defend themselves. One example occurs when the Chiang Mai troops defeat Chiang Thong.

> When [the Chiang Mai troops] reached the region of Chiang Thong, the villagers trembled like stricken fish. They did not wait to show their faces but closed up their doors and windows, and scattered in panic into the forest. / Neither big villages nor small put up any resistance. People hid, or scrambled and staggered away in flight. The Chiang Mai troops gave chase, shooting the villagers down to roll in the dirt. (168–69)

Apart from physical violence of this sort, sometimes the victors show their aggression by rape, pillage, and other forms of violence that cause hardship and mental anguish. When Lao prisoners are being swept down to Ayutthaya by the Thai troops, the women lament as follows:

Oh, unending misery	roaming far from home
heavy poles bending	wending through the wood
tall grass, dense thicket	papyrus clumps and reeds
grimy sweat floods down	toil and trudge ahead
eat rice with salt alone	drink sweat not water
morning meal comes	later evening meal at nightfall
can't ever stop at all	Thai bash and thrash us
can't even have a pee	they seize us for a feel
knocked flat, goods fall	trawled into the trees
hump us if they can	thump us if we flee
by the road, by the track	jig-jig, jog-jog-jog
up-down, up-down-up	heart will crack, will die. Oh! (689)

Robbers display aggressive behavior that has an element of strangeness or deviance. The thirty-five convicts who are recruited to accompany Khun Phaen to war have all been guilty of wild, violent, and aggressive behavior. Some have been convicted for acts of unusual aggression. For example, Ai-Phuk was "convicted for robbery, forcing the victims to dance a forest dance, and making I-Ma dance naked single-handed." Ai-Mi "stabbed I-Chang while she was pissing. She grimaced and fell down flat, slobbering." Ai-Pan "tied Ta-Jai and Granny Rot by the neck, and singed off all their hair." Ai-Jan "robbed Khun Siwichai and shoved a stick up his arse so he died" (551–52).

This aggression, whether on the part of King Phanwasa, the King of Chiang Mai, overseers, troops, or robbers, is not very surprising. From one perspective, it is just a function of their job, their duty, their situation, or the environment. For example, the king can command the execution of anyone because he has legitimate power to do so. He dispatches an army to invade another country because he has a duty to expand his authority and his dominion. Overseers and army officers have authority to wield power within certain limits in order to achieve a certain objective. Soldiers at war commit violence because the situation demands it. As for robbers, they may have a leaning or natural instinct towards wild, violent, and deviant behavior, or just act in such a way because their profession demands it.

Yet a significant element of this aggressive behavior in *Khun Chang Khun Phaen* seems to arise for other reasons. The characters in general, whether young or old, male or female, tend to display aggressive behavior at all times.

In the case of children, for example, when Khun Phaen, Khun Chang, Nang Phim, and their servants play together, they fall into a quarrel that ends with physical injuries. The incident suggests that a tendency to aggression is present in humans from childhood:

> Children soon turned up in a noisy crowd. Khun Chang's gang gave chase fearlessly. When they caught up with Phlai Kaeo's band, all shouted at one another, and fell to blows. / Noses were smashed. Mouths split. Blood flowed. Some ran off shaking with tears, calling out to their mothers and fathers, shouting and hitting at one another noisily. (15)

In the case of youth, Phlai Ngam, who volunteers to go to war when only fifteen years old, is described as exhibiting aggressive behavior like other characters. His rage or temper sometimes impels him to injure whoever is the cause of his frustration. For example, when Soifa and Simala quarrel, he takes the side of Simala and violently beats Soifa, showing his inability to control his temper and shocking even Simala by his behavior:

> He picked up a stick and went for her, / thwacking her so she was marked all over her back and shoulders. Soifa ran to escape in panic. "Please forgive your wife just this once." / Simala's anger turned to pity. She rushed forward and grabbed the stick. "Why are you hitting her? It'll leave marks." Soifa ran off to her inner room, / closed and bolted the door in fear, and lay down, writhing and sobbing, aching all over, weeping and wailing as if to die. (984)

Later when Phlai Ngam is infatuated with Soifa, Simala becomes the butt of his aggression instead, and his younger brother Phlai Chumphon gets beaten too:

> He took a stick and chased after her, / thwacking her all across her back. . . . [Phlai Chumphon] came up to shield Simala. Phra Wai attacked again violently, / hitting Simala repeatedly, and catching Chumphon with several strokes. (999)

In the case of young women, Wanthong, Saithong, and Laothong all display aggression through anger, quarreling, and physical violence for reasons of jealousy. In other examples, young women show even fiercer aggression. For example, Buakhli tries to kill her husband, Khun Phaen, with poison on the instigation of her father. When Soifa is expelled back to Chiang Mai, she sends Elder Khwat down to Ayutthaya to kill Phlai Chumphon.

In the case of older persons, Thepthong, Siprajan, and Thong Prasi show considerable aggression towards their sons-in-law, towards children in general, and even towards their own children. The most common of such scenes shows the aggression of a mother towards her own child. In the passage where Wanthong refuses to be married to Khun Chang, Siprajan beats, pinches, and thrashes her, and even ties up her hands for a whipping:

> Siprajan jumped up and grabbed a stick. "Your mother's clan! You've got a foul and catty mouth. I'll beat you into dust." She lurched up the stairs to the bridal house, / and hit Wanthong on the flank with a big thwack. Wanthong shrieked and turned sideways. Siprajan pinched her repeatedly, and thrashed her with the stick until the welts showed. / Wanthong asked for no forgiveness. "My husband's dead so I'll follow him. That vile Khun Chang has no more hair than a pygmy owl. I'll have nothing to do with this tribe of shiny skulls." / Siprajan pinched Wanthong's lip. "You difficult child! I'll flay your back into

stripes. He's a very rich man. He'll slap you till your teeth all fall out in a pile. / You've got a coarse tongue and a hard chin. Your words are crude and vulgar, you arrogant girl. Khun Chang is like a goldmine." She beat her back mercilessly while delivering her tirade. (233)

Siprajan told her daughter to put on a white lowercloth and white uppercloth. / Wanthong angrily refused. Siprajan smacked her back loudly. "You difficult, foulmouthed child." She wound a cloth round her. They wrestled together. Siprajan dragged her daughter by the hand. (256)

Siprajan could not tolerate her daughter's sarcasm. She hitched up her lowercloth Khmer-style and danced up and down. "Look here, Wanthong, you have a bad mouth and show no respect." She grabbed a stick and beat her many times. / . . . Siprajan grabbed a rope from the wall, tied Wanthong's hands up to the ceiling, and circled round thrashing her with the stick. (258–59)

Elder Khwat, who is over ninety years old, is still capable of aggressive moods and aggressive behavior, such as when he escapes back to Chiang Mai and reflects on the past:

He noticed the mark of the wound on his forehead where Chumphon had cut him with a saber. His anger rose immediately. "You're able, are you? Let's contest and see. / I'll go down to Ayutthaya to catch and kill you." He leapt up from the bed, tossed away the pillows, and stumbled into the kuti. (1091)

According to the understanding of Thai Buddhists, monks are supposed to have composure in their body, speech, and mind. In *Khun Chang Khun Phaen*, monks and abbots display aggressive behavior and attempt to do physical harm to other people, such as when Saithong goes to find Phlai Kaeo at the *wat* and the abbot finds out:

The abbot gnashed his gums, rolled his eyes, and quivered in anger. He got up, seized a walking stick, strode shakily over, and opened the door with a crash. / Just in time, Novice Kaeo and Saithong ducked behind a water jar. The abbot loped around, thrashing about with his stick, shouting at the top of his voice, "Damn you! Goddamn you!" / . . . "Ugh! That dog-faced novice and his ghost woman have defiled our kuti [monk's residence]." He sat down to pound some betel nut but the pestle remained motionless while he ranted until satisfied. (120)

When Siprajan asks the abbot of Wat Khae to chant at the wedding of Phlai Kaeo and Phim, the abbot mentions his own behavior, which is filled with aggression:

The abbot said, "Is she old enough to have a husband? Only last year I saw her coming to bathe, taking off her cloth, eyes red from crying. / I saw her running around the wat with a *jap-ping* [an infant's amulet] tied on her. They dashed around after one another and broke the trees. Every day I cursed them and chased after them with my walking stick. (158–59)

On the surface, Khun Chang usually appears as a weak, fainthearted, and non-combative character. But deep inside he has a streak of aggression that surfaces when the occasion or situation is conducive. For example, when Phlai Ngam grows up and develops an appearance very similar to Khun Phaen, Khun Chang wants to do him harm: "Every night he thought about killing the child" (464). When the opportunity presents itself, Khun Chang displays his aggression in a violent way:

Seeing this was a remote and quiet spot, Khun Chang hitched up his lowercloth Khmer-style, swung Phlai Ngam down with a thump onto the ground, and laid into him with kicks, punches, pokes in the stomach, slaps, and elbow jabs, delivered with loud grunts. / . . . Khun Chang thought he had crushed the child till his liver ruptured. He made a pile of elephant grass and earth to hide the body, rolled logs over the top, and sauntered home blithely enjoying the forest. (465)

These examples of aggressive behavior are committed both by people who are physically weak and those who are physically strong. Siprajan, Thong Prasi, and nonagenarian Elder Khwat are all elderly and might have grown less aggressive with age, but that is not the case. Young women like Soifa, Simala, and Buakhli are beautiful and gentle in appearance yet are more aggressive than they look. Children whose bodies are not yet fully developed still punch one another violently. Even though Khun Chang is fat and clumsy, his psyche is aggressive enough to attempt the murder of an eight-year old child. The reasons for this aggressive behavior might be hypothesized as reactions to some frustration, but in certain cases the aggression is unusually strong and so frequent that it becomes the character's normal temperament. Psychologists and anthropologists explain very credibly that early upbringing from birth to teenage contributes to constructing the personality or normal disposition of an individual. The local culture also plays a part in developing the emotional side of any individual.

Margaret Mead, currently a renowned anthropologist, explained this causation in detail in her book, *Sex and Temperament*. In one interesting passage, she describes local inhabitants in the northeast of New Guinea, a region of mountains, plains, lakes, and rivers. There are several tribes that live independently from each other, and have distinct cultures developed over a long period even though their villages are not far apart. The first village she describes belongs to the Arapesh tribe in the hills. The houses are mostly built high on cliffs with a beautiful outlook. Mead found that this tribe had a more highly developed society than others. All families were friends to all others, and they treated one another with love and a readiness for self-sacrifice and mutual assistance even though some families were of rather low status. The atmosphere in the village was quiet and peaceful. Life went on smoothly. Women and children could be alone without any fear of danger. The thinking of this tribe was that the world was like a flower garden that had to be carefully looked after in order to be at its best. Apart from lavishing attention on growing crops and keeping animals, they also lavished equal attention on bringing up children. They believed that a mother and father were equal owners of the life and spirit of their children. When a mother was giving birth, the father had to lie beside her and act as if giving birth just like the mother. All the time the child was in the care of the parents, both had equal responsibility for loving and caring for the child. Infants were cuddled. At any time they could not be cuddled, the child was placed in a cradle that was soft and warm to give the same experience. When an infant grew up and began walking, the parents still paid very close attention to guard against any mishap. A female child was betrothed at age seven or eight to a male around six years older, and went to live in her husband's family from that time onwards. The youth had the responsibility for looking after his wife very carefully from then onwards. The girl gradually got to know the husband and his family. By the time of the marriage, she could go through the ceremony without any apprehension, and feel as close to the husband's family as if it were her own. Relations between husband and wife were peaceful since they were as accustomed to each other as if they had been of the same family since childhood. These relations were passed on to their children, who were looked after well because the parents lived in love, harmony, and mutual empathy. This culture had been passed down for many generations, giving the village a peaceful atmosphere. The emotional and social development of this tribe was superior to others in the nearby area.

Only ten miles away from the Arapesh village lay a village of the Mundugumor tribe on both sides of the Yuat River. The river had a strong current that symbolized the emotional state, personality, and society so different from those of the Arapesh that it is scarcely believable. Both the males and females of the Mundugumor tribe had a very harsh and rough temperament. They often fell into arguments and quarrels and did physical harm to one another. They not only hunted people from other tribes to eat as food but often ate people of their own tribe too. An atmosphere of hatred, fear, and bloodthirstiness dominated the village. Margaret Mead believed this difference resulted from infant upbringing. She found that the outlook of this people was a key reason in shaping this personality. The women of the tribe did not want to have children because they believed children were a source of pain and hardship for them and so hated their children from birth. Children were brought up in a harsh and cold atmosphere with no displays of love or warmth, either physical or emotional. Before the child could walk, the parents would put the child in a crude and hard basket. When drinking milk from their mother's breast, the child would be held in an uncomfortable position. All the time they were growing up, they heard only rough speech or crude abuse, and were often violently beaten. The upbringing that the infant received and the social environment that the infant experienced from an early age created feelings of fear and hatred towards the world. The child gradually learned how to adjust in order to survive. Only strong children could survive through to youth. The institution of the family had little meaning in the society of this tribe. A son could become the rival of his father in competition over the same female to the point of trying to kill each other. The females of the tribe had just as aggressive a temperament as the males, and would fight one another with physical force in competition over the same male. Husbands and wives argued and quarreled violently despite the fact they already had children together.

Upbringing and environment in childhood are thus factors shaping the temperament and developing the emotions. The societies described here may be used to draw comparisons with some of the characters in *Khun Chang Khun Phaen*. For example, both Khun Phaen and Wanthong have mothers who display violent emotions through verbal abuse and physical violence. In their childhoods, Khun Phaen and Wanthong were probably brought up in this fashion.

Their childhood experience may have given them a more aggressive temperament. Khun Phaen's experience as a child having to flee from royal seizure and undergo many hardships may have shaped a sense of severe repression and a wish to display aggression towards other people when the opportunity arose or the situation was conducive. Phlai Ngam, who Khun Chang beat up as a child, may have nurtured a drastic death instinct that drove him, after he had grown up, to beat other people such as Soifa, Simala, Phlai Chumphon and Khun Chang in recrimination.

Apart from frustration and experiences that develop a sense of repression from childhood, psychologists also hypothesize that another cause of aggression is a basic psychological need. In *Khun Chang Khun Phaen*, there are many passages of aggressive behavior that do not seem to arise from any frustration and cannot be attributed to any sense of repression developed since childhood. For example, in the passage where King Phanwasa decides to "stay in the forest and round up wild buffaloes," (20) the description of the hunt displays the psychic brutality of human beings intent on killing animals:

> They set an arc of fire. / Murky dark smoke spread through the forest. Flames licked at the trees, burning them to the ground, killing cobras and turtles. / Deer, tiger, bear, boar, rabbit, and other animals had to take flight. Monkey and langur swung away from tree to tree. Throughout the forest, parrots took fright. / Scared by the forest fire and the shouts of people advancing, great numbers of wild buffaloes were seized with panic, and plunged around in all directions. (31)

The aggressive behavior of tormenting animals by hunting is similar to the psyche of people who like to shoot birds or catch fish, who like to play or watch sports like boxing, wrestling, and rugby, and who like to watch bull fighting, cockfighting, and fighting fish.

The mental state that inclines people to like such bloodthirsty things does not arise simply from a sense of frustration or repression developed since childhood. Similarly, warfare does not arise from such causes in every case. Yet the cause may be a stimulus buried in the human psyche that can be more easily expressed when frustration is cited as the cause or excuse. Many people doubt there is any such thing buried in the human psyche. Between the two world wars, Einstein wrote a letter to Freud, the renowned psychologist of that era, asking what was the cause of war. Freud replied that human beings were born with a drive to injure or destroy. Aggressive behavior was a result of this drive, which could be reduced only by releasing its power without any control imposed by mindfulness. Because of this special character, Freud called this drive an "instinct." The main objective of this instinct is to injure or destroy everything in every way in order to "reduce life to its primal state of inert matter." Freud thus coined the term "death instinct." Conversely, human beings have another instinct which fights against this death instinct by trying every possible means to sustain life. Freud called this the "life instinct." One element of this life instinct is expressed in sexual desire. The death instinct is the cause of tension in everyday life.

These two instincts struggle with each other constantly throughout life. The life instinct is generally the victor for most of the time, yet the death instinct triumphs in the end. The struggle between the two lies behind aggressive behavior. Human beings try to divert the death instinct away from themselves by committing actions against other things or other people. For this very reason, we see that all persons are eager to destroy living things. This eagerness develops gradually, as can be observed from the display of anger or brutality in everyday life. The world wars arose from diverting the instinct for self-destruction by externalizing it into action committed against others.[2] Freud added that every individual has death wishes and also murderous wishes buried in the psyche. At the same time, humans have a "pleasure principle" to manage the death instinct by diverting it away from the self onto

2. Sigmund Freud, "Why War? Letter to Professor Einstein," in *Collected Papers of Sigmund Freud*, vol. 5 (New York: Basic Books, 1959).

other people or by transforming it into something less dangerous. The sexual act is a transformation of the death instinct into something less dangerous. The operation of the pleasure principle reduces tension in the human psyche and enables the human being to survive. Hence this pleasure principle is actually a tool of the life instinct.[3]

Freud's theory seems to have some truth in it. In *Khun Chang Khun Phaen* there are many scenes of aggressive behavior where the pleasure principle tries to divert the death instinct, resulting in the aggression diminishing, or humor disrupting the display of aggression. These scenes confirm that the display of aggression is a process that helps to reduce tension in the psyche. For example, when Nai Janson raids the house of Khun Siwichai, there is a scene where the robbers release their aggression and relax by forcing Thepthong and Khun Chang to dance chicken-flapping songs while the robbers provide the music:

> "Hey, mother and child, get up and dance. If you stay still I'll belt you on the mouth. If you don't believe me, try it just once. I'll poke you with a pike butt and then you'll dance!" / Khun Chang and Nang Thepthong said, "We can't dance without a flute and drum." All the robber gang chanted a rhythm, and tootled like flutes. / Mother and son clomped around, looking forced and clumsy. The robbers said, "The boy is jiggling okay, but the mother is hopeless." "Her waist is stiff as a board." / Thepthong took fright. She jiggled and wiggled in all four directions, swaying her shoulders and bottom around to the rhythm, waving her arms clumsily like a mask-play actor so her droopy breasts swung and slapped against her body. Khun Chang jumped up and down frenetically like a big monkey. (45)

Subsequently the robbers "showed off their power by firing guns, and whooping through the woods, dropping lots of goods without bothering to pick them up" (93). Thepthong and Khun Chang then

---

3. Sigmund Freud, *Beyond the Pleasure Principle* (New York: Bantam, 1959).

went out to recover the remaining property and continued to count among the wealthy families of Suphanburi, suggesting that the robbers carried out their raids for pleasure to reduce tension according to Freud's psychological theory rather for any desire for goods and property.

The fact that virtually every character in *Khun Chang Khun Phaen* of any age and gender displays aggressive behavior shows that the death instinct plays a major role in human behavior. Most swear words, sayings, and proverbs that come from the past and are still used in everyday speech tend to have some association with death. In *Khun Chang Khun Phaen* there are many passages referring to death. For example, adults give newly married couples advice or blessings such as "Look after each other until death" (1184). The death instinct also has a major role in the behavior of Khun Phaen and Wanthong throughout the story. In a passage where each of the couple is complaining about the other lacking commitment, both refer to death, though in ways that are interestingly different. She says: "If he doesn't turn up tonight, I'll . . . *hang myself*" (136). And he says to her, "Oh Phim, how could you abandon me so easily? I'd have to *stay in the monkhood until death*, with no one else from now on . . ." (137). From the viewpoint of Freudian psychology, she has a death wish that is stronger than her life wish. She is considering self-destruction, the ending of her life. Meanwhile, he has a life wish that is stronger than his death wish. He does not contemplate self-destruction.

Yet Khun Phaen is under some influence of the death wish, and unconsciously refers to death all the time. When he places himself at the service of Muen Han, he says: "I want to live in your lair and shelter under your protection from now on. If your lordship is kind and merciful, I'll be your servant *until death*" (1182). And a little later he tells Muen Han, "I have in mind to devote myself to you *until death*, and I expect you to feed and protect me" (1187). In addition, there are many passages where Khun Phaen says he will "fight to the death," which in psychological analysis is a form of words showing that the speaker has a wish to die and also a wish to kill.

"Oh my beauty, my utmost love, now that I've come, please don't chase me away. I'm ready to *fight to the death* without a care for my own life. My jewel, please don't go on so." (103)

"Fair, gentle Phim and you are the two nearest and dearest to me. My heart is pledged and will never weaken. I'll *fight to the death*. Don't imagine my love will fade." (119)

Throughout Khun Phaen's life, his life instinct tries to divert the power of his death instinct outwards onto something or someone. For this reason we find that Khun Phaen has an aggressive temperament like other people. His aggression is sometimes expressed through anger, as a form of "displacement" in Freudian theory, sometimes through destructive behavior visited on a house pillar or an embroidered curtain, and on some occasions through actions so violent that someone is killed for reasons of either duty or emotion. Khun Phaen could be said to display every type of aggressive behavior except self-injury or self-destruction. This is clearly different from Wanthong. Her psyche is the opposite of that of Khun Phaen. Her death instinct triumphs over her life instinct. Her psyche is inclined to desire death more than survival or the destruction of others. This psyche is expressed through her thoughts, words, and deeds. She thinks about killing herself by various methods:

Really, he wanted to jump on me for fun. I was angry but it had no effect. Today I'll take a knife and *stab myself to death* to erase the shame. (99)

Night came and there was still no sign of Phlai Kaeo. "I think he's tricked me. If he doesn't turn up tonight, I'll say farewell to Saithong and *hang myself*." (136)

She constantly uses phrases about dying or killing herself:

I felt very hurt and I burst into tears. We went two rounds with me bent double and him trying to raise my head and pull the clothes off me. *I'd rather die* than go on living. (99)

I'd be afraid of being in the same house. *I might not die but my back would be dripping blood.* (103)

How will I survive sleeping alone? Who'll hug me to sleep against the cold? You used to be so close beside my body. Husband, lord, and master, *your wife will die.*" (182)

If another man asked for me, and Mother gave me over to him but he wasn't to my liking, *I'd tell her to kill me* rather than force me against my will. I wouldn't beg for mercy. (95)

"It's a pity you don't listen. *Are you going to kill me here in this field?* (97)

Phim prostrated and wai-ed Phlai Kaeo. "They're coming! Please go. They'll see us. *Do you want to kill me?* Have mercy and go quickly!" (98)

As noted above, the special nature of the death instinct is to seek ways to injure or destroy. If the life instinct triumphs, the drive to injure or destroy is diverted outside the body onto something external. But if the life instinct loses, the drive leads to self-destruction, which is the strangest form of aggression. Those who display this type of aggressive behavior tend to be people with a weak psyche, incapable of helping themselves, or people affected by something in their childhood upbringing. For instance, there are children who like to be hurt a little by hitting on the back to induce sleep,[4] a simple expression of the

---

4. Swami Satyananda Puri [Prafulla Kumar Sen], *Phet khu* [Couples' sex] (Bangkok: Thai-Bharat Cultural Lodge, 1941), 167.

death instinct. Wanthong may have been accustomed to pain since childhood. When frustration acts as a stimulus, she has to release her internal tension by causing herself to feel pain, meaning that her death instinct triumphs over her life instinct. For example, when her mother gives her to Khun Chang:

> At this, Wanthong collapsed in grief on the spot and screamed out loud, "This is not right! Beat me to death, I don't care. / When I'm born again in my next life, I've no desire to enter your womb. Not ever! Not for hundreds and thousands of eras. What kind of mother is this? / All you can see is money. It's obscene. You'd give a person to a ghost. Please kill me and let me have done with life." *She beat her chest, boxed her head, and collapsed down flat.* (233)

Challenging someone else to kill her and physically hurting herself are a form of aggressive behavior turned back against the self. When Wanthong suffers extreme frustration, such as at the point where Khun Phaen severs their relationship and threatens to kill her with his sword, she is so mentally stressed that her death instinct does its duty of overwhelming her life instinct and she attempts to relieve the mental tension by self-destruction:

> "Death is finer." She dragged over a rope, raised her hands, and prostrated three times. "In this life, I've lost you, Phlai Kaeo. / In fear of shame, I'll die and wait for you. May we meet again in the next life. Don't let Khun Chang have even a hint." She ducked behind a curtain, reached up, / grasped a pillar, and climbed onto a roof beam. With two hands, she tied the rope tightly round her neck, and let her body swing, making the roof sway. (274)

Leopold von Sacher-Masoch, an Austrian intellectual, wrote several novels describing torture, pain, and various forms of injury. He argued that all these were a form of "happiness," especially pain suffered for the sake of sexual pleasure, which he considered the ultimate happiness. His most famous novel, *Venus in Furs*, describes the deviant sexual relationship between himself and a wife named Mme Wanda von Dunajew. She inflicts pain, which he suffers to achieve the ultimate pleasure from lovemaking. The deviant behavior includes pinching, scratching, biting, and whipping. Both take pleasure from the experience. These strange goings-on exposed to public view made this book attract both extreme interest as well as widespread criticism. Psychologists such as Freud adopted the story as a case for analysis involving the death instinct. He analyzed that, in Masoch's case, the death instinct combined with the sexual instinct, which in Freud's theory was an instinct for survival, but which could not be expressed in a direct manner, probably because of the social environment or some experience in childhood, and hence rebounded back on the self. Because Masoch showed exceptional sexual deviation, Freud labeled such behavior as "masochism."[5]

Another group of psychologists argued that people with a masochistic mentality were not happy to suffer only physical pain for sexual pleasure but liked to suffer mental pain too, meaning that they liked to be abused, disparaged, and ridiculed in harsh language, especially by a spouse.[6] Maslow and Mittlemann summarized masochism as a form of sexual deviation in which only the experience of pain, torture, or shame can create pleasure and especially sexual pleasure. Verbal abuse, beating, or physical abuse heighten the emotions, and without pain lovemaking is not pleasurable. For this reason, masochists constantly seek to be harmed and tormented. They like to punish themselves, to feel wronged and shamed, and they often complain that they wish to die. They like to hurt themselves by bumping their head against a wall, pulling out their own hair, or biting their own tongue or lip. When they feel extremely frustrated, they may even injure themselves to death.

---

5. Nathaniel Thornton, *Problems in Abnormal Behavior* (Philadelphia: The Blakiston Company, 1946), 108.

6. Walter J. Coville, Timothy W. Costello, and Fabian L. Rouke, *Abnormal Psychology* (New York: Barnes and Noble Inc., 1965), 135–36.

According to the psychological theory above, Wanthong appears to have a psyche which leans somewhat in the direction of masochism. Apart from complaining that she wishes to die, she challenges others to hit, whip, or kill her, she contemplates killing herself in the future, and at one point she does indeed attempt to do so. Wanthong also behaves at many other points in ways that suggest she has this psyche. For example, sometimes prior to making love, Wanthong acts evasively by pushing, hitting, and pinching until the male resorts to force with the result that she suffers pain. This behavior accords with a masochistic drive:

"I admire your beauty and I caress you with a good heart. It was you, poor dear, who needlessly tried to escape, / and my fingernail grazed you accidentally when you swiped me away. You were shoving, pinching, and hitting out. I'm sorry you got scratched." (103)

He hugged her, kissed her, and stroked her back lovingly. "Calm down. I love you. Don't be angry." / Wanthong scratched, pinched, twisted, and squirmed. "Stop making love to me. I won't let you have me. . . ." / "I thought you said you weren't afraid of falling off [the horse]. How come you're hugging me so tight now, pinching so hard you'll leave a mark? We've reached a place to stop and rest." (367–68)

Wanthong's vacillation between Khun Phaen and Khun Chang, which results in a belief that she has two husbands, causes her to feel shame and dishonor and to appear in court several times. Yet Wanthong is able to tolerate this, to whichever side she is pulled. From one angle, shame is perhaps a device for stimulating her sexual feelings, heightening her sexual pleasure. She lives with Khun Chang for as long as fifteen years quite happily even though Khun Chang fills her with hatred and disgust. Perhaps living with someone hated is a way to release masochistic feelings. At the conclusion when she is unable to choose which of the two men she will live with, a masochistic tendency may have a part to play in the situation. A subconscious impulse may incline her psyche to seek happiness from more pain, and hence she chooses the ultimate happiness that her instinct demands: "to be put to death."

I have described various expressions of aggressive behavior by the characters throughout the story of *Khun Chang Khun Phaen*, both major and minor instances. It seems that psychology is part of almost every passage and every character in this story. The psychological factor that influences almost every character is the death instinct that directs them to behave throughout in various ways that injure or destroy other characters or themselves. The protagonist, Khun Phaen, is not excluded from this law of nature. In general we can see that he is a good character; loyal to the king to an exceptional extent; respectful towards his mother Thong Prasi, and responsive to her advice; extremely loyal and grateful to his patrons such as Phra Phichit and Busaba to the point of threatening to injure his son Phlai Ngam for failing to show them proper consideration and respect; courteous, gentlemanly, loving, and caring towards his women including Wanthong, Saithong, Laothong, and Kaeo Kiriya; kind and attentive towards animals such as his horse, Color of Mist, even going to visit him after he is released from jail and the horse is very old. Such positive qualities ensure he is a "hero in Thai literature" in every age and period, appreciated and admired more than heroes of other works.

There is evidence in the historical work, *The Testimony of the Inhabitants of the Old Capital*, that Khun Phaen may be based on a real person from the Ayutthaya era, an accomplished soldier who led an army to attack Chiang Mai successfully.[7] But Prince Damrong cautioned that there are no sources to show that Khun Phaen's life and family were anything like the story, which was probably a local folktale that was passed down by word of mouth for many generations,

---

7. See Prince Damrong's preface in *Khun Chang Khun Phaen*, 1342–45.

becoming lengthier and more elaborate over time.[8] Hence there is a problem in evaluating whether the role of Khun Phaen, especially his personal and family life, corresponds to real life or not. In general, his behavior can be analyzed by psychological theory, especially theory on aggression, as shown above. Khun Phaen expresses aggression in thought, word, and deed no less than the other characters. Indeed, Khun Phaen's aggression could be called more clear-cut and more violent than that of others. Because he has many fine and positive qualities, readers are not so aware of his violence. His aggression appears from childhood to old age, suggesting that the character may be based on a real person, and that his personal life in the tale may mostly be modeled on a true life story. Hence applying psychological analysis to every angle and aspect of Khun Phaen's character may help us to understand his temperament and disposition more fully, and to understand this literary work more deeply than before.

The authors of the tale refer to Khun Phaen in childhood as follows:

> Now to tell of Phlai Kaeo and Khun Chang. Both went out to play along with their servants. When they met, Phlai said amiably, "Let's go and buy liquor to drink together." / Phlai Kaeo took a swig. Khun Chang gulped until his head swam. (14)

This passage shows that Khun Phaen is already a practiced liquor drinker, not a fitting habit for a child of five or six. In addition, when Khun Chang, Khun Phaen, and Nang Phim play a game of "husband and wife," we can detect the sexual instincts according to Freudian psychology even in childhood:

> Phlai Kaeo made a *weird* suggestion, "Let's play at husband and wife." Khun Chang cried, "I like that!" / Phim said, "You misfit with an ugly scraped head! I won't play." Phlai Kaeo said, "Let's

---

8. See Prince Damrong's preface in *Khun Chang Khun Phaen*, 1346.

play. It's nothing. Khun Chang can be the husband. / I'll creep in and steal you from his side." (14–15)

The Thai word used for "weird" (อุตริ, *uttari*) suggests that Khun Phaen was an odd child, someone who encouraged his friends to feel their sexual instincts. Khun Phaen's experience as a child is an important key for better understanding his mental state from birth, namely that he has a death instinct whose power is diverted into aggression to injure or destroy. As his life instinct is more powerful, his aggression is diverted away from himself onto other people and things in order to reduce his internal mental tension. When Phim "lay down on the ground and baldheaded Khun Chang lay beside her, pretending to be asleep," Khun Phaen "jumped in between them, hitting Khun Chang in the middle of his bare skull" (15).

Khun Phaen has a disposition to be aggressive towards others which is a feature of every person to some degree, but in Khun Phaen is remarkable. The fight scene shows that his aggressive behavior was present even from childhood, and that it was aroused especially by sexual feelings. The vision of Phim lying beside Khun Chang seems to have immediately stimulated his sexual impulse. His sexual feelings are different from those of others in the sense that they propel him to cause harm or pain to other people, such as when he hits Khun Chang's skull in this scene. When he grows up, such behavior continues and intensifies. For example, when Wanthong has gone to live with Khun Chang, and Laothong is separated from Khun Phaen, his sexual desire propels him to consider abducting Wanthong and to prepare in advance to kill Khun Chang should he obstruct the attempt:

Now to tell of Khun Phaen, great romancer, whose famed mastery made heads bow and tremble in every city, as much in awe of him as of a fierce lion. / While asleep in his bed at midnight, he started awake with an unsettled heart. He had been sleeping alone for many days and felt randy thinking of his wife. / . . . The more I think about this, the more I'm losing my mind. This accursed

Khun Chang did all that! If I can't repay him to my satisfaction, it'd be better to die than continue living. / I'll go and kidnap my Wanthong. If Khun Chang comes after me, I'll kill him." (316)

According to psychological theory, every person displays some aggressive behavior from childhood onwards. Some children like crushing cockroaches, chasing cats, or shooting birds, and some animal-lovers will hug a cat or dog so tight that it hurts. As people grow up, such direct displays of aggression diminish, but this does not mean that the disposition has disappeared completely from the psyche. Rather, there is a substitution or "displacement" into another form, perhaps taking up an occupation that involves inflicting pain such as teacher, policeman, or jailer. Because these occupations are involved with the external world, they offer opportunities to inflict pain on others without offending against morality or social standards. For example, a teacher can beat or scold a student, a policeman can shoot or manhandle a criminal, and a jailer can whip a convict. People who displayed unusually aggressive behavior in childhood may be brutal towards people who fall under their power in the course of such duty. Khun Phaen displays aggression from childhood. When he grows up, he displaces his aggression by becoming a soldier. In the course of duty, he fights fearlessly and his ability is fitting and admirable. But Khun Phaen fights in a violent, vicious, and bloodthirsty fashion. For instance, he is capable of killing his own fellow officers. In the passage when he flees into the forest with Wanthong, King Phanwasa commands two officers to give chase:

Khun Phaen slashed masses of people until he suddenly came upon Khun Ram face to face. / Khun Ram thrust with a long pike but landed only a glancing blow on the shoulder that spun Khun Phaen around. Khun Phaen lunged forward into the fray, and slashed Khun Ram down from his elephant onto the ground. / Khun Phaen leapt down from his horse, and hacked Khun Ram's shoulder, felling him, doubled over. Khun Phaen slashed again, and Khun Ram tumbled forward, convulsed, and died in a pool of blood. "One down, you meddler!" / Khun Phetinthra came to help with his pike raised in challenge. He thrust into Khun Phaen's chest but it was as impenetrable as iron or diamond. / Khun Phaen leapt onto the elephant and swung at Khun Phet's neck, which severed like a plucked flower, staining Khun Phaen's sword red with blood. He remounted his horse and galloped into the thick of the army. (406–7)

In the campaign against Chiang Mai, in order to take their clothing as disguise for infiltrating the city, Khun Phaen kills a Lao father and son who are walking along a road singing happily.

Khun Phaen slashed and Phlai Ngam struck. The heads of the Lao father and son were lopped off, and blood spurted from the necks in a torrent as they fell to the ground dead, / eyes rolled up, faces blanched, and blood streaming out. Khun Phaen and Phlai Ngam were pleased as could be. (610)

From one angle, Khun Phaen simply wants to do his duty, which is normal in warfare. Yet it is significant that when he has killed them, seen the pool of blood, and seen them writhing in the throes of death, Khun Phaen is "pleased as could be." This feeling may be interpreted as an unconscious show of happiness or jubilation following the needs of his death instinct.

Apart from these displays of aggressive behavior as a warrior, Khun Phaen has many others as a husband experiencing frustration, such as displays of temper:

"I hate Khun Chang so much I could writhe to death. He gets his way so often it's become a habit. / He dragged Wanthong off to partner and possess. Because I've given my word that I won't escape, he thinks I can't cut his head off. Now he's tried to kill my son like an ox or horse. Does the villain think I'm scared of him? / This evening I must go to his house and chop his head so the blood flows. A man dies where he dies." He gnashed his teeth and worked himself up into an aggressive rage. (481)

"If Wanthong is sleeping with him, I'll slash both their throats, / and those of Siprajan and Thepthong too. They were involved and I won't let them live. I'll treat them like dogs with crooked tails, as they deserve. Those old ladies who asked for her hand too." (282)

I'm known as an able person. Tomorrow I'll go to Suphan, / split open his chest to secure my revenge, and kidnap Wanthong away into the forest." With this thought he leapt up in excitement . . . (330)

His aggression is expressed not only in thought, but also sometimes by committing violence against someone or something:

He kicked them off the bed, one after the other. "Why should I let you live?" / He raised his sword to cut them in two . . . (283)

Khun Phaen punched, elbowed, and kicked Khun Chang away, then stood shielding her. (438)

"You're going to die, Wanthong. You cannot live." He drew his sword, raised it to strike, and stamped his foot on the boat. "I'll grasp you by the hair and cut you dead!" (273)

As he admired the scene, he thought of Wanthong, / and slashed the curtain to ribbons. . . . / In rage, he cut down the curtain, ripped it to shreds, and tossed it aside. / . . . Looking at the curtain, his heart raged like a roaring fire. Suddenly he raised Skystorm, slashed the curtain to ribbons, / and chopped it into a heap of hundreds of shreds. (344–45)

Khun Phaen also displays aggressive behavior even when he is old enough for his two sons to be fully grown. When he gets angry at Phlai Ngam for mistreating Simala, he loses his temper and shows aggression towards his son:

> Khun Phaen was extraordinarily angry. "Hey, Wai! Come here and fight with me. / I'm no longer your father. That's final. Though I'm old, I'm not afraid. Dead or alive, for better or worse, I'll slash you—and your stupid wife too. Watch out. / Where are you hiding up there?" He picked up lumps of brick and hurled them to clatter against the bedroom, several times over. Phra Wai stayed inside the apartment and kept perfectly quiet. (1026)

Most interestingly, Khun Phaen's aggression is rather violent. He even concocts a plan with Phlai Chumphon to kill Phlai Ngam, his own son:

> "The fact that you made a giant figure to send to me shows that you have powers and knowledge. Please make soldier dummies, disguised as New Mon, and send them down here. / Have them charge down and invest Doembang, which is not far from Suphan. The news will spread to Ayutthaya. King Phanwasa will probably send Wai to do battle, / and will probably recruit me to go along to help him. You and I can cooperate to attack Wai in a pincer, and slash him to pieces. Then you escape back to the north." (1031)

When Phlai Chumphon comes in disguise as planned, King Phanwasa does indeed send Phlai Ngam out to fight him and Khun Phaen does follow the plan to kill him, but Phlai Ngam survives:

> As enraged as if struck by lightning, Khun Phaen spurred his horse to race forward like a windmill, shouting out from a distance, "Hold him tightly, Chumphon! I'll slash him myself!" / Phra Wai looked up and saw his father. In fright, he released

his brother's neck, and leapt onto his horse to escape, but lost his balance, and Chumphon stabbed at him. / The pike hit his chest but broke without piercing. Phra Wai rode his horse away. Khun Phaen furiously charged in from an angle.... / ... Phra Wai rode his horse straight across the plain—face drawn, hungry, aching, and out of breath—and went straight across the river at Wat Thamma. / People who saw him ran away in shock, crying, "Catastrophe!" "We're dead for sure!" "Phra Wai's army is routed!" The whole city was seized with fear. / ... Phra Wai dismounted and entered. / He prostrated, shaking with fear, hungry, aching, and with face drawn. He waited in silence without saying anything. / ... "Their army chief and I fought one on one, slashing and chopping at each other many times at close range. I did not realize it was my own brother, Phlai Chumphon, until I saw Khun Phaen race out. / He called for Chumphon to capture me. My father intended to slash me dead. I managed to get away alive but I can't escape royal authority." (1051–52)

From these examples of his behavior, Khun Phaen could be called a very aggressive person, indeed quite terrible. The fact that Phlai Ngam is so fearful shows that he knows full well that his father is quite capable of killing his own son. The son of someone else might not show such fear in the knowledge that a father would not be so condemnatory and vindictive towards a son. Although Khun Phaen is a good person with many fine qualities, he also has a disposition to be aggressive at all times. From one angle, he has a complex character like ordinary people in real life who have both good and bad sides. In Freudian terms, Khun Phaen's superego has a considerable influence on his life. His loyalty to the king, his sense of gratitude, his gentleness, and his gallantry all make him a character that is generally admired. But he lacks self-restraint and often allows his emotions or baser instincts to dominate his psyche. He thus behaves in various aggressive ways on the impulse of instinct without any ability to impose control. In psychological terms, his id dominates his ego and his superego.

The same is true in matters concerning sex. Khun Phaen's sexual instinct is sometimes expressed without self-restraint. Even when he is wearing a novice's robe, he chases women, such as the case of Saithong. Other examples could be understood more clearly through psychological analysis. In Freudian analysis, the terms "sexual instinct," "life instinct," and "libido" have a similar meaning, that is, a sexual desire to create a living thing or to go on living for some time, with a mechanism to reduce tension in the psyche in line with the pleasure principle. These instincts fight against another type of instinct, namely the death instinct. In some such struggles, the sexual instinct combines with the death instinct that seeks to harm and destroy, resulting in sexual perversion. If the death instinct triumphs, this sexual perversion rebounds against the self, resulting in masochism or pain inflicted on the self for sexual pleasure, as noted above. But if the life instinct triumphs, the sexual perversion is directed outward against others, especially those of the opposite sex, causing pain and torment to the other for the sexual pleasure of the self.

The example of such perverse behavior is de Sade (Donatien Alphonse François de Sade), known as the Marquis de Sade, a French intellectual. De Sade served as a soldier for a time, and later was jailed many times for crimes including murder. While in the Bastille prison, he wrote several plays and novels including *Justine* (1791) and *Juliette* (1798) which are about the sexual deviation of inflicting pain on others for the sexual pleasure of the self. De Sade described this behavior very clearly since he shared this disposition in an intense form. Subsequently he was confined in a mental hospital where he died.[9]

Freud took de Sade's name to describe this deviant mental state as sadism. In general terms, a sadist is someone who derives the greatest pleasure by inflicting extreme pain on the partner during lovemaking. Pain may be inflicted by whipping, pinching, hitting, scratching, biting, and so on. Some psychologists include using verbal violence

9. Thornton, *Problems in Abnormal Behavior*, 106.

on the partner as well.[10] Some people gain satisfaction by inflicting physical and mental pain on the partner at the same time. If this deviation takes an extreme form, it becomes almost a mental illness, as found among disturbed serial rapists and those who murder and dismember their victims. As a major feature of sadism is the liking of the sight of blood, it may lead to bizarre forms of murder such as disembowelment, cutting out the heart, liver, kidneys, and so on. All stem from the sexual deviation of sadism. This deviant emotion can appear at any age from childhood to old age. It may first appear in a weak form such as tormenting animals and gradually become more intense by stages until it finally involves taking life.

As noted above, Khun Phaen tends to display aggressive behavior often as a result of the redirection and externalization of the power of his death instinct. At the same time, his well-known sexual license shows that he has a very strong sexual instinct. According to Freudian psychological theory, if these two instincts combine, his destructiveness and his sexual feelings will find expression in various kinds of behavior associated with his love life. For example, Phim complains:

> "*Tugging at my clothing* with your *heavy hands* is so rude. Having such a fine fellow as a husband, I'd be afraid of being in the same house. I might not die but my back would be dripping blood. / *Just grabbing my hand or holding my arm, you hurt me.* You've got *sharp fingernails that draw blood.* Just teasing, you leave *lots of scratches.* Please go away at once. I don't care for you." (103)

Her words may contain some truth. She may be complaining from the heart that Khun Phaen has "heavy hands" that "hurt me" to the extent that she fears "lots of scratches" and her back "dripping blood." This shows that Khun Phaen inflicts pain on her as part of showing his love. He has "sharp fingernails," nails so long that he can inflict pain and draw blood. Interestingly, when she feels maltreated, she threatens

10. Thornton, *Problems in Abnormal Behavior,* 107–8.

him, "However much I pinch, you don't hurt. If you grab with your fingernails, I'll break them clean off," and he replies, "Breaking my fingernails shows you don't really love me. Even with one *chang* of money, you can't find love equal to that fingernail." (104) Khun Phaen's reply is problematic. Why does he love his fingernail so much that he allows other parts of his body to be damaged but not the fingernail, which he states has a value of over one *chang*, a large sum of money at that time? Up to this point in the story, Khun Phaen has not used his "heavy hands" to "hurt" any other partner, only Phim. With Saithong, Phim's maid, he behaves in a similar way:

> "Pretending it was accidental, he touched her breast. When she did not react, he grasped with his full hand." (136)

When Khun Phaen inflicts pain on Saithong, she complains in an odd way:

> "Are you really so insistent? Do you want to raise a scandal all over the house, sir? I've talked to you nicely, but you still pester me. I don't know what to do. Here, I'll scratch you so it shows, right now! / Oh, who would want to be in my place? All this pinching and teasing is uncouth and shameful." (142)

This passage shows that he hurts Saithong by pinching and teasing, namely by using his fingernails as in the case with Phim. However, as noted above, Khun Phaen has a complex character with both good and bad sides. By the same token, in love scenes he displays both violence at times but also gentleness at other times, and he can be very caring, for example:

> Phlai Kaeo smiled. "Darling Phim, they [her breasts] rise and shine at the touch of moonlight. Let me wash you to feel good. I won't be rough on your skin but soft as a spider's web." / Phim sat close to him with a smile and stretched out her arms. Phlai

Kaeo hugged her tightly to him and caressed her gently with his hand. (138)

With these thoughts, he stepped down from the bed and tiptoed slowly away, glancing around. At the sound and tremor of his footfalls, Phim turned over. He edged back to her side, / hugged her close to his chest, rocked her back and forth, and cradled her back to sleep. "Don't you want to nap, Phim? Though we did it until the sweat flowed, still you don't sleep." / He opened a sandalwood fan and fanned her. "Relax and have some rest, dear Phim." (140–41)

He edged up next to her and lightly touched her breast without pressing hard. / They embraced and lay down side by side on the bed. He kissed her head very gently, and hugged her tightly against his chest. (142)

These actions are clearly mutually conflicting yet they are the actions of one single individual and may be reconciled in psychological theory. His caring and gentleness are expressions of love made deliberately with full awareness. But his violent teasing that causes pain to the partner is done unconsciously, performed at the dictate of instincts buried deep in the psyche to inflict damage. Perhaps this disposition arises from a combination of his death instinct and his sexual instinct. In particular, when Khun Phaen hurts his partner by pinching or scratching with his fingernails enough to leave marks and sometimes to draw blood, it appears that he has a mental disposition to show his love in deviant ways, by inflicting pain on the other to achieve the sexual satisfaction of the self, similar to sadistic sexual deviation. From this point in the story forwards, Khun Phaen's mental deviation increases. This may occur because he has the opportunity to go to war, and causes the death of many people. After the war is over, he may still have the desire to kill or injure people at the behest of his internal instincts. His aggressive behavior increases. He carries a sword that he brandishes and threatens to kill Wanthong, but luckily she is able to flee inside her house. His psychic state, stimulated by mental frustration, has an opportunity to give full expression to his instinct for aggression. He calms down for a few days but then becomes more violent again and returns to find Wanthong at Khun Chang's house. He splinters a pillar of the house with a knife as a sign of his aggression, and then slashes a curtain. When he sees the pair sleeping together, he kicks them off the bed and "raised his sword to cut them in two" (283). But the working of the ego following the pleasure principle restrains the badness of the id and diverts his desire to kill. He modulates his violence into a wish to inflict "shame" on the other side instead, a clear result of the operation of the pleasure principle. At the same time, his action can still be interpreted as a symptom of sadism because he has the intention to inflict mental pain on others:

> He pulled a cord out from a curtain. "Although I've decided not to put you to death, you'll still get what you deserve, you scourge. I'll fix you with this rope." / With his foot, he pushed the two of them together, and wound the rope tight around their prone bodies. He trussed them with lengths of the rope, tightened the bonds with splints, and tossed the end of the rope up onto the roof. / Then he wrapped them in cloth like a corpse. "Tcha! You vile lot, that's what you deserve." (284)

His actions cause Wanthong to feel ashamed, giving Khun Phaen satisfaction. He leaves the room and summons other people to gather outside Khun Chang's room and calls on Khun Chang and Wanthong to come out, which they cannot do as they are tied up:

> Wanthong recognized her husband's voice and shivered in growing panic. With the two of them tied together, she felt helpless, and was too ashamed to call out. (286)

Later, after Laothong has been taken away into the palace and Khun Phaen is ordered by the king to patrol the forest, Khun Phaen experiences great mental anguish because he has no opportunity to release his sexual feelings at the behest of his life instinct and no opportunity to express his aggressive desire to cause damage at the behest of his death instinct. He thus travels through the forest with the intention to "forge a sword, buy a horse, and find a spirit son" (316). Searching for these three devices of destruction may be analyzed in psychological theory as a substitution for the feeling of hatred provoked by his lack of opportunity to express aggression through violence. During the search, as frustration intensifies in his psyche, his mental state becomes aggressively destructive to an unusual extent, as in this description of his mood:

> In search of what he needed, he delved into every nook and cranny, passing through villages of Karen, Kha, Lawa, and Mon, and sleeping along passes through the mountains. (317)

While he is blundering around the forest in an unusual state of mind, he comes across Buakhli. In terms of psychological analysis, Buakhli is an individual who has great meaning for Khun Phaen, because he is experiencing intense frustration both in his work, which means his future in royal service, and in his love life, which also means his future. When Khun Phanwasa was angered by his petition for the release of Laothong, Khun Phaen was reduced to patrolling the forest, a post with no rank or significance that he may hold forever with no end in sight. In his love life, the future means the descendants he should have with either Wanthong or Laothong to carry on his lineage, but he is not living with either wife. This is thus a period of great frustration for Khun Phaen. When he meets Buakhli, he invests all his hope in her. They get married and live together until she becomes pregnant. He grows happier because his former frustrations can now be repressed in his subconscious. This significance of Buakhli is the reason why she must be killed. Her attempt to poison Khun Phaen triggers the frustration buried in his subconscious to burst out. He kills her in a mixture of love and hatred, stabbing her chest and then slicing open her belly to take the infant from her womb. Some psychologists propose that the sadistic sexual deviation of hurting can become violent to the point of murder, because love and hatred coexist in the subconscious. Because of this unconscious ambivalence towards the sexual partner, the expression of love and pain become associated.[11]

Before the murder, Khun Phaen expresses his love for Buakhli for the last time:

> He embraced, fondled, and aroused her. Buakhli was not at all dismayed. He hugged her tightly, kissed, and caressed her so that she trusted him completely. (1192)

His behavior prior to the murder suggests that Khun Phaen kills her in an ambivalence of hatred and love. The passage shows the conflict between love and hate in his psyche:

> Late at night when everyone was sleeping quietly, he blew a Subduer formula to immobilize people, and got up to get things ready. / He hastily put his devices, three candles, a flint box, sacred thread, and yantra cloths in a sidebag. / He grasped a tooled knife with a coral handle, and went straight to Buakhli. He parted the curtains and turned up the mosquito net. The lamp shed a dim light. / He stood up on the bed beside her and examined her sleeping form with a great sigh. "I didn't know such a body could have no heart. That she could kill her husband is unthinkable." / He raised the knife to strike but felt a pang in his heart, changed his mind, and relaxed his arm. Then he thought again about her giving him the poison. "Don't hesitate! Take her life." (1193)

---

11.   Coville et al., *Abnormal Psychology*, 135–36.

Eventually hatred, frustration, and especially the desire to inflict harm arising from the death instinct, join forces in an outward display of violent aggression:

> He plunged the knife into her chest, piercing right through. She writhed and died. Red blood spurted out and spread all around like the killing of a buffalo. (1193)

However this violently aggressive behavior does not end with Buakhli's death, because the main point of Khun Phaen's frustration is in Buakhli's womb. He has wanted a son for some time. From his first meeting with Buakhli, he hoped to have a son with her:

> He saw Buakhli in the shelter. She was just of age, with an eye-catching slight figure, beautiful fair complexion, and attractive bearing. / His heart skipped a beat in sheer delight. Some merit drew him strongly to her. He set his heart to fall in love, and wanted her as his partner. / On looking at her closely, he saw that she fitted the requirements of the manual in every way. If they were to have a first child together, he would certainly get the son he wanted. (1176)

When she dies, the child he wants is still in her womb. Driven by the power of his long-standing subconscious desire to have a child, Khun Phaen behaves in a rather deviant and aggressive way:

> He cut her belly wide open, and severed the umbilical cord. Examining the baby, he was happy to find it was the male he wanted. / He lifted the infant out of her belly. "Come, my Goldchild. Go with your father." He picked up his big sidebag and hung it round his neck. He wrapped the son in a cloth, and slung him on his shoulder. (1193)

In the next scene, he "roasts the Goldchild." The image of Khun Phaen sitting and roasting the Goldchild in an old *wat*, in the bright red light of candles, with the sound of fat dripping from the body to hiss in the fire as he turns the body over and back until it is seared dry, is a frightful, hair-raising scene, whether viewed through a lens of astrology or common sense.

> Opening the door, he walked quickly away from the village through the forest to Wat Tai. He closed the door of the preaching hall, shot the bolt inside, and inserted battens to secure it tight. / He put down the sidebag and took out his flint box to strike a flame and light candles. He stuck pieces of victoriflora wood in the ground to make a frame on which to lay the Goldchild. / He put a yantra cloth with a Narayana design of mighty power over his head, another with a Racha design on his lower body, another with Narai Ripping the Chest on his middle, and one with Nang Thorani on the ground. / He drove amora wood into the earth as pillars of the four directions, attached more yantra cloths as flags, and circled them with sacred thread. As a canopy he put a cloth with the design of Indra's breast chain. Everything was prepared according to the manual. / To light a fire on the ground below, he made a bundle of goodwood, armorbark, and shieldvine. He meditated to focus his mind, and sat grilling the Goldchild, / heating the whole body, turning it over front and back so the fat dripped and sizzled. Just as the dawn brightened and a golden sun rose, it was dry and crisp as he wanted. (1194)

Khun Phaen's behavior in killing Buakhli and roasting the Goldchild is a *saiyasat* rite following an old belief. General readers may think that Khun Phaen does nothing unusual as he is merely acting on an ancient belief; the killing by slicing open her belly and lifting the infant out of the womb is not an act of brutality because, as the description of the roasting recounts, "Everything was prepared according to the manual." But from the angle of psychological theory, the perpetrator of such an act is not in a normal state of mind. What stimulated Khun Phaen to kill Buakhli was the frustration that arose when Buakhli acted disloyally by trying to poison him at the behest of her father. This action created acute tension in Khun Phaen's psyche. His mental state thus was seeking some means to lessen or ease this tension through the operation of the pleasure principle. Since childhood Khun Phaen had found that he could ease his own mental tension by hurtful or destructive actions to inflict pain on others. In this instance, the tension in Khun Phaen's mind was extreme, perhaps the most extreme he had ever experienced. The destructive or hurtful behavior needed to reduce this tension was thus more violent than at other times. In addition to his desire for a son, Buakhli's disloyalty has stimulated the frustration in his subconscious to an exploding point. Khun Phaen thus behaves following the desire of his instincts without any self-restraint. The sexual deviation in his psyche that was explored above perhaps also contributed to Khun Phaen becoming a murderer of unusual brutality. Perhaps his death instinct was aroused by his intense frustration, creating a mental deviation for a time.

However, as the cause of his frustration goes back to Wanthong, his aggressively destructive behavior continues. He breaks into Khun Chang's house, takes Kaeo Kiriya, enters the room where Khun Chang is sleeping with Wanthong, and slashes three curtains to shreds. On the sight of the couple sleeping together, he repeatedly raises his sword to slash them, but is checked each time by Goldchild:

> He raised his sword. "Lay bare his neck. I'll slice it to pieces!" /
> Goldchild intercepted the sword, and then prostrated in apology.
> Growing ever angrier, Khun Phaen kicked Goldchild off the bed,
> but the spirit came between them and would not yield. / "Hold
> off! Cool down. Don't kill him, Father. Don't you fear the power
> of the Lord of Life?" Khun Phaen ground his teeth and growled
> back, "No! I don't fear his power. / The wrong Khun Chang did
> me deserves a response this dire. I'll split open his chest with my
> sword. Back off and don't interfere! This is not your business. If

I kill him secretly who'll catch me?" / Goldchild replied, "Don't make him die, just so hurt and ashamed that blood flows from his eyes. If you slash him dead, the gods may ensure you're arrested, and the story will spread around." (345–46)

The role of Goldchild here, if analyzed in the light of psychological theory, seems to represent the operation of the ego, which controls the instinctive desires of the id. The destructively aggressive behavior to destroy or injure other people, which is a symptom of a deviant mental state, is soothed by the sight of the child that Khun Phaen has taken from Buakhli's womb. The extreme act of killing his own wife by slicing open her belly and seeing his own child diminishes Khun Phaen's frustration and momentary sexual deviation. Hence the Goldchild is a symbol of his self-awareness or his realization of good and bad, right and wrong. After Khun Phaen has acted badly on the impulse of his id from his deviant subconscious psyche, the Goldchild appears in front of his face to forbid him from unconsciously doing anything else. The exchanges between Khun Phaen and Goldchild in this passage metaphorically represent the struggle of his conscience or superego that controls the ego to triumph over the unconscious evil-doing of the id. The superego gains a partial victory, terminating Khun Phaen's intention to kill, but he remains partly under the power of the id, which is under the direction of both the death instinct and the life instinct. His need to display aggressively destructive behavior is still present in his mind, but is diverted into making Khun Chang "just so hurt and ashamed that blood flows from his eyes." His sadistic tendency to inflict pain or shame on others still has a role in Khun Phaen's behavior in this passage, and it continues to appear throughout the story. He abducts Wanthong in order to hurt Khun Chang and to inflict both mental and physical torment on Wanthong by making her face hardship as a vagrant in the forest for a year. He makes Wanthong feel ashamed that she is batted back and forth between the two men. All the time they are together, Khun Phaen repeatedly speaks to her sarcastically about the past. When he is in jail, his aggression to inflict pain on others does not diminish. He goes on a rampage, injuring the warders until they are subdued and fearful. When he leaves jail, he goes to war against Chiang Mai and brutally kills two Lao peasants. At the conclusion of the story, Khun Phaen still displays deviant aggressive behavior by being brutal and callous enough to plan the killing of his own son, as discussed above.

The examples presented here lead to a conclusion that virtually every character in *Khun Chang Khun Phaen* has subconscious aggression buried in the deep portion of the psyche. This aggression finds expression as thought, word, and deed in many forms according to the situation, circumstances, and the pressure of experience from childhood. The aggression of the principal characters, Wanthong and Khun Phaen, can be clarified by psychological theory. Wanthong's aggression is expressed through self-injury or self-destruction. Some of her behavior appears to have an element of sexual deviation combined with this aggression, resulting in a masochistic desire to inflict pain on the self to attain sexual pleasure. Compared to other characters, Khun Phaen has a more intense form of aggression that is directed towards harming or destroying external things. Many aspects of his behavior suggest his aggression is combined with a sadistic sexual deviation of attaining sexual pleasure by inflicting pain on the partner. Both Khun Phaen and Wanthong have rather deviant psyches that dictate extremely aggressive behavior. One of them commits the murder of a woman with a child near to delivery. The other tries to kill herself and acts in ways that result in her own death.

This essay has applied Freudian psychological theory to analyze the temperament and behavior of literary characters. Classic literature created for public entertainment, such as *Khun Chang Khun Phaen,* deserves to be highly valued. It provides a detailed and multifaceted record of the roles, behavior, and temperament of the characters that can be analyzed and clarified by psychological theory. This literature is of a realistic nature. The fact that its content is susceptible to psychological theory, as demonstrated here, suggests that the characters in *Khun*

Chang Khun Phaen, especially Khun Phaen and Wanthong, may have been based on a true-life couple. This argument provides support for Prince Damrong's suggestion, based on historical analysis, that Khun Phaen was a prominent soldier of rare ability who led an army to war against Chiang Mai and gained victory to the satisfaction of the king. In addition, psychological analysis can explain some of the characters' behavior that earlier studies have found to be puzzling or irrational. For example, Khun Phaen's killing of Buakhli and creation of the Goldchild are usually explained simply as an ancient practice, but analysis based on psychological theory suggests that the creator of this passage was someone with a mental inclination towards destructive aggression and the sadistic sexual deviation of liking to inflict severe pain on the opposite sex. The scene must have been created and passed down by people of a similar mentality, because someone with a normal state of mind would not be aggressive to the point of killing his own wife and child.

Applying psychological analysis to reveal the profound mental state of the characters in this way may give rise to a misunderstanding that such analysis destroys the literary value of a work. But in the writer's opinion, this approach and analysis does not destroy its literary value but helps to bring out its value from another angle. The authors, editors, and compilers of *Khun Chang Khun Phaen* collectively had the literary skills and artistic understanding to create an example of literary excellence that has survived down through later generations. The excellence of the work lies not only in the well-known qualities of its poetry, its didactic value, and its capacity to entertain, but also in the fine-grained detail of its plot and characterization. Consistently from start to finish, the characters behave realistically, in keeping with their mental disposition. Though *Khun Chang Khun Phaen* is the handiwork of many authors, there is a harmony of every word, verse, and passage. For example, Khun Phaen is shown to have an outwardly directed aggressive temperament from childhood through to old age. The plot is realistic in nature because aggression is a mental state that humans have from birth. Society and environment help to develop that aggression and to redirect, divert, reduce, or increase its power, but its origin stems from the instincts in the human psyche that subconsciously dictate various forms of human behavior. Hence, this critique of aggression in the characters of *Khun Chang Khun Phaen* does not destroy the literary value of the work but highlights a truth that many may not grasp, in the same way that humans in general may not be aware of the truth that aggression, bloodthirstiness, and the desire for death are buried in the psyche of every human being of any race or language without limitation of age or gender.

KHUN CHANG KHUN PHAEN AND THE MORAL LANDSCAPE OF THE *THREE WORLDS* COSMOLOGY

Warunee Osatharom

This chapter is shortened from two articles: "Krung lae mueang nai rueang lao nangsue kham klon sepha Khun Chang Khun Phaen: Phumithat lae kan sue khwam mai mahanakhon lae nakhon chonabot nai Traiphum" [Capital and city in *Khun Chang Khun Phaen*: Landscape and the communication of great cities and provincial towns in the Three Worlds], *Thai khadi sueksa* [The journal of the Thai Khadi Research Institute] 8, 1 (October 2010–March 2011): 89–181; and "Nakhon chonabot mueang thongthin nai thana phuenthi thang sangkhom jak kan sueksa nangsue kham klon sepha khun chang khun phaen chabap phim" [Rural places and localities as social space from the study of the printed edition of *Khun Chang Khun Phaen*], in *Ruam botkhwam nak wijai sathaban thai khadi sueksa nai wara 42 pi* [Collected articles of researchers of the Thai Khadi Research Institute for the 42nd year], Bangkok: Thai Khadi Research Institute, 2012, 1–45.

Khun Chang Khun Phaen[1] is a literary work in verse from the early Bangkok era that has had lasting popularity down to the present day. Extracts are still found in secondary school textbooks on the Thai language, and the story has been adapted as novel, film, and cartoon.

---

1. Throughout this article, *Khun Chang Khun Phaen* means the standard printed "library edition" of the story, edited by Prince Damrong Rajanubhab and first printed in 1917.

Because the work has many realistic details on everyday life, it is often classified as folk literature and studied as evidence on the society and culture of its time. Much less attention has been given to studying the meanings that are buried in the plot of the work and elements used in the structure of the story. One striking feature of this construction is the realistic and detailed geography of Siam that forms the setting for the tale.

In this article, I argue that the plot and characterization of *Khun Chang Khun Phaen* are designed to convey a Buddhist morality that was a key part of the ideology of the early Bangkok state. This morality is found in several works of the time including recensions of the Three Worlds cosmology, a genre of didactic literature, and most strikingly in the design and decoration of Wat Phra Chetuphon Wimon Mangkhalararm (Wat Pho). One technique that is shared between *Khun Chang Khun Phaen* and works based on the Three Worlds cosmology is the use of geography or landscape to ground moral teaching in the real world and everyday life.

Khun Chang Khun Phaen: From oral tradition to written work of court literature

Most poetical works from the First to the Third Reign of the Bangkok era (that is, from 1782 to 1851) were in the form of *nirat* travel odes, *jataka* tales, collections of moral sayings, and stories in which the leading character is a king or high noble. In only two works are the central characters ordinary people: *Raden landai* (a satirical spoof of court literature) and *Khun Chang Khun Phaen*.

Khun Chang Khun Phaen originated from a folk tale passed on by recitation. Prince Damrong Rajanubhab speculated that the folk tale was based on a true story, known in the Suphanburi region. In the early nineteenth century, two writers, Sunthon Phu and Nai Mi, traveled to Suphanburi and recorded the local people's assertion that the main characters of the tale, Khun Chang, Khun Phaen, and Phim/

Wanthong, were local people who had lived in the area. Sunthon Phu named several wat on the west bank of the river including Wat Phrarup, Wat Pratusan, and Wat Takrai. He stated that the homes of Khun Chang and Nang Phim were in this area, while the family of Khun Phaen lived around Wat Khae. He reported that local people, who believed that Suphanburi was the birthplace of these characters, had pointed out these places to him.

Possibly Prince Damrong's speculation that the work was based on a true story came from this knowledge. However, Prince Damrong believed that the Ayutthaya version of the tale had disappeared and been rewritten from the Second Reign (from 1809 to 1824) onwards for recitation during the royal hair-cutting ceremony at court. At this point of the tale's transition to written literature, the poets may have inserted events, customs, and facets of everyday life into the story, in order, as Prince Damrong notes, to make it "appear realistic" (1354), that is, real for the early Bangkok era.

One key aspect of this realism is that the names of towns, villagers, and routes of travel in the tale correctly match those on the map. The routes are described in great detail, including landmarks passed and time taken. Prince Damrong himself "once tracked down the various places referred to in the *sepha* and found that most are correct." He concluded that the authors "had to know a certain amount of geography" (1354). Readers can follow the routes today. These place names were probably inserted at the point when the oral version was converted into written literature. If so, the insertion of these names must have had a purpose.

Khun Chang Khun Phaen is thus not only the only work of court literature whose main characters are ordinary people, but also the only work where the events and characters are set into a landscape of Siam in the Ayutthaya era, including the capital city and several other towns. Although the tale is set in the Ayutthaya era, this setting belongs to the early Bangkok era when the work was written down. The court intended that the places should convey a certain meaning.

The landscape of *Khun Chang Khun Phaen*

The towns mentioned in the tale can be classified into principal and secondary towns as follows. The principal towns are those associated with the main characters. They include Suphanburi, Kanchanaburi, Sukhothai, Phichit, Ayutthaya, Chiang Thong, Chomthong, Chiang Mai, and Vientiane.

Secondary towns are those mentioned along the way in journeys. They include Phetchaburi, Kui, Pran, Marit, and Tanaosi in the south; Ang Thong, In(buri), Phrom(buri), Chainat, Paknam Koeichai, Nakhon Sawan, and Lopburi in the center; Phitsanulok, Phichai, Satchanalai, Sawankhalok, Rahaeng, Tak, Thoen, Lampang, Lamphun, Phrae, and Nan in the north; and Vientiane, Nong Bua, Phu Wiang, Khorat, Dong Phaya Fai, and Saraburi to the east and northeast.

The routes followed during the tale include: Suphanburi-Ayutthaya, Kanchanaburi-Ayutthaya, Suphanburi-Kanchanaburi, Phichit-Ayutthaya, Ang Thong-Ayutthaya, Ayutthaya-Chiang Thong, Chiang Mai-Ayutthaya, Ayutthaya-Chiang Mai, Vientiane-Ayutthaya, and Chiang Mai-Vientiane.

Place names in Siam in the early Bangkok era are listed in two other places. First they are found in the register of civil and military officials in the *Three Seals Law*, a collection of old and existing laws compiled in 1805. Second, they are found in various manuscripts that present the Buddhist cosmology of the Three Worlds. These documents include: several illustrated accordion books that are variously believed to originate in the late Ayutthaya, Thonburi, and early Bangkok periods; a version of the cosmology entitled the *Traiphum lokawinitchai*, commissioned by King Rama I in 1791; and murals and inscriptions on the walls of Wat Phra Chetuphon (Wat Pho), dating to the Third Reign (1824–51).

Most of the place names found in *Khun Chang Khun Phaen* can be found in both of these listings. Their appearance in the law code confirms that these places truly existed and were part of Siam of that era. Their appearance in the various Three Worlds texts suggest that these places in the tale have not only a worldly meaning as the setting for the lives of the characters, but also a religious meaning within the Buddhism of that era.

The landscape of the Three Worlds

The second or royal version of the *Traiphum lokawinitchai*[2] describes the eternal cycle of the world's destruction and recreation, and attributes this cycle to the good and bad deeds of humans in the world. It also describes the geography of the universe in two different ways.

The first of these follows the cosmic geography found in an earlier version of the Three Worlds and in other Theravada Buddhist texts. At the center is the holy mountain, Mount Meru. On the peak of the mountain is Tavatimsa (Dawadueng), the heaven presided over by Indra. Above Tavatimsa are various other heavens and the realms of "immaterial factors." Below are the nether regions inhabited by the *asura* demons. Around Mount Meru are the Satthaboriphan, the Seven Ranges of mountains, and the Sithandara Ocean. Beyond them are the four large continents, many smaller land masses, and the *prajanta prathet* the "Outer Country." Finally, there is a wall marking the outer limit of the universe.

Among the four continents, the Jambu Continent (Chomphuthawip) to the south of Mount Meru is distinguished from others as the only continent where Buddhism has taken root. Here is found *machanima prathet*, the Middle Country, where the Buddha lived (in his current and past lives), along with his family, disciples, and the *chakkavatin*, the wheel-rolling emperor who governs the people and makes them observe the five precepts of Buddhism. The Middle Country is not spatially defined, but includes any area where Buddhism flourishes.

---

2. Phrabatsomdetphra Phutthayotfa Chulalok [King Rama I], *Traiphum lokawinitchai chabap thi 2 (Traiphum chabap luang)* [Second or royal edition of the *Traiphum lokawinitchai*] (Bangkok: Fine Arts Department, 1977).

Fig. 1. Mount Meru surrounded by the Satthaboriphan mountain ranges and the four great continents in the Ayutthaya Traiphum manuscript

It may expand and contract depending on the merit of the emperor. The text names the *solot mahanakhon*, sixteen Great Cities where the Buddha has lived in his present and past lives, sometimes as a human and sometimes in the form of various animals. The list of sixteen begins with Varanasi and includes many places that figure in the life story of the Buddha and in the *jataka* tales. Ranged beyond these cities are another sixteen *nakhon chonabot* or Upcountry Cities. This list includes Kampotrat, which may refer to the Khmer country.

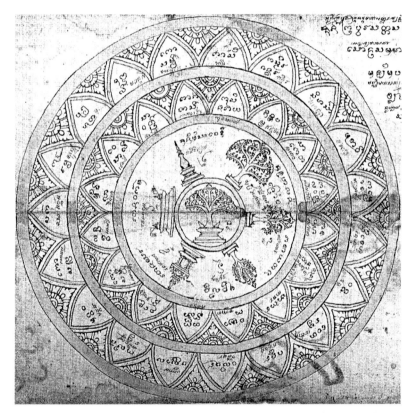

Fig. 2. The Jambu Continent from the Lanna-script Traiphum scroll showing the Great Locations of the Buddha's life at the center, surrounded by the Great Cities and Upcountry Places

The Middle Country is a special place where human beings have the opportunity to do good deeds, accumulate merit, and thus improve their status in future lives. At the same time, humans are subject to worldly attachments (*kilesa, kilet*) including greed, anger, and delusion, which may give rise to conflict. For this reason the people in the Great Cities and Upcountry Cities agree that the person with the greatest merit should become king, with the duty "to enforce the law," uphold the Ten Royal Virtues, and select people to serve as viceroy, ministers, nobles, artificers, and soldiers. The king and this ruling class carry out their duties in return for food and necessities of life which "all the people" provide as recompense for making the society peaceful and content so that they may accumulate merit and attain the ultimate objective of enlightenment.

Fig. 3. Map of the Buddhist world in the Thonburi Traiphum scroll, showing Ayutthaya on the eye-shaped island in the center

The geography described in the *Traiphum lokawinitchai* is illustrated in several accordion books from this era showing exactly the same locations. The illustrations of the cosmology that appear in the final leaves of the various scrolls are very similar and closely match the description in the *Traiphum lokawinitchai*.

In the Thonburi Traiphum scroll, the plan in these last folds shows Ayutthaya with other known places where Buddhism has spread ranged around, including Kampotrat, Lawaek (an old Khmer capital), and Lanka. These plans are at one and the same time a representation of the world as known, and a representation of the "world of Buddhism."

The Three Worlds and Wat Pho

Another important Buddhist achievement of the First Reign was the renovation of Wat Phra Chetuphon (Wat Pho). The architecture scholar, Chatri Prakitnonthakan, has shown that the design and decoration of the wat is based firmly on the cosmology found in the *Traiphum lokawinitchai* and the Traiphum scrolls.[3] This cosmology has two distinctive plans that are layered in the same space.

The first plan identifies the new capital and country of Siam with the Middle Country, the center of the world of Buddhism. The fall of Ayutthaya in 1767 had been a shock and a tragedy that discredited both the old dynasty and the old theories of kingship. The chronicles written in this era attribute the fall to the failure of the late Ayutthaya kings to rule as Buddhist kings. The renovation of Wat Pho, along with the reform of the Sangha, compilation of key Buddhist texts, and passage of laws enshrining Buddhist principles all projected the new Siam as the Middle Country of the Three Worlds, the special area where

---

3. Chatri Prakitnonthanakan, "Symbolism in the Design of Phra Chetuphon Wimonmangkhalaram (Wat Pho)," *Journal of the Siam Society* 102 (2014): 1–39; see also Samoechai Phunsuwan, *Sanyalak nai ngan jitakam thai rawang phutthsatawat 19–24* [Symbolism in Thai murals in the 19th–24th centuries BE] (Bangkok: Thammasat University Press, 1996).

Buddhism flourishes, and where the citizens have the opportunity to accumulate merit and advance towards enlightenment. The king is identified with the wheel-turning emperor of the Three Worlds who gains legitimacy because of his superior stock of merit, adherence to the Ten Royal Virtues, and dedication to protecting and promoting Buddhism for the benefit of the citizens.

In this plan, the ordination hall of Wat Pho is the *sisa phaendin* or Head Realm of the world of Buddhism. At the focus of the Head Realm is the bodhi-tree throne where the Buddha sat after gaining enlightenment, symbolized by the main Buddha image in the ordination hall, which is appropriately in meditation pose, not the pose of subduing evil. After attaining enlightenment, the Buddha sojourned and meditated for a week apiece in Seven Great Places. The six of these, other than the bodhi-tree throne, were represented in the two preaching halls that are placed to the east and west of the ordination hall. (Only two can now be clearly identified.) In the life story of the Buddha, there are Eight Great Incidents. These are represented through images and murals in the two preaching halls placed to the north and south of the ordination hall.

In the texts, the Middle Country is said to have the shape of a *taphon*, a drum that tapers slightly at both ends. Around the ordination hall, linking the four preaching halls, there are two levels of cloisters. Seen from above or in plan form, they resemble the shape of the *taphon* with tapering ends.

The inner and outer cloister respectively represent the Great Cities and Upcountry Cities of the Middle Country. In a Khmer-language version of the Traiphum scroll made by King Mongkut for the Cambodian court, the plan of the Jambu Continent is not rendered in the usual circular form found in such texts, but in a square plan. The plan very closely matches the plan of the inner part of Wat Pho, with the names of the Great Cities and Upcountry Cities written in boxes in that part of the plan matching the cloisters. In the renovation of Wat Pho in the Third Reign, the roof was raised by two cubits, and in this new upper register were painted images and names of 374

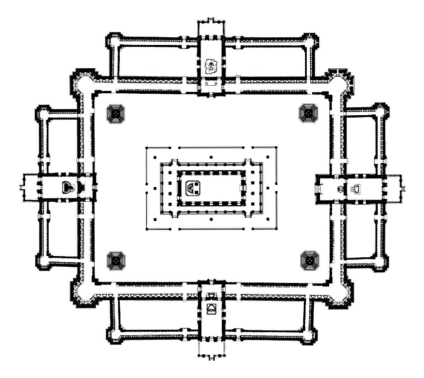

Fig. 4. Probable ground plan of the ordination hall and cloisters at Wat Pho in the First Reign

Fig. 5. A *taphon* drum

cities or provinces subject to Siam, with the placement matching the compass directions (i.e., cities in the east are written on the wall to the east). The images have since disappeared, but 194 of the 374 names have survived.[4]

Fig. 6. The Jambu Continent in the Khmer-language Traiphum scroll

In the Three Worlds geography, beyond the Middle Country lies the Himavanta Forest with mountains, oceans, and the abode of animals. At Wat Pho, this is represented by the area between the cloister and the bounding wall. The surface of this courtyard represented the Sithandara Ocean. In the renovation of the First Reign, a group of five stupas was placed in each of the four corners of this space,

4. Niyada Laosunthorn, *Prachum jaruek wat phra chetuphon* [Collected inscriptions of Wat Pho] (Bangkok: Amarin, 2001). See also Prince Dhani Nivat, "The Inscriptions of Wat Phra Jetubon," *Journal of the Siam Society* 26, 2 (1933): 153–55.

representing the Satthaboriphan, the mountain ranges of Himavanta. The renovation in the Third Reign added another thirty-one stupas and several *khao mo*, artificial hills. The four continents other than the Jambu Continent are represented by four angled pavilions at the corners.

In the *Traiphum lokawinitchai*, the animal life of the Himavanta is related through *jataka* stories. In Wat Pho in the First Reign, all 550 *jataka* stories were recorded in murals in the *sala rai*, satellite pavilions against the bounding wall.

The renovation of the Third Reign added a new area to the west, which completed this representation of the Three Worlds geography. The reclining Buddha in the northwest corner represented the Lanka continent. The reclining form of the Buddha image is seen to originate from Lanka, and in addition its pavilion has murals based on the Lanka chronicle and a bodhi tree grown from a seed brought from Ceylon. The central part of this western section with four stupas and a scripture hall represents the Jambu Continent. The preaching hall to the south represents the realms of hell, with murals on that theme.

The plan of Wat Pho thus depicts the geography of the Three Worlds, centered on the Head Realm in the ordination hall, surrounded by the Middle Country, the world of Buddhism, represented by the surrounding preaching halls and cloisters. Inscribing the place names of Siam in these cloisters identified these with the Great Cities and Upcountry Cities of the Three Worlds.

A second aspect of the plan of Wat Pho concerns Indra. In Buddhism, Indra is the deity that protects Buddhism, appearing many times in the story of the Buddha's life in this role. King Rama I chose to identify his realm with Indra, rather than Vishnu (and to a lesser extent, Siva), who had been more popular among Ayutthaya kings. He incorporated Rattanakosin, meaning "Indra's jewel," in the title of the city; was crowned in a hall named after Indra; and probably placed an image of Indra on the frontage of Wat Pho. In some Buddhist texts, Indra is not a permanent deity but a human who is reborn as a deity because of accumulated good deeds, and who is replaced by another similar human when his merit is exhausted. King Rama I had commoner origins. His use of the symbolism of Indra was another way to legitimize his rule as a king based on merit not lineage, as well as emphasizing Siam as the center of the Buddhist world.

The plan of Wat Pho can be read in a second way with a focus on Indra. The Tavatimsa Heaven, where Indra presides, is located on the peak of Mount Meru, represented in Wat Pho by the presiding image in the ordination hall. The mural behind the image, depicting the Three Worlds, gives special emphasis to the Tavatimsa Heaven.

Prince Poromanuchit Chinorot, who oversaw the renovation of Wat Pho in the Third Reign, left an explanation of the inscriptions:

To preserve images from the floor	on the blue walls, to the top
In sixteen parts	many
On beams going round clockwise	in all four directions
All the known subject towns inscribed	quickly done
Three hundred cities altogether	and another seventy
Plus four cities, inscribed	areas and districts
Complete with boundaries	the frontiers of Siam
To honor the great Buddha	the golden one[5]

In sum, the design of Wat Pho positions Siam as the Head Realm at the center of the Middle Country in the Jambu Continent within the geography of the Three Worlds. This design identifies the Kingdom of Siam in the Bangkok era as central to the world of Buddhism, a domain where Buddhism is protected and promoted under the reign of a righteous king, giving opportunity to its citizens to accumulate merit, improve their standing in future lives, and advance towards enlightenment.

---

5.   Somdetphramahasammanajai Kromphra Poromanuchit Chinorot, *Khlongdan patisangkhon wat phra chetuphon* [Verse on the Renovation of Wat Pho] (Bangkok: Mahachulalongkorn University Press, 2009), 26.

Morality of the Three Worlds

The *Traiphum lokawinitchai* contains a section called *manutkatha*, the Discourse on Humanity, which describes the principles and goals of human existence for those who live in the various cities of the Jambu Continent and have the opportunity to accumulate merit in the course of their lives.

Since life is a cycle of death and rebirth, existence in this life is determined by conduct in previous lives, while future lives are determined by conduct in this life. All conduct can be classified as good or bad. Merit is accumulated by avoiding bad actions and choosing good actions. Actions to be avoided are outlined in the precepts (do not kill; do not steal; etc), and in a general instruction to avoid worldly attachments that give rise to greed, anger, and delusion. Actions to be chosen are outlined in the teachings (dhamma) including general principles such as adhering to honesty and gratitude.

To aid the citizens of the Jambu Continent in the task of avoiding bad conduct and selecting good conduct, this Discourse presents easy-to-follow lists of actions for specific human circumstances, such as the proper conduct of a true friend, the improper conduct of a false friend, the proper conduct of women in general, the attributes of a good wife and good husband, the attributes of a bad wife and bad husband, and so on.[6]

In the renovation of Wat Pho in the Third Reign, the cloisters, which metaphorically represent the Middle Country of the Buddhist World, were not only used to inscribe the 374 Great Cities and Upcountry Cities of Siam but also to inscribe instructions on good conduct and bad conduct similar to those found in the *Traiphum lokawinitchai*. These instructions were inscribed in verse on the pillars of the cloisters at the behest of King Rama III so that "people who lack wisdom and experience"[7] could read and gain the knowledge to conduct themselves

---

6. Rama I, *Traiphum lokawinitchai*, 255–414.
7. Niyada, *Prachum jaruek*, 493.

in ways that would bring them rank and reward in the present-day world. The instructions fall into two codes, the first describing conduct for ordinary people, and the second for the king and other members of the ruling class. The first code specifies good and bad conduct, and the resulting merit or demerit, for various groups of the ordinary people.

The five actions of a bad wife include: thinking of killing her husband to be with a lover, greedily coveting the husband's property, and scolding or browbeating the husband like a slave. The four actions of a good wife include: showing respect and deference to the husband, sharing happiness and hardship, being obedient to the husband as master, and bearing no grudge even if beaten. The six actions of a sinful person include: drinking liquor, walking in a lonely place, getting drunk at entertainments, being a gangster or tough, having bad friends, and being lazy. The code also specifies the consequences of these actions.

The code pays special attention to friendship. A bad friend is someone who does not speak straightforwardly, who makes contact only when in trouble, who stands idle when he could solve a problem, who speaks deceptively and inconsistently, and who flatters. By contrast a good friend is wise and dependable, helps to look after property, does not abandon a friend in trouble, does not think of doing harm to a friend, does not disclose a secret to others, shares happiness and hardship, helps to solve problems, and gives good advice on upholding the precepts.

Another section recounts the four types of prejudice, namely prejudice arising from love, anger, fear, and delusion, and offers advice for avoiding the five dangerous sins, namely choose good conduct, do not covet the property of others, avoid bad carnal behavior, do not lie, do not criticize and scold, make the mind transparent, solve problems without grudge, and avoid misunderstandings.

Another section deals with ways to earn merit as a lay person including: acquire thorough knowledge, follow the teachings for lay persons, fulfill duties in the family, behave properly towards parents, pursue an honest occupation, give good advice and assistance to relatives and friends so they earn merit and avoid sin, show gratitude to teachers, avoid doing harm to animals, see value in every life, be tolerant, overcome idleness, and pay no attention to gaining or losing rank.[8]

For noble officials, there is a specific code for serving the king: avoid acting in any way that makes the king ill at ease; be especially attentive when the king is angry, and do not be angry in return; be a loyal and trustworthy servant, never disobedient; know how to remain humble and composed; do not dress flashily or untidily; stay at a lower level; do not presume to be equal; do not sit on the throne; wait to be invited to speak; do not be too close or too distant; do not infringe on royal authority; show gratitude; know court behavior such as not entering the royal cloister; and take care over emission from the nine orifices (ears, eyes, nose, mouth, urethra, and anus).

In addition, there are instructions on how noble officials should behave towards others including parents and people in general, such as: be honest; show respect; show gratitude; see the virtue of other people; repay debts of gratitude to parents and teachers; have a sense of right and wrong; maintain good manners; show restraint and do not accuse anyone before the king; consult monks, Brahmans, experts, and learned people in order to know how to perform good deeds; follow the precepts; pay respect to elders; give alms; give to the poor; and do not look down on the poor.

Nobles must be knowledgeable about disciplines needed for government such as: astrology; astronomy; the arts of war and the placement of an army; understanding past and future, right and wrong, sin and good; looking after property; providing for oneself and family; bringing up children and preventing them from making bad friends.[9]

The code concerning the conduct of the king was inscribed on the pillars of the doorways leading to the outer cloister on all four sides. One part has instructions on the king's conduct in everyday life, such as: do not overindulge in carnal pleasure, do not hold back

---

8. Niyada, *Prachum jaruek*, 385–462.
9. Ibid., 462–73.

urine or feces, do not stay up at night often or sleep more than twice during the daytime, and know the auspicious directions for various bodily activities (sitting, sleeping, standing, walking, etc.) and avoid the inauspicious ones. In addition there are instructions on behavior for longevity, such as: rest after completing government work so the body is strong, do not travel after finishing work in the afternoon, and do not walk or play immediately after eating. Other items have advice on maintaining personal health, such as: wash face and rinse mouth after waking from sleep; wear clean clothes; comb hair; do not sleep more than twice during the day, and do not sleep naked; wash feet and coil hair; and avoid sex on days such as Songkran (Thai New Year), birthday, and holy days.

Another section prescribes conduct for leadership, especially in war. The king should display bravery, prudence, and knowledge of strategy and tactics in order to conserve his troops. He should live with the troops, share with them, keep good time, be fair and just with high officers, and copy the behavior of animals that stick together in herds. The king and the noble officials should adhere to discipline; abide by the law; show gratitude and friendship; be honest even with enemies; and lie only to save one's troops, avoid danger, help a friend, or achieve victory.[10]

Besides these inscriptions in the cloister, three other works of moral instruction were inscribed in the pavilions around the stupas in the western extension during the Third Reign. These three are *Kruesna son nong* (Krishna Teaches a Sister[11]) and *Pali son nong* (Pali Teaches a Brother[12]), composed by Somdet Phra Poromanuchit Chinorot, and *Khlong lokaniti* (Verses of Worldly Wisdom) composed by Somdet Phra Dechadisorn.[13]

10. Niyada, *Prachum jaruek*, 476–94.

11. Krishna giving advice to Draupadi, wife of the Pandava brothers in the Mahabharata epic from India.

12. A monkey king from the Ramayana instructing his brother Sukrip/Sukriva on the proper behavior of a royal servant.

13. Phraya Dechadisorn (1793–1859), a son of King Rama II with a daughter of

Two verses explain these inscriptions. First, in the cloister:

These inscriptions carved on stone
on pillars of the cloister halfway around the building
are provided by the king with the royal intention
for people who lack wisdom and experience
to study, remember, and practice
these various actions with perseverance
so they may be blessed with wealth, fortune,
rank and riches in the present day[14]

Second, in the pavilions at the western end:

I the resplendent great king	of the Ram lineage
Pass on these inscribed tablets	to communicate
The most sought-after	advice to be followed
In hope that people will	read, understand and remember the verses[15]

King Rama III offered this advice to his people so that they might conduct themselves as good people to earn merit in the present-day world, and avoid or desist from bad deeds that would load them with bad karma in this and future worlds.

In the *Traiphum lokawinitchai*, such advice appears in the Discourse on Humanity, which prescribes the principles for those living in the Great Cities and Upcountry Cities of the Middle Country in the Jambu Continent, the domain of Buddhism. In Wat Pho, this advice is inscribed in the cloisters that also contain the images and inscriptions of the towns and cities subject to the Kingdom of Siam.

Chaophraya Phrakhlang Hon; he was in charge of the Department of Scribes during the Third Reign.

14. Niyada, *Prachum jaruek*, 493, emphasis added.

15. Ibid., 638.

In Theravada Buddhist culture, one important medium for teaching principles of good conduct are the *jataka* tales, which use stories of the previous lives of the Buddha in the human world to give examples of meritorious conduct. In Wat Pho, the *jataka* tales were illustrated in the sixteen satellite pavilions that represent the Himavanta Forest, along with the four great continents and many minor land masses.

In the various Traiphum texts and in the *jataka* tales, the geography of continents and cities provides a landscape in which humans conduct themselves in ways good and bad, thus earning merit or demerit and bearing the consequences in the cycle of death and rebirth. These texts and tales are illustrations of Buddhist teachings on worldly conduct. They can be read or listened to for advice.

The same technique is found in *Khun Chang Khun Phaen*. The geography of the capital, provincial cities, and villages of Siam provides a landscape in which humans from many stations in life conduct themselves in ways good and bad, thus earning merit or demerit and often bearing the consequences in the course of the plot.

The landscape of *Khun Chang Khun Phaen* as social space

Ayutthaya and the provincial towns that appear in Khun Chang Khun Phaen are places that existed in reality in early Bangkok and at the same time are models of the Great Cities and Upcountry Cities of the Buddhist world in the cosmology of the Three Worlds. They form the social space in which the characters create the plot, by living their lives under the power of karma and its consequences. This is the same technique that is used in telling the history of Buddhism. In the story of the Buddha, his disciples and important figures in Buddhism, both in past and current lives, live according to Buddhist principles in the Great City and Upcountry Cities of the Three Worlds texts.

Ayutthaya in the tale represents the capital city of Siam, or the abode of the wheel-turning emperor in the Three Worlds. The other major locations in the tale (Suphanburi, Kanchanaburi, Phichit, etc.) are equivalent to the Upcountry Cities. They are the social spaces where the principal characters in the tale, who are mostly common people or low-level nobles, live their worldly lives as human beings whose fate is determined by worldly attachment and the karma that they make. Beyond is *Prajanta prathet*, the Outer Country, the world beyond Siam.

Ayutthaya, capital of the Middle Country

The Great City in the Jambu Continent lies in the Middle Country where the Buddha was born, along with his disciples, and the wheel-turning emperor who protects and promotes Buddhism. Ayutthaya in *Khun Chang Khun Phaen*, or Krungthep Mahanakhon in the kingdom of Siam, is ruled over by King Phanwasa, who is portrayed as a *rajathirat*, a king of kings, similar to a wheel-turning emperor.

The landscape of Ayutthaya is not very clearly described in *Khun Chang Khun Phaen*. Only a few streets, palace buildings, and a ferry crossing are mentioned. The population is described as consisting of many ethnic groups such as "Thai, Chinese, Mon, Burmese, Kha, Lao, and Lue" (559) and "adults and children, Chinese, Farang, Khaek, Kha, Mon, and Lao." (766) But the common folk of the city have roles only as an audience, watching the king's soldiers leave for war and return from war, waiting for the outcome of a royal audience or court proceedings, and watching spectacles presented in the palace courtyard. These crowd scenes are ways to emphasize the portrayal of the king.

The king represents the city. Just as one of the plans of Wat Pho symbolizes the Tavatimsa Heaven, so the Ayutthaya of King Phanwasa is compared to the heavenly realm of Tavatimsa. One of the invocations that announce an appearance by King Phanwasa in the tale makes this comparison explicit by comparing his palace to the Vejjayanta (Wetchayan) Palace of Indra in the Three Worlds:

> The king of the city of Thawara Ayutthaya, a world like heaven,
> resided in a brilliant jeweled palace surrounded by all his consorts
> and court ladies, / like Lord Indra of mighty power ensconced in

the resplendent Wetchayan, surrounded by heavenly angels, and regaled by his booming drums. (172)

When King Phanwasa enters audience, the comparison continues by mentioning Indra's Bantukamphon throne and the Parichat tree, a landmark of the Tavatimsa Heaven:

Amid a thunder of gongs and drums, and a fanfare of conches and horns, the king looked as sublime as Lord Indra seated on his immense glittering throne, / Bantukamphon, the seat of stone, with all the gods arrayed around, under the resplendent Parichat tree and the many-tiered ceremonial umbrellas of Indra. (173)

The fact that King Phanwasa is a "king of kings" is announced in the opening lines of the tale:

Paramount throughout the world, his writ unfurled far afield, A source of joy, like heaven revealed, a shield and shelter of the commonalty. / Dependencies diverse within his power did cower in awe of such authority. All lands around the sacred city in humility clasped hands, heads bowed. / The sovereign holder of the royal wealth, perfect in health, with happiness endowed, Ten Royal Virtues duly avowed. The common crowd as one was joyful. (1)

His power extends far and wide. Many other lands willingly subject themselves to his authority. He rules according to the Ten Royal Virtues. All these attributes match those of a king of kings or wheel-turning emperor in the Three Worlds. Another feature of such an emperor is the possession of seven "gem" (i.e., perfect) attributes. At least two of these have parallels in the tale. Khun Phaen is like a "gem soldier," ever ready to volunteer and win victories over enemies. When the beautiful Princess Soithong of Vientiane is presented to King Phanwasa, she is described like the "gem woman" of the Three Worlds.

In the political geography of the time, smaller states were bound to place themselves under larger states for protection against enemies. The King of Vientiane explains to his queen why he has decided to place his country under the protection of Ayutthaya

> The prestige of the Thai monarch is known far and wide. If we ask to depend on his protection, I think our plea will be well received. Don't they talk about the reputation of the King of Ayutthaya, upholder of the teachings, / and how his power extends in ten directions over all countries and languages? If we present Soithong to him, and Chiang Mai ever attacks, / the Ayutthaya army will come to our aid. They won't leave us to die because their illustrious king is just. (500–501)

In the missive sent to Ayutthaya along with the princess Soifa, the king emphasizes the same points:

> "In the missive, the King of Wiang [Vientiane], ruler over the royal wealth of the city of Si Sattana, upholder of truth and religion, pays respect to the King of Ayutthaya, /*the great, who resides under a tiered white umbrella loftier than that of any monarch in all directions.* He begs to present tribute of gold to the king of the capital of Si Ayutthaya, / who has such renown that every country quails and submits, who protects the mass of the populace and soldiery so they are joyful, / *who upholds the Ten Royal Virtues, and who governs with justice and honesty.* / As the King of Lanchang wishes to request the protection of your royal power until his dying day, he begs to offer his daughter as a servant to the royal foot of the great and glorious king, descendant of a brilliant royal line. Your humble servant pays homage." (505–6, emphasis added)

King Phanwasa is portrayed as a just ruler in the politics among states. When Chiang Mai has been defeated for the second time and its king and people have been swept down to Ayutthaya, King Phanwasa acts according to royal virtue by deciding not to impose the penalty of execution for revolt:

> His city is of primary rank and outside the dominion of the capital of Ayutthaya. Now that he's submitted and agreed to offer tribute, he should not be put to death. (713)

King Phanwasa reasons that Chiang Mai was not "in revolt" as it was not formerly subject to Siam. Moreover, as Chiang Mai has now agreed to render tribute, "If I were to execute him in revenge, who would trust Ayutthaya in the future?" (713). But the release is conditional, ". . . if he acts improperly again, he should be punished with his life." The King of Chiang Mai thus gives his word: "let me be a servant of the foot of Your Majesty, and keep my word to act with rectitude until death" and "let me depend on the bodhi-tree shelter of your accumulated merit from now on" (715). The king then orders his officials "to take the ruler of Chiang Mai to swear loyalty and drink the waters of allegiance," so he becomes a tributary from then on and promises to "maintain friendly relations forever according to the example of other countries' rulers" (716).

Through the course of the tale, King Phanwasa is portrayed as fitting the role of a king of kings. According to the Traiphum, it is the duty of the king to ensure the happiness of the populace. As the first subject in audience, the king receives reports:

> "The rains and the river flow are good." "The first and second crops of rice are plentiful." "The people are happy every day." The king laughed heartily at these reports. (504)

The king is also shown in his role at the summit of the judicial process. In many cases, he assigns this responsibility to the appropriate judicial officials. The process of law is portrayed as complex and oppressive. The common people try to avoid becoming entangled in court cases because it requires time and money to achieve a result. However, the law is a worldly matter where morality should prevail, and hence it is an opportunity for the king to display his qualities. In two cases where a decision is difficult because of inadequate or conflicting evidence, the king commands the use of ordeal by fire and water to reach a decision. In both cases, the result of the ordeal is seen to be just; the guilty party fails the test.

The king is also seen involved in the royal traditions of court, such as organizing processions, receiving a diplomatic mission, distributing rewards and promotions, and sponsoring royal weddings and cremations.

While King Phanwasa is portrayed as a king of kings, the King of Chiang Mai serves as a contrast, a ruler who fails to follow the moral rules prescribed for kings because he is governed by worldly attachments of greed and delusion. When he hears of the beauty of the Vientiane princess, he becomes obsessed by the idea of having her as a consort and agonizes over the means to achieve this aim:

> He could not decide, and pondering over this problem plunged him into turmoil, unable to sleep during the night. / He lay with his hand flung across his forehead. "How can I arrange this romance?" (494)

Because of his failure to abide by moral principles, he loses his power and status. He ceases to be a "primary ruler" and becomes a tributary to Ayutthaya. His daughter is separated from him, and kept in Ayutthaya to serve as a hostage for his loyalty. He suffers a loss of face when King Phanwasa refuses his offer for her to become an Ayutthayan royal consort and instead marries her to Khun Phaen's son. As he leaves Ayutthaya to return home, the King of Chiang Mai reflects on his fall:

> In the past, there were all kinds of pleasures and dazzling possessions. Every city quailed before me. / Falling in love with

Soithong was a mistake that brought enormous misfortune. I lost my home, lost my city, and gained torment. My beloved child cannot return with me. (729)

Upcountry Cities: Landscape of everyday life

The Upcountry Cities in *Khun Chang Khun Phaen*, including those associated with the principal characters such as Suphanburi, Kanchanaburi, Sukhothai, and Phichit, are not described in any detail. In each place only a few *wat* are named. On the population, there is more detail. In Suphanburi and Kanchanaburi, there are both Thai and Mon. In Ang Thong, we find Khmer and Lao. In the forest and hills there are hill people including Karen and Lawa, who also appear as slaves and servants in the Upcountry Cities. The agricultural workers and household slaves of Wanthong are Lawa. So are the people who have commercial dealings with Khun Chang over eaglewood, a high-value export product in early Bangkok. Karen in hill villages also grow cotton. In their flight to the deep forest, Khun Phaen and Wanthong visit a Lawa village that grows "sweet potato and taro. . . . gourd, aubergine, chili, dry plantain, and sparrow's brinjal" (386).

The people of the Upcountry Cities differ from those of the capital, Ayutthaya, who are Kha, Chinese, Jek, Khaek, and Farang, besides Thai, Mon, and Lao. No Karen or Lawa are mentioned as inhabitants of Ayutthaya. They are truly people of the provinces, of the forest.

Unlike any other literary work of its era, *Khun Chang Khun Phaen* portrays the everyday life of ordinary people including the cycle of birth, ageing, sickness, and death as well as education, raising children, ordination, courtship and marriage, house-building, and everyday matters of food and clothing.

The people in the Upcountry Cities include both law-abiding citizens and those involved in criminal activity. The latter are strikingly numerous. Stealing cattle appears to be common. Siprajan's brother-in-law, who is mentioned only briefly, "was interested only in stealing buffaloes" (11). Ai-Thit, servant of Simala, who is sent back to Phichit to report on the love charm, follows "the route, which he could recall from his time as a buffalo thief" (1014). When he reaches his destination, Phra Phichit addresses him as "you jailbird," and asks, "Did you come looking for some fun thieving buffaloes?" (1015). Stealing buffaloes was not a serious crime if Phra Phichit describes it with the term "fun." The roll call of the thirty-five convicts shows they have committed a great variety of robberies in places all over the west and center of Siam. The father of Khun Chang is killed by a robber gang that is large, highly organized, and well connected to other robber gangs.

One other striking feature of the Upcountry Cities is the role of lore or supernatural powers, including invulnerability and fighting skills. As a youth, Khun Phaen is educated in lore by three teachers who are all abbots. Although lore is not part of Buddhism, the two coexist very closely. Khun Phaen learns about mantras and supernatural fighting skills at the same time that he studies Buddhist texts including *jataka* tales. His son, Phlai Ngam, has no monk-teacher but studies from Khun Phaen's library with some help from his grandmother. His curriculum includes "the teachings, meditation, the Formulas on Extinction for summoning and suppressing spirits" (484), meaning both Buddhist texts and lore.

Khun Phaen, his son, and other characters learn lore for worldly purposes. They need the skills for their careers as soldiers. They also use them for their careers as lovers. When Phlai Ngam visits his father in jail, Khun Phaen tells him, "No pursuit surpasses the pursuit of knowledge. In the future when you grow up, you'll reap the benefit" (482).

In *Khun Chang Khun Phaen*, the power of any individual's lore depends not only on diligence in study but also on that individual's conduct. As a result, that power is not constant over time. Before executing his plan to abduct Wanthong from Khun Chang's house, Khun Phaen refreshes his lore because he fears its power has declined. When Khun Phaen and Phlai Ngam infiltrate the Chiang Mai palace, Khun Phaen tells his son not to touch the sleeping palace ladies because "to be expert in warfare, you shouldn't dally with women" (662).

Lore is used for both good and bad purposes, by both good and bad people. Nai Janson's robber gang that robs and kills Khun Chang's father behaves in exactly the same way as soldiers in the service of the king. They are invulnerable and skilled in lore. They are well armed with "pikes, swords, flintlock guns, powder horns, fuses, and Ho spears" (41). Before the raid, they hold a ceremony: building an eye-level shrine; placing their weapons and protective devices on the shrine; making offerings of "liquor, rice, food, sweets, incense, bright candles, krajae-sandal, and fragrant oil"; and then summoning a wide variety of gods and spirits to instill power in their weapons and protective devices. Their command of lore, their weaponry, and their ritual are no different from those of Khun Phaen and his son when they are serving as soldiers of the king. The skills of lore are used both by those who serve the state and those who are enemies of the state.

When Khun Phaen is preparing to leave for war with the thirty-five convict volunteers, he holds a similar ceremony. The procedure with the shrine, offerings, and summoning of spirits and deities is exactly the same with only one key difference. At the end of the long list of spirits and deities summoned, Khun Phaen also calls on "the supreme Three Jewels, our eternal fathers and mothers, our teachers and preceptors, and the royal command [meaning the king]" (566–67).

The skills of the robber gang and the military detachment are the same, but their *intent* is different. The robbers intend to take property away from other people, possibly also killing or doing harm to their victims. These are bad deeds, violations of the precepts. By contrast, the intent of soldiers is to serve the king, the highest authority, the king of kings, the ruler who upholds the teachings, the emperor. Winning a war on behalf of the king spreads his power far and wide and embellishes the name of the country. The accumulated merit of the king means that the service of the soldiers qualifies as good deeds. As already noted, lore does not prevent the thirty-five convicts from being captured and jailed because their actions have violated the precepts, but their service as soldiers of the king results in them gaining freedom and social status.

The most striking examples of the use of lore in unethical ways are Elder Khwat and Muen Han. Elder Khwat is known to be "adept with lore and exceptional powers" (723). He has also been ordained as a monk in Chiang Mai. However, he does not abide by the disciplinary code. In particular he drinks liquor. He helps Soifa by making a love charm, a practice that is strictly forbidden by both law and moral teachings. The love charm creates chaos in Khun Phaen's family. However, Khun Phaen's son Phlai Chumphon is able to rescue the situation by getting Khwat drunk, so he spills the truth. Later in the story, Phlai Chumphon defeats Elder Khwat in a contest of lore. This shows that lore loses its power and sacredness if the user is not moral.

The same message is found in the story of Muen Han. He is versed in lore and invulnerable. But he also is a professional criminal who has robbed and killed many people and thus carries a weight of bad deeds. When it comes to a contest, his lore is no match for Khun Phaen.

In the Second Reign there was a policy to encourage low-level officials to establish villages in the forest and hills to extend production of goods that the capital wanted from the forest. In the Third Reign it was found that some such villages had become robber lairs so the policy was revoked. The story of Muen Han's lair might be based on real life. Muen Han has the title *muen* from the *sakdina* system, which would convey command of some *phrai*. He has some twenty soldiers who have invulnerability. Their village, Ban Tham, "was large, and teemed with cattle, buffaloes, elephants, horses, and servants. Houses were crowded together, and furnished as well as any princely palace" (1175). His own house reflects his high status as "There were throngs of young Lao and Thai girl servants, all just of age and good-looking. The sitting halls were spread with soft mats, pillows, and carpets, and strewn with items of gold, silver, nak, and nielloware" (1175). We learn that he has contacts with the local officials of Suphanburi who come to ask for his daughter's hand.

But the village is also a lair, defended by a fence of felled trees. It is a place of refuge for "people who had stolen elephants or fled from their masters." Officials or masters who try to chase them down risk being captured and buried alive. Interestingly, the village has no *wat*, no monks. At the marriage of Khun Phaen with Muen Han's daughter, no monk is present and "there's no *wat* here for prayer chanting. We make offerings to the spirits in the ancient way" (1182). The fact is a sign that this place does not follow the Buddhist principles that frame the story.

When Muen Han demands that Khun Phaen participate in the robbing activity of the settlement, Khun Phaen's refusal states clearly the difference in *intent* between a soldier and a robber in the use of the same skill: "I won't steal elephants, seize people, rob houses, or go in for any other banditry. Yet if there's any danger, I'll bear the brunt so you're not affected" (1187).

This refusal prompts Muen Han to try to kill Khun Phaen. He asks his daughter to give him poison, and gains her consent by promising, "We'll set you up with a new husband and hand you all the property. We'll make sure it's a gentleman of good lineage with heaps of money to keep you happy" (1190). She agrees out of greed, thereby acquiring bad karma with fatal and near-immediate results: "now that her father had mentioned heaps of money, her mind became fixed on possessions, and selfishness shaped her thinking. She was fated to die" (1190).

The morality here follows that expressed in the inscriptions of Wat Pho about the behavior of a bad wife. One of the points is "doing harm to a husband or planning to kill him in order to be with another lover." One of the instructions in the cloister of Wat Pho even describes the poison method that Buakhli uses:

A woman who uses violence or covert trickery   on a man
Who has crooked intentions   morning and night
Who waits for a fever or fatal sickness   a bad fortune
Who administers a poison too   be careful of such things[16]

But when Muen Han attacks Khun Phaen and is defeated, Khun Phaen spares his life because he recognizes a debt of gratitude: "you fed

---

16. Niyada, *Prachum jaruek*, 664.

and supported me in your house, giving me rice, curry, chili, and salt. For that kindness, I won't execute you. / Also your good wife, Sijan, gave me cash and clothing. If I didn't think of these things, your life would be dust. This time it's not your fate to die" (1197).

Ban Tham is thus a complex social space. It harbors criminals who do harm to others, but also serves as a refuge for those who flee oppression by state or master.

Karma in *Khun Chang Khun Phaen*

Among the *Verses of Worldly Wisdom* in Wat Pho, one excerpt emphasizes that all human actions are determined by karma:

Do not blame freemen, lords,	or gods
Do not blame the mountains	or open spaces
Do not blame relatives	or friends
Blame only the karma made yourself	and sent to yourself[17]

Although people with various kinds of expertise might explain events according to this expertise, the truth is that karma is the determinant:

A doctor divined a fever,	a wind of virtue
An astrologer said powerful stars	were to blame
A sorcerer said spirits were in control	and blamed them
A philosopher said it was just karma	made by yourself[18]

Differences in the status of people in society as well as the tribulations of everyday life can be traced back to karma:

---

17. Niyada, *Prachum jaruek*, 659.
18. Ibid., 660.

Rank and title come from	merit made
Dangers arise as fruit of karma	made before
Study and remember	that the karma one makes oneself
No one can avoid	throughout the world[19]

Even the power of mantras and other supernatural skills depends on the accumulated merit or demerit of the practitioner:

Using lore and mantra for luck	see the result
Do anything to achieve an affect	anything
But if the merit of the person	is low then
That mantra lore	declines every day[20]

The characters in *Khun Chang Khun Phaen* are examples of humans whose lives fall under the law of karma. Their fate, both happy and tragic, is determined by the merit or demerit of their actions. Often this fate is revealed in advance in the narrative. For example, in their childhood the three principal characters, Phlai Kaeo (who becomes Khun Phaen), Khun Chang, and Nang Phim (who becomes Wanthong), play a game of "husband and wife" that prefigures what will happen in their adult lives. The narrator of the story then comments that "the envoy of the gods" engineered this event:

Dear listeners, all of you, please do not suspect that this has been made up. No. Children's play is strange. Should it come true, well, the envoy of the gods makes it happen. / Whatever children play is not wrong. To call it bad is only a mouth speaking. This story comes down from ancient times, and there is a text in Suphan. (15)

Sometimes this already determined future is revealed by astrology. For example, when Phlai Kaeo as a youth prepares to leave the novitiate,

19. Niyada, *Prachum jaruek*, 682.
20. Ibid.

his abbot-teacher casts his horoscope. He discovers that Phlai Kaeo has been involved in a love affair with Phim, and he predicts that "you'll marry as you intend, set up house together, and build up some wealth, but it won't last" (133). He even foretells that Phlai Kaeo will be jailed for ten years and that Phim will have a new husband. Despite this knowledge, Phlai Kaeo does not avoid this fate. He is so overwhelmed with love that he continues with his plan to disrobe and marry Phim, thus setting in motion the love triangle that is the core of the story.

When Phlai Kaeo goes to war, he wins a victory in Chiang Thong, and his troops chase the fleeing enemy northwards, looting and causing havoc in the villages along their way, as was the custom of the time. Only at Chomthong does Khun Phaen constrain his troops to be orderly. This exception was arranged by the gods so that Phlai Kaeo would gain his second wife, Laothong, daughter of the Chomthong headman.

> The gods induced Phlai Kaeo to have this idea so he would get Laothong to love. So by chance, here the troops were kind and helpful. They passed in and out freely. (204)

Phlai Kaeo's acquisition of Laothong as a wife plays a crucial role in the plot as her appearance provokes Wanthong to quarrel with Phlai Kaeo resulting in him abandoning her and presenting an opportunity for Khun Chang to become her second husband.

The characters of *Khun Chang Khun Phaen* are aware of the cycle of life, death, and rebirth. Before Phlai Kaeo leaves for the war in Chiang Thong, he, along with his wife and mother each plant a Bodhi tree sapling and pray that their sapling act as a signal of their condition.

> "If I pass away and cannot survive, may this bodhi tree of mine die. If I'm sick, may the bodhi tree sicken in the same way. / If I'm hale and hearty with no suffering, may this bodhi tree be leafy, lush, and shady for all to see." (191)

All three then make a joint prayer which shows their belief in the cycle of life:

> Should any one of us die, may that person go happily to heaven above, to be born again in the next life. May we meet together with certainty for hundreds of ages and thousands of eras into the future until attaining nirvana. (192)

The characters are also aware of the role of good and bad deeds in determining their future. After Khun Phaen has been jailed, he is visited by his mother, who tells him that Khun Chang has tried to kill his son. When Khun Phaen vows revenge, his mother cautions him: "Why go on creating karma by bad deeds?" She advises him to accept his current fate with the words, "In a time of bad fortune, you must act humbly." And she consoles him that "there's an ancient saying that mortal humans can rebound from hardship seven times" (481). In other words, his current situation is a result of the "bad fortune" that he has accumulated by bad deeds in the past, but if he behaves properly the influence of this bad fortune will diminish. Later in the tale, another character sums up the law of karma:

> Nobody born as an ordinary human being can escape sorrow. It depends on karma made in the past. When a time for happiness is over, sorrow begins. / When a time for sorrow passes, then happiness returns again. This has been the nature of things forever. There's no need for fear. (724)

Even though the characters may be aware of the law of karma, they are powerless to defy it. While Khun Phaen is in jail, his young son is taken to be presented to the king. The son's face reminds the king of Khun Phaen.

> He felt pity and was about to pronounce a pardon for Khun Phaen but karma was destined to influence the king's disposition. / His

mind veered to a verse from an outer drama that he could not complete. His head spun and his thoughts drifted away. He forgot to make the announcement as intended, and instead returned inside to the royal bedchamber. (491–92)

As a result, Khun Phaen festers in jail for several more years, fulfilling the prediction of the abbot, cited above.

The power of karma also proves inexorable in the tragic final scene. The king condemns Wanthong to death for failing to respond to his command that she must choose between her two husbands. As time for the execution approaches, her son proposes to attend on the king and ask for a reprieve. Khun Phaen calculates Wanthong's horoscope:

"It looks like a violent death. Saturn is in conjunction with her ascendant, and the Crow appears in the Coffin. This is a time when the monkey reaches into a hole and is eaten by a crocodile. / Someone with this position cannot survive."

The son responds:

"I can see it all—bad fate, life, and death. But I must still repay her kindness and my upbringing. I'll say a couple of words in appeal for her, then it depends on her own merit and karma." (811–12)

The son attends on the king and wins a reprieve. He mounts a horse to speed back but the executioner misunderstands that this must be a messenger sent to expedite the execution and carries out the sentence immediately. Khun Phaen explains to his devastated son, "She had to die as fruit of her karma. . . . Wanthong's life had reached its end" (816). According to the Three Worlds texts, the length of any person's life is determined by the accumulation of good and bad deeds. Even the proper and meritorious acts of a son for his mother, or the orders of the king, the supreme authority in the land, cannot disrupt the law of karma.

Several of the characters suffer an untimely death. In each case this is attributed to their unusual karma. Khun Phaen's father is executed for an error on royal service. As a friend consoles him just before the execution, "When the time comes, it comes. . . . / Who lives to prop up the sky, year in, year out?" (33). Khun Chang's father is brutally murdered by a robber gang while his son is still a young child. On viewing the body, his wife asks, "Truly, what karma made you die such a violent death, naked on the ground in the middle of a forest? Maybe in a previous life you skewered a fish, and so in this life you've been skewered to death too" (47).

Karma also determines the ups and down of characters in their current life. While in jail, Khun Phaen meets thirty-five convicts who all have exceptional skills of invulnerability and other supernatural powers. As we learn from a roll call, all have committed serious crimes, killing many people and stealing a great deal of property, thereby violating the basic Five Precepts of Buddhism. For these bad deeds, they have been captured and imprisoned despite their powers. Being sent to jail is a worldly equivalent of being sent to hell beyond death. This parallel is clearly expressed in a passage where Wanthong visits a jail, finding a scene very similar to the portrayals of hell in the depiction of the Three Worlds in temple murals and manuscripts:

> Wanthong steeled herself to enter the jail. She saw people suffering gruesomely, with thin bodies like creatures in hell. They looked ugly and frightful, making her scalp crawl. . . . / They had scabies, boils, running sores, stench like corpses, / and hairy lice crawling on their skulls. (772)

However, when Khun Phaen is released to lead an army to war, he requests that the thirty-five convicts be pardoned to accompany him. This is attributed to the fact that their bad karma has diminished through their punishment: "For their karma, they had been imprisoned a long time. But now the ending of that karma caused a change for the better." (553)

As Khun Phaen asks for their release to be his troops, so they become like men who have "volunteered to serve the king until death." Being a soldier in the service of the king is a good deed that earns merit. Winning this war on behalf of the king spreads his power far and wide and embellishes the name of the country. The accumulated merit of the king means that the service of the soldiers also qualifies as good deeds. On their victorious return from the war, the thirty-five are upgraded to the status of *phrai* (freemen) and given special exemption from various taxes.

Kings are not immune from the law of karma. The second war with Chiang Mai is provoked when the King of Chiang Mai so desperately desires the beautiful young daughter of the King of Vientiane that he seizes her while she is traveling to Ayutthaya to be presented to the king there. In the ensuing war, Chiang Mai is defeated. The king, his family, and many of his subjects are hauled down to Ayutthaya. The king explains to his assembled consorts, "This heap of karma that we've made between us has now caught up with us all. Don't cry. Face up to the karma first without fear." (681)

Fate controls the life of the characters. Happiness or sorrow depends on karma made by the individual. This principle, which is the principle found in the description of the Jambu Continent in the Three Worlds, drives the whole plot of *Khun Chang Khun Phaen*.

Good and bad characters

The characters of *Khun Chang Khun Phaen*, who live in the realistic landscape of Siam of that time, experience life realistically, subject to emotions and worldly attachments, driven by love, greed, anger, jealousy, and delusion. Those that perform good deeds and accumulate merit are rewarded with happiness, achievement of their goals, and advancement of their status in life, while those that perform bad deeds and accumulate demerit fail to achieve their goals and meet with sorrow and tragedy.

The principal characters in *Khun Chang Khun Phaen* can be classified into two groups: those who enjoy the fruit of their good deeds, including Khun Phaen, Phlai Ngam, Phlai Chumphon, and Kaeo Kiriya; and those who face the consequences of their bad deeds, including Khun Chang, Wanthong, Elder Khwat, Buakhli, and Soifa. Here I will present a few examples from each group.

Khun Phaen

Khun Phaen is subject to strong emotions of love and anger that occasionally lead him into difficulty, but overall he is an example of a good character. He is portrayed as physically good-looking, which, according to the Three Worlds, is a result of good karma accumulated in past lives. He is brave, intent on becoming a warrior like his father, and thus ordains as a novice in order to study lore (supernaturalism or magic). He twice leads an army to defeat Chiang Mai on behalf of his king and is rewarded each time with wealth and a rise in his social status. He is portrayed as a loyal servant who twice volunteers when no other noble will come forward:

> "My liege, lord over my head, my life is beneath the royal foot. I beg to volunteer, Sire, / to attack Chiang In and Chiang Thong and fulfill Your Majesty's wish without fail. As long as I live, I will not shrink from battle." (178–9)

In the works of moral instruction of the era, volunteering for royal service in war was identified as a meritorious act. In *Pali Teaches his Brother*:

Volunteer when there is war	do not give any thought to fear
Fight the enemies to repay	the merit of the lord without fear of danger
Give no thought to survival	even death is not reason to lament
Fame of the Thai will spread	proclaimed famously across the world[21]

---

21. Niyada, *Prachum jaruek*, 619.

And in *Verses of Worldly Wisdom*:

Volunteer to fight for the king	until death
Volunteer to serve your lord	without letup
Volunteer to battle for mother-in-law	do not shrink or lose heart
These three things hold steadfastly	until the world ends[22]

Even though Khun Phaen has lore to loosen chains, make dummy soldiers, be invisible, and even use a love mantra on the king, when he is sent to jail by the king he does not try to escape:

It's like the time my father was punished. When the king gave no pardon, he didn't try to escape. I'll suffer even to death if that's the penalty. (454)

He is sent to jail after he petitioned for Laothong's release soon after being given a pardon himself. The presumption implied in the second request provoked the king's anger. In *Pali Teaches His Brother*, there is advice on proper timing for such petitions that Khun Phaen had failed to follow:

If the channel is good, speak	if not, do not address the king
Be careful not to provoke anger	and suffer being burnt and tarnished[23]

The equanimity that Khun Phaen exhibits even after the king executes his father, jails Khun Phaen himself, and executes his wife exemplifies the virtue of honesty and loyalty to the king. The *Verses of Worldly Wisdom* prescribe as follows:

Love and be loyal to the ruler	be just
If he is angry do not speak	attend on his feet

---

22. Niyada, *Prachum jaruek*, 681.
23. Ibid., 618.

Be very loyal like	a dog
Do not neglect the king	keep your mind straight[24]

And similarly, *Pali Teaches His Brother* advises:

If the king is angry do not be angry back   do not speak improperly
So as to provoke anger and punishment   show restraint[25]

Khun Phaen thus has the three qualities that appear in the Code of Royal Service, namely: do not contemplate evil towards the king, perform royal service without worrying whether it will inspire royal trust, and do not show anger to the king.

Khun Phaen is portrayed as a good husband in a traditional society that accepts polygamy. Although he has more than one wife, he looks after all of them. When Laothong is detained in the palace, he takes the risk of petitioning for her release because he had promised her parents in Chomthong that he would look after her. In this context, Khun Phaen refers to the Buddhist principle "But there's an old saying: Sacrifice money but not morals, sacrifice anything but your word" (449).

Khun Phaen is thus portrayed as a good person who is a good royal servant, brave, honest, and loyal to king, and also a good husband who tries to take care of several wives. At the same time, he is a human being subject to worldly attachments of love and anger that draw him into a whirlpool of hardship and sorrow.

Khun Chang

Khun Chang is ugly, fat, short, bald, pot-bellied, and goggle-eyed. The *Traiphum lokawinitchai* relates that when the Buddha was asked by a Brahman what caused differences among humans on such dimensions as appearance, longevity, healthiness, and wealth, the Buddha replied

24. Niyada, *Prachum jaruek*, 681.
25. Ibid., 619.

that all arose from the accumulation of good and bad deeds in past life.[26]

Khun Chang breaks the first precept by trying to murder Khun Phaen's son, and he breaks the third precept by coveting another man's wife and conspiring with his mother-in-law to force her into his bridal house.[27] He does not behave towards Khun Phaen as a good friend. When Khun Phaen entrusts Khun Chang to undertake his duties as a page while he visits a sick wife, Khun Chang immediately informs the king and compounds the offense by claiming Khun Phaen climbed over the palace wall. Soon after, he concocts a charge that Khun Phaen has gathered an armed band intent on raising a revolt. His behavior at many points fits the description of the "behavior of an evil person" described in the *Traiphum lokawinitchai*, namely "praising someone to his face while slandering him behind his back, acting well to his face while gossiping maliciously behind his back."[28] Among the qualities of a bad friend listed in the cloister of Wat Pho are being tricky and speaking deceptively, while one of the six sins of friendship is doing violence to a friend.[29]

Khun Chang's behavior is driven by his worldly attachments of love for Wanthong and anger at Khun Phaen. However, in the plot of *Khun Chang Khun Phaen* the fruit of this karma falls on Wanthong, the only woman that he loves, so he is deprived of her permanently when she is executed.

Wanthong

Although physically attractive, Wanthong is a woman dominated by emotion. She is hot-headed, argumentative, and stubborn. She refuses to bow to anyone she does not agree with, including to Khun Phaen over Laothong, or to her mother over her marriage to Khun Chang.

---

26. Rama I, *Traiphum lokawinitchai*, 255–58.
27. Ibid., 262–63.
28. Ibid., 396.
29. Niyada, *Prachum jaruek*, 417.

She always resists. She fails to follow the instructions on being a good wife delivered by her mother before her marriage to Khun Phaen:

> You must make no mistake that moves the man to malice. / A cool head is mistress of the house. Follow what I've always taught you. Both inside and outside the house, in whatever situation, be careful to pay respect to your husband and heed him. / Don't be jealous and make accusations that cause a scandal. Don't go ahead of your husband; it's not appropriate. I brought you up in the hope you'll do well. I pray you'll be blessed with constant happiness. (164)

The drive behind her behavior is her strong love for Khun Phaen. When Khun Phaen goes away to war and Khun Chang spreads a rumor that he has been killed, she resists the pressure from Khun Chang and her mother-in-law to be married to Khun Chang. When Khun Phaen returns and she expects to return to her old happy state, she instead explodes with jealousy at the appearance of Khun Phaen's new wife, Laothong. In the ensuing quarrel, Wanthong ignores Khun Phaen's pleas for restraint and rebukes him with strong words. Khun Phaen accuses her of not acting as a good wife:

> "Eh! Enough! Too much, Wanthong. You show no respect for your husband. You're stubborn, wrongheaded, thoughtless. Even if you don't fear me, at least show me a little respect. / For better or worse, I'm your husband, but you don't seem to want me to be. Don't overdo it or I'll get angry. Don't lose the fish by beating the water in front of the trap. / If you love yourself and fear shame then calm down. Don't make a row or you'll lose face. If you don't listen to me and keep on, you'll be shamed in front of the townsfolk. Wait and see." (272)

Wanthong's actions have violated the code of a good wife as laid down in the *Verses of Worldly Wisdom*:

A good wife is like a slave, knowing	how to manage a household
Submissive to her husband like	a younger sibling
Ready to offer advice and warning	like a mother
Whenever her husband is angry	*she bears it with deference*[30]

Her actions also violate those in *Krishna Teaches His Sister*:

| Do not copy a rough woman | who is jealous, angry, and quarrelsome |
| Or refuses to submit to her husband | stubbornly stares and talks back without fear[31] |

And they violate the five rules of a good wife in the *Traiphum lokawinitchai*:

First, be loyal and loving to the husband; do not let your mind stray away; do not look at any other man except him; behave in a straightforward manner towards him both to his face and behind his back.[32]

According to the same text, a good wife cannot have two husbands. When the matter comes to a court case, Wanthong's own evidence is ruled as inadmissible precisely because of her simultaneous attachment to two men:

"This woman in the middle is impetuous. She finds herself in the wrong but has no fear. / She loves her lover so she sides with him. She lives with her husband and so she sides with him. The evidence is muddled and hence inadmissible." (443) Wanthong is subject to the four forms of prejudice listed and condemned in the *Traiphum lokawinitchai*, namely prejudice based on love, on anger, on delusion,

---

30. Niyada, *Prachum jaruek*, 683, emphasis added.
31. Ibid., 608.
32. Ibid., 512.

and on fear. As the section of this teaching about prejudice based on love notes, "such a person will bend with the power of love, turning right into wrong and wrong into right." In his speech condemning her to execution, the king notes, "You cannot say which one you love! Your heart wants both of them so you can switch back and forth, having a reserve deeper than the deep sea" (800).

Although Wanthong's actions contravene the moral code, she is portrayed as a woman who is steadfast in her love for her husband and son, and who is strong-willed in asserting her own opinions and fulfilling her own needs, as far as was possible for a woman of her time. As a result she is a memorable example of a bad woman that is still discussed and analyzed down to the present day.

Khun Chang Khun Phaen is a tale of ordinary people set in the landscape of cities and towns of the Siam of its era. In the same way that the display of the cities and towns of Siam in Wat Pho is set in the space occupied by the Great Cities and Upcountry Cities of the Jambu Continent in the Three Worlds manuscripts, so the characters of the tale are representative of the inhabitants of the Jambu Continent in the Three Worlds. The karma that they accumulate through their own good and bad deeds drives the plot of the tale and determines the fate of the characters.

Conclusion

Khun Chang Khun Phaen developed from a folktale passed on by word of mouth to become a written work performed at the royal court. The cast of principal characters, who are mainly common people or minor nobility, probably did not change in this transition from oral to written form, but the work acquired a new moral landscape. This was an era of didactic literature on morals including sayings, teachings, and advice in works like *Verses of Worldly Rules, Pali Teaches a Brother, Phleng yao thawai owat* [Long song of advice], *Sayings to Teach Ladies*, and *Lady Noppamat*. This literature was used to bring up young people in the court and urban society. The moral teachings in this literature also appeared in the inscriptions of Wat Pho, the royal *wat* renovated by King Rama III to strengthen the ideology of the Bangkok kingdom. This ideology is expressed in the plans of the city, of the royal palace, of Wat Pho, and of Wat Suthat, which were all established as symbolic centers of the cosmology in the Three Worlds texts.

When *Khun Chang Khun Phaen* was revised in the Second and Third Reigns, the work was adjusted to align with this ideology. Thus *Khun Chang Khun Phaen* was no longer simply a folktale about common people recited to entertain audiences in local towns, but became a means of propagating the ideology of the Buddhist state and society that the early Chakri court aimed to establish. The message about the laws of karma is told through the story with characters, including common people and kings, who commit good and bad deeds and who are visited with the consequences. This story is set in a detailed landscape of places including the capital, provincial towns, and routes passing through villages, the deep forest, and lands beyond Siam's borders. This landscape closely matches the one found in the Three Worlds texts with its Great City and Upcountry Cities in the Middle Country, its villages and the Himavanta Forest further away, and the Outer Country beyond.

Thus *Khun Chang Khun Phaen* is not only fine literature but a medium for the moral message in the cosmology of the Three Worlds. This message, which is deeply integrated into the plot and characterization, shapes reactions to the work right down to the present day.

SPACE, IDENTITY, AND SELF-DEFINITION: THE FOREST IN *KHUN CHANG KHUN PHAEN*

David C. Atherton

Introduction

Roughly one-third of the way into the classical Siamese narrative poem *Khun Chang Khun Phaen*, the poem's hero Khun Phaen makes a remarkably drastic decision. Although still a young man, he has already lived a life full of dramatic ups and downs and twists of fate. Born as Phlai Kaeo into a noble family of privilege, while still a child he loses everything when his father is executed on the king's orders. He is educated as a novice monk, marries the woman he loves, and is rewarded with the noble title "Khun Phaen" for leading an army to victory over Chiang Mai. But his return from war with a second wife prompts a quarrel with his first wife, Wanthong. Before long he is separated from both wives and banished from court to patrol the forest frontier, while his fat, ugly, boorish, and privileged rival Khun Chang takes Wanthong as his own wife against her will. It is at this moment that Khun Phaen makes his drastic decision. Lamenting the fate that has befallen him, he decides that "to be completely destroyed is better than to go on living."[1] First he will acquire magical items to make himself more powerful than he has ever been. Then, in the dead of night, he will steal into Khun Chang's house, take back his first wife

---

1. "Banlai sia yang di kwa mi chon." *Sepha rueang khun chang khun phaen: Chabap hosamut haeng chat* [Khun Chang Khun Phaen, National Library Edition] (Bangkok: Sinlapa Banakhan, 2001), 1:279.

Wanthong, and escape with her into the forest. If anyone attempts to pursue them, even the forces of the king, he will strike them down dead.

Why does the text present the forest as the only space available to Khun Phaen at a moment when he feels that being "completely destroyed is better than to go on living?" What can he hope to achieve in this forest? In other words, what exactly *is* this forest, and how does it function in the poem?

By looking at the ways that the forest and other spaces (the social spaces of state, village, and home) function in the poem in relation to the construction of identity, I will argue that the forest is a space that at one level implicitly correlates to the individual. Through what I propose is a unique relationship between the forest and words in the poem, the forest provides Khun Phaen with the ability to define his identity in terms of his own subjective inner world and to evade, or even defy, the externally imposed constructs of society.

The forest of the nineteenth century

What was the nature of the space that Siamese of the time designated as the "forest," at its most straightforward, non-literary, non-metaphorical level?

Until the mid-twentieth century the forest for most Siamese was something very near at hand. In the early nineteenth century the population of what we now think of as Thailand was a mere fraction of what it is today; the total combined population of Bangkok and the Central Plain as late as 1840 has been estimated at between only 230,000 and 410,000.[2] While increasing amounts of land came under cultivation, enormous swathes of it remained wild, and these uncultivated areas were largely forest, whether in the form of bamboo

2. Based on B. J. Terwiel, *Through Travellers' Eyes: An Approach to Early Nineteenth Century Thai History* (Bangkok: Editions Duang Kamol, 1989), 250–51.

thicket, stands of trees and shrubs, or thick jungle, interspersed with swamp, dry scrub, and grassland. This vast hinterland existed right at the edge of human habitation, just beyond the edge of cultivation. A mere sixty kilometers from the very rural capital city of Bangkok, wild elephants still "acted as a deterrent to the expansion of settlement" into the twentieth century.[3] With the forest so close at hand, human interaction with the forest was substantial.

Yet penetrating deep into the forest was difficult and dangerous; the growth was thick and full of wild animals and disease. Human habitation in the early nineteenth century consisted of mere "islands of settlement" in the midst of a much larger sea of uncultivated land,[4] and so while Siamese may have interacted extensively with the forest, most did not find their way into it too deeply, though they often had to cross patches of it simply to get from one settlement to another. As a result, the forest was a natural dwelling place for bandits and societal outcasts, who could live close enough to cultivated areas to prey on or benefit from them but could just as easily vanish into the thick protection of the forest growth. Aside from bandits, areas of the forest were also home to non-Siamese peoples such as the Lawa and Karen, who were perceived by the Siamese as culturally very different from themselves, but with whom there was some interaction and trade. The dangerous realities of the forest play a key role in the story of *Khun Chang Khun Phaen*: the fathers of all three main characters meet their deaths in ways that are explicitly related to the forest.[5]

3. Pasuk Phongpaichit and Chris Baker, *Thailand: Economy and Politics*, 2nd ed. (New York: Oxford University Press, 2002), 7.

4. Pasuk and Baker, *Thailand: Economy and Politics*, 7.

5. The death of Khun Phaen's father occurs in the forest on orders of the king, the father of Khun Chang dies in the forest at the hands of a forest bandit, and the father of Wanthong dies as the result of a fever caught in the forest during an expedition to trade with non-Siamese forest-dwelling peoples.

A conceptual model: Forest versus society

In the above descriptions of the Siamese forest, we can see a juxtaposition between inhabited, cultivated lands grouped into political entities, and a vast forest hinterland beginning wherever those lands ended. Philip Stott has characterized this traditional division as one between *mueang*, or state, and *pa*, or forest.[6] Stott characterizes the center of the traditional Tai city-state as a "princely capital" that formed

> the "merit-heart" of the *muang*, from which the "umbrella" of merit . . . spread to the very edge of the intermontane basin. . . . Above all, the effectiveness of this "umbrella" . . . depend[ed] on the merit (*bun*) of the king himself.[7]

Stott's characterization of this political entity follows the mandala[8] and galactic polity[9] models of premodern Southeast Asian state structure, in which polities formed around relatively stable centers, from which power extended outwards towards undefined, ever fluctuating borders. In Stott's model, this "light" or "heat" extends only as far as the mountains that surround the cultivated fields around the center. Beyond that frontier at the edge of the "controlled and benign Nature" of the fields,

---

6. Philip Stott, "*Muang* and *Pa*: Elite Views of Nature in a Changing Thailand," in *Thai Constructions of Knowledge*, ed. Manas Chitakasem and Andrew Turton (London: School of Oriental and African Studies, 1991), 145.

7. Stott, "*Muang* and *Pa*," 145.

8. O. W. Wolters, *History, Culture, and Region in Southeast Asian Perspectives* (Ithaca, NY: Cornell University Southeast Asia Program Publications, 1999), 27–40.

9. S. J. Tambiah, *World Conqueror and World Renouncer: A Study of Buddhism and Polity in Thailand against a Historical Background* (Cambridge: Cambridge University Press, 1976), 102–31.

rise the mountains that hem in the mental map of the *mu'ang*, for here is a forested land, the *pa thu'an*, which is filled with spirits, wild animals, and non-Tai peoples. Such regions lie outside the essential social organization of the *mu'ang*, outside the "umbrella" of merit emanating from the king, and outside controlled and benign Nature. Here we have a crucial contrast between Tai "civilized" space and Nature beyond normal social control.[10]

The forest lies beyond the "light" or "heat" radiating from the king at the center of the social polity and therefore, in Stott's characterization, is not merely a neutral space containing a large number of trees and animals, but a realm of "wilderness, savage and barbarous." He refers to the forest specifically as *pa thu'an*, which has overtones not only of wildness but of illegality; the term emphasizes "the barbaric character of the forest, which lies outside the civilized and lawful lands; such regions are wild, uncontrollable, and full of 'energy.'"[11]

We can therefore conceive of the nineteenth-century Siamese forest as a space considered separate and distinct from the social space of the *mueang*, which was a space of cultivated lands as well as villages, towns, and cities. The unifying power or merit emanating from the king at the center of the *mueang* did not penetrate into the forest, which was a dangerous space of wild animals and disease, a cover for bandits and those wishing to escape society, and also a site of spiritual power for ascetic monks. The forest was not distant, but existed right at the edge of cultivated land, and while most people did not penetrate too far into its depths, they could not help but interact with it, whether passing through it on the way to another settlement, or searching for valuable forest products at its edges.

10. Stott, "*Mu'ang* and *Pa*," 146.
11. Ibid., 144.

Society, the hierarchy of social space, and the forest

In *Khun Chang Khun Phaen,* society itself exhibits a complex architecture of its own based on different spaces within the overarching "umbrella" of the *mueang.* By space I do not mean simply physical locations, but the full assortment of constructs and concepts connected with a particular location, similar to the way in which the forest as a space is both a physical location and, conceptually, a hinterland full of dangers and abundance. Thus the "space" of the home includes, for example, the concept of the family, as well as the individual's identity within that family. In each of these spaces the identity of a human being is constructed in different ways; at the same time, each space appears to have a unique relationship with the space of the forest. Yet in all encounters between these spaces and the forest, a negotiation is always involved, whether characterized by antagonism, ambiguity, or accommodation.

The social sphere itself consists of a hierarchy of spaces descending downward from the overarching state (*mueang*) through the village (*ban*) and the house (*ruean*).

The state (*mueang*)

David Wyatt describes *mueang* as

> a term that defies translation, for it denotes as much personal as spatial relationships. When it is used in ancient chronicles to refer to a principality, it can mean both the town located at the hub of a network of interrelated villages and also the totality of town and villages which was ruled by a single *chao,* "lord."[12]

While the *mueang* as an "umbrella" incorporates all other layers of the social hierarchy (village and house), we also see it operating

---

12. David K. Wyatt, *Thailand: A Short History* (Chiang Mai: Silkworm Books, 1984, rpt. 1991), 7.

as a constructed space that defines identity in particular locales, particularly those spaces that correspond to government or royalty, such as the capital, in particular the royal palace, or in the cities. However, as a space defining identity, the *mueang* is not limited to these explicitly "state-related" locations: in fact, the "space" of the *mueang* can enter into the other levels of the hierarchy.

In the space of the *mueang*, identity is largely based upon class, which in turn is largely determined by proximity to the king. Premodern Siamese society was loosely divided into four classes: members of the royal family, nobles/officials, *phrai* (sometimes translated as "freemen" or "indentured peasants"), and *that* (often translated as "slaves").[13] *Phrai* and *that* had no identity within the political space of the *mueang*, which was explicitly concerned with officialdom and government. The "nobility" was not hereditary; status as a noble was conferred exclusively by the king through the conferment of a rank and title. In this sense, *phrai* could enter the realm of the *mueang* by receiving a rank and official position from the king, and similarly, nobles could be removed from the political space of the *mueang* through the loss of official position. Entering the space of the *mueang* as an official involved an explicit separation with one's identity in other spaces:

> [N]o official was known by his personal name, which he dropped immediately he was appointed to any office, but was known only by the titles connected with that office. Thus it was that officials were soon forgotten when their places had been filled by others. A result of this was that distinguished though nameless officials were seldom long remembered to serve as a model and inspiration to those who followed . . .[14]

13. H. G. Quaritch Wales, *Ancient Siamese Government and Administration* (New York: Paragon Book Reprint Corp., 1965), 21–68; Pasuk and Baker, *Thailand: Economy and Politics*, 7–9.

14. Wales, *Ancient Siamese Government*, 38.

Thus in the space of the *mueang* identity is defined explicitly by the king, and in terms of rank and title, in an almost anonymous way, disconnected from the individual personality of the holder of office. This *mueang* identity is then represented through the new name as well as through insignia, privileges, and gifts and servants bestowed by the king. Thus we can conceive of the space of the *mueang* as a space associated with authority, government, officialdom, rigidity, precision, rank, and order, and dominated exclusively by the figure of the monarch. This is a space explicitly separate from the other levels of social space, and strictly opposed, in all of its characteristics, to the wild, uncontrolled, uninhabited space of the forest.

Not surprisingly, the poem depicts the *mueang* as explicitly antithetical to the forest; when the two spaces come into direct contact, the encounter is usually violent. One example of this opposition comes near the beginning of the poem when the king decides that he will go to the forest to hunt buffalo. As the king's officials prepare for the king's progress into the forest, one of them is assigned the task of preparing a road; he is instructed to make it smooth and level, remove all the undergrowth completely, and make it eight *wa* (fathoms) wide. Roads are elements of the *mueang*. They are the strands that link the disparate parts of the *mueang* together, physically and symbolically. The forest is the natural enemy of roads. It overgrows the paths humans cut through its growth, encroaching through its natural abundance of life upon the arteries of the *mueang*, and obstructing travel and communication between these different parts through its thick growth and many dangers. The construction of a road is therefore crucial to the king's progress into the forest. The procession into the forest itself appropriately resembles an invasion force; the retinue includes a collection of royal elephants, an array of foot soldiers, a cavalry contingent of the finest, most elegantly harnessed horses, and an assortment of noblemen atop elephants.

The forest, however, appears more uncooperative with this endeavor than other social spaces would be. The corvée laborers preparing the hunting site in the forest resist performing the tasks they are assigned, work slowly and in a disorderly manner, are motivated only by the beatings they receive from their supervisors, and slip away into the forest to hide and rest any chance they can get. In other words, despite the impressive representation of the extension of the king's authority into the forest's space, in the forest that authority is visibly weakened, and the forest itself provides the cover that allows for evasion of that authority. Ultimately the hunt proceeds poorly as well. Thus we see the forest as a space in which *mueang* order and authority remain extremely tenuous and volatile, despite large-scale attempts to represent them as otherwise. This is in sharp contrast to the stability of *mueang* authority in the capital and palace, or even the lower spaces within the "umbrella" of social space.

The village (*ban*)

The *ban* is a far more intimate space than the *mueang*; it comprises a community whose members refer to each other by their birth names and in which there is more room for the expression of individual personality. As opposed to the exclusive space of the *mueang*, the village as a space accommodates both those with and without official rank; membership is determined by residence and acceptance by other community members rather than through formally conferred status. The sheer impersonality of the *mueang* is lessened in the village, but one's perceived place within the community of the *ban* still matters, and gossip can be a powerful and deadly force. Whereas the king is the final arbiter of authority in the *mueang*, one's perceived standing in the eyes of other members of the community largely determines one's position within the *ban*. Thus elements of personality such as perceived appropriate behavior, wisdom, or charisma, can play a role in the formation of one's identity in the village, as well as external elements such as wealth and rank. The rich Khun Chang, for example, holds a more ambiguous position in his community than he might, because the fact of his enormous wealth is counterbalanced by the common perception of him as an oaf and fool.

The home (*ruean*)

Each *ban* is comprised of a number of *ruean*, or homes, and the space of the home is the next unit of space in the hierarchy. The *ruean* is the most intimate of the social spaces; the unit of the *ruean* is the family, and official rank or wealth plays no role here, as all family members share the same status as a family unit. The ultimate authority within the family is the father, and in addition to the wife and children that make up the family, a household may also include servants and, at a more ethereal level, guardian spirits. Identity within the family is determined in relation to the other family members; an individual is a father, mother, husband, wife, son, daughter, brother, sister, or grandparent, and is usually addressed as such by the other members of the family.

The poem also depicts the interaction between the space of the house and the forest, but the negotiation between the two is strikingly different from the violent antagonism between the *mueang* and the forest. Rather, we find a domesticated, ordered, and enclosed reflection of the forest *within* the space of the *ruean*. This elaborate look within the space of the home occurs in the crucial moment when Khun Phaen comes to Khun Chang's house in the night to kidnap Wanthong, one of the most famous episodes of the entire poem and widely considered one of the most beautifully composed.

Penetrating the house compound, he climbs up to the house, close to Khun Chang's bedroom, and lands among the potted flowers of an ornamental garden on the terrace. The garden, intriguingly, is described in poetry that resembles that used to describe the forest; the flowers are grouped in ways that allow for maximum alliteration and internal rhyme in the poetry, as in the first stanza:

> There were flowerpots (*krathang*) in rows with *kaew, ket*, and
> *phikun* mixed together (*kaem*).
> *Yisun* and *masang* interspersed (*saem*) were arranged brightly
> (*sawai*).

Samo was tied and arranged into pretty forms.
Takhop and *khoi* were selected (*khat*) to alternate appealingly.[15]

Whereas in the forest such linguistic order seems fantastical, as we shall see in the next section of the paper, here it seems natural: a garden, after all, is a space in which order has been brought to nature. The structure of the poetry, while highlighting the poetic beauty of the flowers, reminds us of their orderliness, and of the human artifice that has been applied to them. Unlike the catalogues of plant names that appear in the forest, where names of trees and flowers can be listed without a single word of narrative interruption, the listing of flower names here is punctuated with phrases, such as "mixed together," and "arranged brightly," that remind us, despite the resemblance to descriptions of the forest, of the constructed nature of this garden. Unlike the wild vastness of the forest, this garden is ordered through human craft, and contained by the walls of the inner house.

Khun Phaen proceeds deeper into the house and approaches the bedroom where Wanthong and Khun Chang are sleeping. In order to enter the bedroom, however, he must first pass beyond three hanging tapestries embroidered with exquisite skill by Wanthong. The first of these tapestries depicts, with stunning beauty, an elaborate version of the Himaphan (Himavanta) forest, the mythical forest on the outskirts of human habitation in the Buddhist cosmology of the Three Worlds. Like the garden, this, too, is a representation of a domesticated version of the wild forest. Wanthong's weaving, for all its beauty and detail, is static; moreover, it is bounded by the edges of the tapestry. Like the garden, the tapestry represents nature brought under control and contained within borders, and then contained, in turn, within the space of the house. After admiring this tapestry, Khun Phaen unsheathes his sword and cuts it to shreds, symbolically liberating the forest from its static, bounded depiction and underscoring his violation of the ordered spaces and social relationships of the *ruean*.

15. *Sepha rueang khun chang khun phaen*, 1:310.

He then proceeds into the bedroom, kidnaps Wanthong, and escapes with her out into the unbounded wilds of the forest itself.

In the poem's construction the household is thus the level of the social hierarchy that provides the most accommodation for elements of the forest, which within the space of the house appear controlled and domesticated. In this space, humans exert control over nature, but the negotiation appears to be a relatively peaceful one, as opposed to the dramatic representation of difference involved in the interaction between the *mueang* and the forest. If, as this essay will ultimately argue, the poem constructs the forest as the space that accommodates subjective, self-defined identity, there appears to be an implication here that within the social hierarchy of spaces, the intimate space of the home provides the most accommodation for an individual's subjectively defined identity—though that identity nonetheless remains mediated through interaction with others.

The many social identities of Phlai Kaeo/Khun Phaen

Most of the events of Khun Phaen's life involve either the pursuit of legitimacy at all levels of the hierarchy, or the unexpected loss of that legitimacy—showing, perhaps, how precarious identity can be at any of society's levels of space. Understanding his travails at the various levels of the hierarchy will help us to understand Khun Phaen's eventual decision to take the drastic step of leaving society behind altogether and escaping to the forest with Wanthong.

As a child he is born as Phlai Kaeo into good standing at all levels: his father is a nobleman favored by the king, and the family therefore has rank and prestige within the *mueang*. The family also has good standing within the local village community, and the marriage between Phlai Kaeo's parents is a happy one. All of this falls apart when Phlai Kaeo's father, through no fault of his own, runs afoul of the king and is executed. Phlai Kaeo's world is shattered at every level of the hierarchy. He has not only lost a channel of access to the *mueang* through his father, but he carries the stigma of being the son of an executed man. At the village level, he and his mother have to flee their *ban* and start over in a new community to avoid capture and imprisonment by the king's troops, as all of the executed man's property reverts to ownership by the king. The family structure has also been shattered with the removal of the father, the central figure of family authority. It is perhaps no surprise that the one space open to Phlai Kaeo and his mother in this moment of rupture at every level of society is the forest. As the king's troops come to confiscate the possessions of the executed man and force his wife and son into palace servitude, the two are able to slip away, with almost no possessions, and seek refuge in the forest; Phlai Kaeo spends the first night of his new, shattered life sleeping in a tree.

Phlai Kaeo and his mother eventually make their way to Kanchanaburi and slowly begin the process of building a new life. Through agriculture and trading his mother slowly establishes herself. She earns the respect of this new community for her hard work, and so the shattered family, with the mother now filling the role of both father and mother, becomes established at the level of the *ban*. Phlai Kaeo becomes a novice in a local monastery and distinguishes himself as an expert pupil, quickly mastering all of the knowledge the abbot imparts to him. He moves to Suphanburi to continue his studies at a larger temple, and he also becomes adept at reciting the *jatakas*, particularly the prestigious and popular Mahachat (Great Jataka); this ability earns him praise from the community. Phlai Kaeo meets his childhood playmate Phim Philalai, now a beautiful young woman, and falls in love. He seduces her, leaves the monastery, and marries her, beating out his rival Khun Chang.

At this point Phlai Kaeo is a complete success at the level of the *ruean* and the *ban*. He is a dutiful son, a talented student, a respected member of the community on his own merits, and he has succeeded in establishing a family through his love marriage to Phim. At the level of the *mueang*, however, Phlai Kaeo remains a nobody; he has no rank, no title, and he is completely unknown to the king. Soon, however, he is brought to the king's attention. The king needs someone talented to lead an army against Chiang Mai. The king remembers Phlai Kaeo's valiant father and wonders if he left behind any children; Khun Chang, seeing an opportunity to remove his rival, tells the king of Phlai Kaeo's marvelous skills as a warrior. Phlai Kaeo must part with his new wife only three days after their wedding, but he leads the troops to victory, and when he returns to Ayutthaya he is given the noble title Khun Phaen. "Khun" designates one of the lower ranks of the noble hierarchy and "Phaen" is a royally provided name; with the conferral of this noble title he achieves legitimacy at the level of the *mueang*. At last he has regained all that he lost as a child, and he is successful once again in all three levels of the hierarchy: state, community, and home.

Interestingly, the rupture that destroys this newfound success at all levels first occurs in the space of the *ruean*. Khun Phaen returns from battle with a second wife, Laothong, sparking a jealous quarrel with Phim (who has changed her name to Wanthong). Khun Phaen and Wanthong are estranged. As a result of Khun Chang's trickery, Khun Phaen also loses Laothong and is banished by the king to patrol the forest frontier. Khun Chang takes his opportunity to force Wanthong into marriage.

Khun Phaen's identity at this point becomes extremely ambiguous at all levels of the social hierarchy. He still has a wife, but he has no access to her. He has not lost standing in his village community, but he is banished from it. He still maintains an identity within the *mueang*, but despite retaining his rank he has been exiled to the edge of the forest, the space most antithetical to the *mueang*, where that rank has the least meaning. Khun Phaen, who up to this point constructed successful identity at each of these levels largely on his own merit, suddenly finds his identity negatively redefined by others.

Interestingly, no part of the hierarchy we have examined necessarily provides a space in which the individual defines his or her own identity. At the level of the *mueang* one only comes into existence through rank conferred by the king; in the village, identity is determined in the eyes of other members of the community, and in the home an individual's identity comes from position within the family structure. There is no space in the social hierarchy that is explicitly for the individual, where internal definitions of identity, based on such subjective elements as emotions, feelings, memories and personal desires can come into play; this subjective space of self-definition of the individual *as an individual* may be reserved for that person's inner world, separate from the external interactions involved in the construction of identity within *society*, which by its very nature necessarily will always involve mediation and translation through interaction with others.

A desire to take his identity into his own hands leads to Khun Phaen's drastic decision to steal Wanthong back from Khun Chang and escape with her into the forest. All of his efforts to achieve a successful identity within society have thrown him into an ambiguous limbo, and he decides to turn his back on society and return to the space that offered him refuge the last time his societal identity was shattered. In the forest, free from the definitions of *mueang*, *ban*, and *ruean*, he may be able to reach for a more subjective, intimate success: the ability to live in a state of personal happiness with the woman he loves, free from societal definitions. In that case, he will be attaining a complete inversion of the social hierarchy, which places the impersonal at the pinnacle and provides almost no space for the explicitly personal, intimate, or subjective.

The forest and words

The space of the forest as constructed in the poem is vastly different from the poem's other spaces. This statement is true at a variety of levels. It is a physically different space, made up of untouched, wild nature rather than nature transformed through human labor. There are no human structures; Khun Phaen and Wanthong do not have a roof, a bed, or a mosquito net, but sleep on the ground beneath a banyan tree. It is not a social space—or it is social in the most reduced sense of "society." Barring two encounters with troops sent to seize them and one visit to a Lawa village for supplies, Wanthong and Khun Phaen interact with no one but each other. Thus we might say that as far as the two of them are concerned, the forest is an intimate space rather than a social space. There is no hierarchy involved, there are no rules, there are no observers keeping watch; there are only two individuals.

However, the forest is also a very different space from the other spaces we have examined in another way. As a poetically constructed space in the poem, the forest is unique. Words work differently there, even the descriptive words of the poem's anonymous omniscient narrator. While alliteration, internal rhyme, and wordplay are a key element of the *klon* poetic meter, in the spaces of society these usually operate within certain bounds. The narrative mode of the poem is highly mimetic; while poetic devices and wordplay enrich and augment the narrative throughout, they remain largely beholden to the meaning of that which they are describing, and this meaning usually will not be sacrificed to sound. In the forest, however, these restraints become looser. Meaning suddenly becomes secondary to sound, and words are allowed to play with a flamboyance and vivaciousness, often delighting in sound for sound's sake, that we do not see in the poetic construction of other sections of the poem.

Once the forest becomes the focus of poetic description, a vast reservoir of vocabulary is suddenly available to a poet in the form of endless and varied names of trees, plants, flowers, and animals. Moreover, many of these names are not simply new words, but may be compounds of, or homonyms for, words that exist in other contexts as well (such as "morning glory" or "palm" in English, as opposed to hydrangea or hibiscus). This fact opens up tremendous possibilities for wordplay, puns, and innuendos.

Not only is all of this vocabulary suddenly available to poets composing verses about the forest, but *the fact that it is the forest* aids them immensely as well: it is a separate space. As in the real forest, there are no rules: poets can utilize the names of trees for their sounds without feeling beholden to any claims to realism. In the forest, words can be allowed to play for the sake of their sounds, and in a sense that playfulness, the almost wild unleashing of words, will be fitting for a wild and fantastical space such as the forest.

The freedom allowed in the poetic descriptions enables a certain freedom for the characters as well, and the loosening of rules concerning meaning parallels the loosening of constraints concerning identity, which the characters experience by leaving the social space. As the connection between word and meaning becomes more flexible in the forest, there is more space for a character to take steps towards defining himself or herself. The forest, it appears, is a space of the individual in a way that the *mueang*, the *ban*, and the *ruean* are not.

Words and power

In order to understand the implications of the unique nature of words in the space of the forest, we must first look at the tremendous sense of power connected with words in the poem up to this point, particularly within the social space.

Khun Phaen is famous for his mastery of the arts of invulnerability; the poem is full of dramatic scenes in which attacks on his body fail to cause him any harm. Rather, it is words that cause Khun Phaen the most damage. Like his father, who possessed similar powers of invulnerability but had to submit to death at the word of the king, Khun Phaen, despite his tremendous powers, is often at the mercy of the king's orders. At a word from the king he loses his wife Laothong and is banished to the forest frontier, and later in the poem the orders of the king confine him to prison for years; he remains in the prison, bound by an oath, despite having the physical means to escape. Khun Chang, helpless before Khun Phaen's physical powers, repeatedly uses words as his weapon of choice against his rival. It is the twisted words of Khun Chang that cause Khun Phaen to be separated from Wanthong three days after their wedding, that cause Khun Phaen to lose his second wife Laothong, and that later cause the king to send a military force to pursue Khun Phaen and Wanthong into the forest.

Khun Phaen and Wanthong's marriage falls apart in a spectacular outburst of heated words, and the gossip of neighbors contributes to the decision of Wanthong's mother to force her into marriage with Khun Chang.

Despite Khun Phaen's frequent helplessness in the face of words, he is in many ways a master of words himself. His powers stem from his control of mantra, and the proper incantation can open locks, turn him invisible, summon up fierce spirits, or cause a woman to fall helplessly in love with him. Even without resorting to mantras, Khun Phaen is a famously smooth sweet-talker in the bedroom, yet also a master of malicious puns and hurtful wordplay in his spats with his lovers. As a novice monk he gains renown for his mastery at reciting the Mahachat. Thus to some degree, Khun Phaen, while a victim of words in some instances (and most often in the space of the *mueang*), is also a master of them in others.

In keeping with this relationship between words and power, names and titles in particular can change the fortunes and destinies of those upon whom they are bestowed. It is in receiving the noble title "Khun Phaen" that Phlai Kaeo finally achieves legitimacy in the space of the *mueang*. Wanthong, too, acquires the name by which she is best known midway through the story; pining for Khun Phaen, who has left for the battlefields of Chiang Mai only three days after their wedding, she has wasted away so much that a fortune teller warns that she must change her name if she hopes to survive. Leaving behind the old name of Phim and adopting the new name, Wanthong saves her life.

Power over words and names can give individuals the power to define themselves. The very ability to change one's name, whether as a measure taken to save one's own life, as in the case of Wanthong, or as a sign of newly conferred legitimacy and respect, as in the case of Khun Phaen, may be a sign of a character's ability to grow, change, and mature. Wanthong changes her name at the moment she first faces the adult grief of womanhood as a wife; Khun Phaen receives his title at the moment he fulfills the heroic legacy of his father and enters the space of the *mueang* as one of its members. Of the three main characters of the story, the only one who never changes his name, Khun Chang, is the one who remains static as a character—always an inconsiderate and ugly oaf, from the moment he is born bald to the moment he leaves the main story of the poem.

The linguistically flexible forest

From the moment Khun Phaen and Wanthong first enter the forest, names and meanings appear to take on a far more flexible, perhaps even playful relationship. Having journeyed across rivers and fields, they enter the forest just before dawn. A beautiful description of the moon, flowers, and then the rising sun leads to a passage about the activities of the forest animals as day breaks.

> A group of monkeys (*ling*) ran about beneath the branches of the *langling* tree.
> Some monkeys (*lang ling*) slipped and chased each other, running wildly.
> Some monkeys (*lang ling*) snatched at lemurs and climbed the *langling* tree.
> Crows (*ka*) became dizzy (*long*) and descended (*long*) into the branches of the *kalong* tree.

> Crows (*ka*) clung to every twig of the *pheka* tree
> The crows (*ka*) snatched flowers (*kanika*) and were lost in admiration of them.
> Flocks of crows (*matka*) disturbed all the crows of the forest (*kadong*)
> In the vines (*kafak*) the crows descended and made their nests (*rangka*).

> A tiger (*suea*) peered out, walking stealthily behind the tiger-eye tree (*ta suea*)
> The broad (*kwang*) shade of a deer-ear tree (*hukwang*) provided shelter to a herd of forest deer (*kwangpa*)

An elephant (*chang*) pushed over elephant-cane (*oi chang*) in a
row
Mynahs clung to *phikun* branches, eating.[16]

These are remarkable stanzas, not simply because of the flamboyant activities of the animals, nor only because of the elaborate wordplay, but because in these stanzas the names of the animals involved and the plays on those names *dominate* the action. Loosed from any pretensions to mimesis, the potential for linguistic play contained in the words comes to dictate the construction of the scene, as the objects of description are put to use to allow the words to explore their own possibilities.

The description of the monkeys in the first stanza shows this phenomenon very clearly. The play of the stanza relies entirely on the pun between the homophones *langling* ("some monkeys") and *langling* (a type of tree). There appears to be a large number of monkeys scrambling below and through the branches of what must be a rather sturdy tree. Yet a *langling* is actually a *pinanga*, "a small or medium-sized ornamental palm" (McFarland). Clearly the poet here was not concerned with the image of a real *langling* tree, but realistic depiction here is beside the point: the focus is on the words and the play that the words allow, more than the actual image that they describe.

The second stanza takes the wordplay a step farther. Its sounds are as follows:

Phe-ka ka kao thuk kan king / kanni-ka ka ching kan chom long
Mat-ka ka kuan luan ka dong / kafak ka long tham rangka.

Not only does the passage include numerous words that include the sound /ka/, but the first three lines are composed in such a way that in each of them the sound "*ka ka*" (onomatopoeia for the crying of crows) is repeated. Thus the verse, while describing the activities of

---

16. *Sepha rueang khun chang khun phaen*, 1:336–37.

crows, also succeeds in "cawing." Many of the words (particularly the ones with /ka/ sounds in them) are doing double, or even triple duty. The first "*ka*" of the first line of the stanza, for example, forms part of the name of the *pheka* tree, repeats the word for crow ("*ka*") thus adding to the sense of numerous crows in the scene, and combines with the following "*ka*" to reproduce the sound of cawing. This very multiplicity of possible meanings highlights the fact that hiding behind a word or name can be a wide range of possible meanings.

The passage demonstrates that in this poetically constructed forest words and names function differently than they do in the realm of society. In the *mueang*, a title can summarize the entire identity of an individual in that space; it functions as a label that indicates where each individual fits into the well-ordered schema of the *mueang*'s space. If one does not possess a title (like Phlai Kaeo before becoming Khun Phaen), that absence indicates one's lack of access to the *mueang*'s political space. In society a person's name and the names of his parents and his wife's parents might summarize everything about who he is. In the third stanza of the above passage, we see a similar tyranny associated with names and titles, but here it is entirely playful. A tiger-eye tree's name also tells everything about what it is: it is a tree that must, of course, have a tiger peering out from behind it. The names of trees determine what happens around them. The elephant will no more push down a row of tiger-eye trees than the tiger will enjoy the shade of a deer-ear tree.

The lovers continue their journey to the banyan tree that will form their dwelling in the forest. The site, referred to as Tha Ton Sai ("Banyan Landing"), is described in idyllic terms: an enormous banyan tree spreads its branches, providing shade and shelter next to the lotus-filled pool of a clear flowing stream. Khun Phaen cuts banana leaves to make a bed, and he and Wanthong make love for the first time in the forest.

Throughout the poem, as in most classical Thai works, lovemaking is described not explicitly, but through the medium of *bot atsajan*: "marvel stanzas." In *bot atsajan* sexual activity is described figuratively, through various elaborations on a set of symbolic imagery, usually connected to wind, rain, and water. A typical *bot atsajan* will describe rain suddenly pouring from the sky, waves pounding the shore, fish and shrimps dancing ecstatically, and, perhaps more suggestively, a boat trying to sail up a narrow canal in the stormy weather. This first instance of lovemaking in the forest between Khun Phaen and Wanthong is also depicted through the means of a *bot atsajan*:

> He spoke as he embraced her tightly with desire.
> Thunder burst and rain fell in a thick splatter,
> Hitting the leaves of the banyan tree and slipping down,
> Drenching and washing the bright leaves.
> A breeze blew, setting everything fluttering.
> The tree swayed from side to side, its branches quivering.
> The two caressed and fondled lustily;
> They were content and delighted in the shade of the banyan in
>   the forest.[17]

There is a key difference between this *bot atsajan* and the ones that appear elsewhere in the poem. In the other instances, the figurative imagery is entirely symbolic. When such a scene, drawing upon, for example, the image of a roiling sea, comes to an end, the characters do not sit up to find the floor of the bedroom drenched in sea water; in fact, they may be hundreds of miles from the sea. In this instance in the forest, however, the boundary between figurative poetic imagery and depicted reality has been crossed: the images have stepped out of the *bot atsajan* and begun to affect the actual scene of the lovemaking. The pounding rain of the storm, a typical element of *bot atsajan*, actually riles the branches of the banyan and drenches its leaves, yet once the lovemaking is over the characters are depicted enjoying the shade the tree provides from the sun, apparently confirming the fact that the storm was merely a figurative one.

---

17. *Sepha rueang khun chang khun phaen*, 1:340.

This rather playful and fantastical moment, combined with the elaborate wordplay of the preceding stanzas, appears to confirm that the space of the forest in the poem functions differently from the other spaces, and particularly in its relationship with words. In the forest, we can begin to question the power relationship between words and that which they describe, between signifier and signified. Which is in control? To what degree is this forest implicitly a forest of words as much as it is a forest of trees? To what degree is the presence of the trees incidental to the play allowed by their names or the words that describe them?

Within the word-logic of the poem, therefore, the forest constitutes a natural space of escape for a character like Khun Phaen, who has been limited and hampered in so many ways by the concrete relationship that exists between names, words, and meanings. Not only is he no longer limited by society's definitions or the words of his rival, but we shall also see that there may even be an opportunity here for him to take advantage of this space, where the relationship between signifier and signified is so flexible, and define himself on his own terms, from a more subjective point of view, with the words of the forest itself (rather than society's concepts and labels) as his medium. As though to counter this possibility, society—specifically the *mueang*—makes an incursion into the space of the forest and attempts to define Khun Phaen on its own terms once again.

After Khun Phaen flees to the forest with Wanthong, Khun Chang gathers a force of soldiers and pursues them, but his posse is repulsed by an army of soldiers that Khun Phaen makes from cut grass animated with a mantra. Khun Chang persuades the king to send a larger force. When Khun Phaen refuses to return with them to the capital, two noble officers, apparently convinced of Khun Phaen's guilt and hoping to bait him, heckle Khun Phaen:

He pointed his finger and shouted, "Hey Phlai Kaeo!
You're acting so haughty as though I don't know anything.

Your lineage is worthless.

…

I've known your father and mother for a long time.
Your father's name was Khun Krai,
Your mother is old Thong Prasi.
That year they went to round up buffalo
His Majesty had your father executed.
His head was cut off and stuck on a stake in the highlands,
And all his possessions were confiscated right down to the cows
    of his relatives.
Your mother took you and hid away.
You secretly made your way out of the city
And went to Kanchanaburi.
You lived there with your old woman at Chonkai Hill,
And ordained at Wat Som Yai, you coward.
When you went off to fight Chiang Thong, people said you were good;
You became the talented Khun Phaen.
Things went well for less than a year,
And then you sneaked away to plot rebellion.
You had an affair with your lover and kidnapped her into the
    forest.
I can't associate with you any longer; our friendship is over.[18]

This is an account of Khun Phaen's identity told in society's (and particularly the *mueang*'s) terms. This account of Khun Phaen refers to his family history, the history of his relationship with the state, and his various activities as perceived and related by others ("people said you were good"). It is the very type of socially constructed identity under which Khun Phaen was chafing when he decided to kidnap Wanthong. It is one in which he has no say in how he is defined, and in which the words and opinions of others twist the perception of who he is, in this case constructing an identity as a political traitor.

18. *Sepha rueang khun chang khun phaen*, 1:374–75.

It is significant, therefore, that Khun Phaen's reaction to this account of himself, partially true though it may be, is to become enraged and slay the two men who have thus described him. Moreover, he then launches an attack against the king's troops by means of his grass soldiers, and while the only individuals slain by Khun Phaen himself are the two officers who heckle him, his grass soldiers annihilate all but a few hundred of the king's several thousand men. This is, literally, a case of the forest (in the form of animated grass) defeating the *mueang*, and it marks the remarkable power that is available to Khun Phaen in the forest, particularly in relation to words. He has punished those who would define him in society's terms, slashing them the way he slashed to pieces Wanthong's forest tapestry in Khun Chang's house, and for the first time he has successfully defied the orders of the king, which have bound him so often in the past and which caused the death of his own father. If the unique relationship between the forest and words allows for more maneuverability and power in relation to words, Khun Phaen is clearly mastering that power.

As they ride away through the forest, Khun Phaen points out trees to Wanthong along the way, and in the process he narrates a subjective account of their relationship, playing on the names of the trees. The result is an account of their affair that is strikingly different from the one presented by the two commanders in the language of the *mueang*:

At a clearing among rocks, blossoms bloomed all around. He pointed out to Wanthong, "Look at the flowers. They're captivating."
The light of a bright moon illuminated the sweet sight of blooming sprays. "There's a *smilinglady* smiling in the forest fringe, just like you smiled in the cotton field;
an elegant spray of *hiddenlover*, just like us two hiding away as young lovers; a *secretscent*, perfuming the air, like the fragrance of your delicate cheeks when you were sent to me in the bridal house;
a *lady's fingernail* with its tiny petals open, like your fingers fan and comb for me; and an *eveningbloom* all over the bank of a lotus pond, like I'm all over you, evening and morning too.

There's climbing jasmine twined round *miseryplum* and *parting palm*. After only three days, karma parted us in misery. There's a *jampi* beside a *heartache tree* hanging with *braidflowers*. For more than two years, heartache and gloom were hanging over me.

Fragrance from a cinnamon tree mingles with the scent of a *happyshade*. Enjoying you today sent me such happiness. The air is bathed in the aroma of roses and *waitingladies*. Little lady, let's wait a little—and enjoy a kiss." (384–85; emphasis added)

Compared to society's version of their story, cast at Khun Phaen by the two commanders during the attack ("You had an affair with your lover and kidnapped her into the forest"), this account of Khun Phaen and Wanthong's history and experience of each other is personal, intimate, and subjective. Khun Phaen is giving an account of himself on his own terms, in his own words, defining his identity not through the medium of external factors or society's interpretations, but through his own inner emotions and experiences. The fact that he accomplishes this account of his inner world through the medium of the forest itself, through the very flexibility between word, name, and meaning that defines the forest, is striking. Here the forest truly does appear to be a space for the individual, which acknowledges the vastness and complexity of an individual's inner world as a part of his identity in a way that none of the social spaces appear able to do.

The subjective forest?

In fact, there may be a sense in which the forest itself *is* a reflection of the individual's inner state: the strikingly different depictions of the forest at different moments in the poem—at times of a dark, dangerous, and forbidding space and at other times of an exuberantly idyllic, almost celestial space—appear to relate directly to the subjective inner state of the person experiencing the forest in that particular context.

When Khun Phaen and Wanthong first enter the forest, Wanthong's feelings are in a state of turmoil. She has been estranged from Khun Phaen, forced to marry Khun Chang, and is now being abducted from her comfortable home. She resists leaving at first, and is uneasy on the journey until the lovemaking described above rekindles her passion for Khun Phaen. She fans him as he falls asleep beside her beneath the banyan, but once he is asleep the love mantra begins to wear off, and Wanthong's feelings change. While the forest up to this point is described in terms of extravagant, idyllic beauty, suddenly she sees it in another way. "Alas, look at me now. / I'm stuck, forlorn here in the large forest. / I'll be bait for tigers and ghosts in the middle of the wilderness, / and the forest will be a home to me like a graveyard."[19] She becomes acutely aware of the insects all around her, and longs for the comfort of Khun Chang's home. "From now on I'll really be tainted. / Soon I'll have to stitch together leaves to cover myself. / I've come to wallow in the dust and wind; / I'll grow sadder day by day." She longs to rest, but laments the discomfort of lying on pebbles and sand. "Everything is destroyed. / I've forsaken my house and position to come sleep in the wilderness. / There are no lights but the moon, / and I've left my house for the shade of trees."[20] We can see in Wanthong's account of the forest a reflection of her own inner state. The forest, which moments before appeared ravishingly beautiful, suddenly transforms as she contemplates the difficulty of her position now that she has accompanied Khun Phaen.

That night, however, Wanthong makes a decision to stay with Khun Phaen in the forest, forget the ups and downs of the past, and let their love blossom once again. Once she has made this decision, the descriptions of the forest as it is seen by the lovers return to their idyllic state and remain that way throughout their time there. After they have been living in the forest for some time, there is a description of the forest that appears to mirror Wanthong's earlier dark comparison

---

19. *Sepha rueang khun chang khun phaen*, 1:340.
20. Ibid., 1:341.

between the forest and the house; this time, however, the perspective has completely shifted:

> Though they had only logs beneath them, they were content.
> Though there was no mattress for soft Wanthong,
>   it was like sleeping on an unblemished golden bed.
> They were absorbed in the reverberation of the cicadas' song
>   and were lulled to sleep by the orchestra of the forest playing
>   to the wilds.
> In the darkness, without a candle or lamp to shine the way,
>   the moon cast its clear, limpid light instead.[21]

The contrast between life in the forest and life in a house remains the same as in the previous passage, yet now the perspective has changed and become far more positive. The forest is not a place of hardship; if anything, the elements that seemed so trying at first (the insects, the lack of a bed or light) now are the very things that appear so pleasurable. The depiction of the forest appears to be acting as an outward projection of the inner state of its inhabitants.

Appropriately, when Khun Chang rides his elephant into the forest with his men in pursuit of the lovers, the forest he sees is not idyllic at all. Khun Chang's feelings are in even greater turmoil than Wanthong's when she first enters the forest. He is insanely jealous that Wanthong is with his rival Khun Phaen, and stung moreover that his beloved Wanthong was willing to desert him to go off into the forest at all. He finally locates their hideaway and challenges Khun Phaen to do battle. Khun Phaen soundly defeats Khun Chang's forces and then charges after Khun Chang, who flees on his elephant. The elephant's howdah catches on thorny vines and crashes to the ground; Khun Chang, in fear for his life, flees straight into a thicket of rattan thorns, which catch at his clothes, rip open his skin, and finally trap him altogether, so that later he has to be cut free by his men after the battle is over.

---

21. *Sepha rueang khun chang khun phaen*, 1:387.

He is so badly wounded that he looks "as torn as though a tiger had clawed him all over."[22]

The contrast of Khun Chang's experience in the forest to that of Khun Phaen and Wanthong is striking. For him, the forest is a dark and dangerous place, and it actively works to harm him. In the battle with Khun Phaen, it is not Khun Phaen who defeats Khun Chang, but the forest itself that attacks and wounds him.

It should be noted that only the forest changes as a reflection of the characters' inner moods. Depictions of social spaces such as the royal palace, for example, are always the same. The palace never changes based on the person observing or experiencing it; it is unfailingly characterized by precision, orderliness, and grandeur. Also, while this phenomenon of the "double forest" appears elsewhere in classical South and Southeast Asian literature, its function as a reflection of the inner state of the characters appears to be unique to *Khun Chang Khun Phaen*. In the Vessantara Jataka, for example, the forest aids Prince Vessantara and hinders the crooked Brahmin Jujaka, but this phenomenon appears to be a reflection of the characters' respective merit or moral stature; trees bend low and offer their fruit to Vessantara because of his status as the future Buddha, to help him on his way, not because of his own subjective inner state. In *Khun Chang Khun Phaen*, on the other hand, the forest does not appear to be responding to the characters' respective merit, karma, destiny, or noble identity. It seems, instead, to reflect the very human characters' subjective inner states. If they are happy, the forest appears beautiful. If they are suffering, the forest appears as a place of suffering.

Conclusion

Why, then, the creation of the forest as a space reflective of the individual, and of his or her subjective inner states? What is the significance of

22. *Sepha rueang khun chang khun phaen*, 1:350.

this alternative space in which representation functions so differently from the way it does in the broader social spaces of the poem? One possibility relates to the very nature of poetic composition itself. There is an intriguing echo between the self-definition of the characters within the space of the forest, and the self-definition of the poets who constructed that forest in words. The composition of *Khun Chang Khun Phaen* was carried out collectively, initially with different oral performers specializing in different sections, and later, when the poem became the subject of court composition, with different court poets responsible for different sections (notably in the salon of King Rama II). In both of these modes of composition—whether a professional performer seeking fame for his mastery of a particular section, or a court poet seeking recognition among his peers in the salon—the forest sections of the poem offer a unique opportunity to showcase verbal mastery and individual style. Just as the characters are freed from conventional social restraints in the space of the forest, so too is the poet freed from the conventions of mimetic realism and plot progression that largely pertain throughout the other sections of the poem. The forest, affording release into a realm of heightened poetic wordplay, becomes a site for indulgence in verbal pyrotechnics, offering the poet a rich opportunity to make a name for himself on the basis of innate skill and poetic virtuosity. In this sense, we may conceive of the forest as a space of self-making not merely for the characters depicted as inhabiting it, but also for the very poets who brought it into being.

At the same time, if we consider the poem within a larger social context, we can find echoes between the self-definition afforded the characters in the forest, and larger changes taking place within Siamese society. Nidhi Eoseewong has argued that we must understand early Bangkok literature in terms of the emergence of a new, "bourgeois" culture facilitated by the rise of an export economy and the resulting changes in the more rigid, hierarchical relationships that had previously structured Siam's upper classes. The subjects of this new bourgeoisie were defined as much by their capacity for risk, individual initiative, and cosmopolitan knowledge—all assets in a market economy—as they were by hereditary status.[23] We can see Khun Phaen as a complex embodiment of this emerging ethos throughout the poem: a self-made man of considerable talents and wide knowledge, frequently at odds with more traditional power structures. It is significant that he is most powerful in the alternative realm of the forest, and that his power there appears to be linked to the capacity the forest affords for self-definition and the outward expression of inner states. It may seem strange to consider the forest (rather than, say, the marketplace or the port) as a site for the exploration and expression of a new, "bourgeois," individual subjectivity. However, we can view the forest as a kind of untamed frontier already present within the traditional landscape of the poem: a fallow site absent a regime of established social expectations in which focus could be placed upon the individual.

We can perhaps go so far as to think of the forest in *Khun Chang Khun Phaen* as not only a space in which the individual can achieve a subjective, personal definition of his identity, but as a space that may, at some level, function as a metaphor for the inner world on which that definition is based. Like the conceptual division that exists between the forest and society, in any individual there is always a division between an experience of oneself based on one's own inner world, and the way one is perceived by others through the various lenses of social interaction and construction. In various social contexts an individual may be a father or mother, a friend, a neighbor, a subject; but to oneself one is much more than the sum of all of these things, because within, one has a seemingly boundless world that takes shape in the endlessly shifting collisions between memories, desires, emotions, and imaginings. It is unlikely that the poets who composed *Khun Chang Khun Phaen* explicitly thought of the forest in these terms. At the same time, it is difficult, after examining the forest in the context of words, identity, and the subjective, not to see a parallel between that vast,

---

23.   Nidhi Eoseewong, "Bourgeois Culture and Early Bangkok Literature," in *Pen and Sail: Literature and History in Early Bangkok*, ed. Chris Baker and Ben Anderson (Chiang Mai: Silkworm Books, 2005), 3–146.

unbounded, dark, wild, rich, and beautiful space, and the limitless inner world that exists in some unseen region deep within every human being. The construction of the forest in *Khun Chang Khun Phaen* may reflect a moment in which changing social conditions opened up a new space for interest in and exploration and expression of this inner world.

Khun Phaen and Wanthong eventually leave the forest. Wanthong's pregnancy means that they can no longer remain in a purely intimate space; the addition of a child marks the true creation of a family, with a family's hierarchies and structures, and a family's space is therefore in the *ruean*, in society. Once again Khun Phaen must accept the realities of a socially constructed identity. Once again he will be beholden to the words of the king, and soon he will be imprisoned in jail for many years on the king's orders. Yet, despite the fact that his time in a position of power over the construction of his own identity comes to an end, our exploration of the forest as a space intimately connected with the individual's inner world perhaps allows us now to understand and appreciate Khun Phaen's action in abducting Wanthong and escaping to the forest. In this bold move, at a moment when Khun Phaen feels that his life has reached a point where "to be completely destroyed is better than to go on living," we may see the fear one must face, and the risk one must take, to look inside and attempt to define oneself by giving voice to one's own inner world. We can see the courage it takes to refuse to be defined by others, even at the risk of losing everything, and to attempt to sing of ourselves in our own words, in the hope that another being will somehow, miraculously, understand us as we understand ourselves: vast, boundless, and limitless as the wild forest.

THE REVOLT OF KHUN PHAEN: CONTESTING POWER IN EARLY MODERN SIAM

Chris Baker and Pasuk Phongpaichit

Craig Reynolds has drawn attention to the role of manuals (*tamra, khu mue, khamphi*) as a genre in Thailand's oral and written literature, and hence as a formative part of the Thai culture of knowledge.[1] Manuals, he notes, may be deliberate attempts to impose discipline—telling people how to fight a battle, behave as a monk, or conduct oneself in everyday life—but may also empower individuals by giving them access to knowledge that leads to success or survival. One consequence of the prominence of this genre is a tendency to read other literary works as if they were a manual, scanning these "virtual manuals" for lessons. Reynolds gives as an example *The Romance of the Three Kingdoms*, where the lessons in political maneuvering and battlefield strategy from a turbulent period of Chinese history are mined today for guidance in the warfare of business.

The folk epic *Khun Chang Khun Phaen* is another text that has often served as a manual because of several features. It is an original story, not adapted from an Indian, Chinese, or Javanese source. It was initially developed, not by court literati, but in an oral tradition of storytellers reciting tales for local audiences. Its central characters are not kings and gods engaged in heroic and fantastic exploits, but relatively ordinary people depicted with some realism. The text

---

1.   Craig J. Reynolds, "Thai Manual Knowledge: Theory and Practice," chap. 10 in *Seditious Histories: Contesting Thai and Southeast Asian Pasts*, ed. Craig J. Reynolds (Seattle: University of Washington Press, 2006).

evolved from the interplay between performers and audiences over a long period, possibly centuries. Storytellers incorporated tales, true and imaginary, whose meanings resonated with the audience, and fine-tuned the episodes, characters, and language to satisfy the tastes of different audiences. By this process, the work became a depository of values, ways to understand the world, and lessons for living in it. The tale remained popular because it could be "read" to extract these meanings and lessons from generation to generation.

At a simple level, the text contains lessons for a boy about how to court a girl, and lessons for a girl about how to deal with his attention. At a deeper level, the whole story can be read as a cautionary tale for women in a society where social power rests with men.[2] Several lessons about proper behavior, similar to those found in nineteenth-century manuals, are embedded as speeches in the text. Passages from the tale on the practice of supernaturalism are today reproduced almost verbatim in manuals of *saiyasat* (the science of dark or supernatural power; lore).

One set of lessons embedded in the tale concerns power and politics. Today, this aspect is rarely if ever mentioned or commented upon. Indeed, when we have drawn attention to this aspect of the work before Thai audiences, the reaction has been surprise and disbelief. Yet, the plot in outline is about a young man who is accused of revolt, becomes an outlaw, and in the finale is hauled before the king. This plot resembles those found in popular literature all over the world about an ordinary man confronting wealth and power. The legend of Robin Hood is an example, and the comparison between the two will be pursued below.

In this essay, we discuss the lessons about power and politics in *Khun Chang Khun Phaen*. First, we examine two concepts of power

2. See Chris Baker and Pasuk Phongpaichit, "Gender, Sexuality, and Family in Old Siam: Women and Men in *Khun Chang Khun Phaen*," in *Disturbing Conventions: Decentering Thai Literary Cultures*, ed. Rachel Harrison (London, UK: Rowan and Littlefield, 2014), 193–215.

as represented by the two key characters, Khun Phaen and King Phanwasa of Ayutthaya. Second, we trace the interplay between these two concepts of power throughout the plot. Third, we discuss what the "writing" of these lessons into a literary work tells us about the era when the work was at its height of popularity. Finally, we examine how such literary manuals are read and revised across different eras, and speculate why this prominent aspect of a major literary work is now largely ignored.

Protection: The politics of everyday life

Power in *Khun Chang Khun Phaen* is the ability to protect.[3] Throughout the tale, characters seek protection against risks, dangers, and threats in order to ward off sorrowful hardship and achieve peaceful contentment. They look for someone on whom they can depend, and who will feed or support them. When the father of a main character dies, his servants lament that "we have lost our protector" and fear harassment by local officials (47). When news arrives that Khun Phaen has died during a military campaign, his mother-in-law's first thought is, "who'll protect us?" (228). When a father announces he will give his daughter away to a husband, she protests, "my lord and master, do you no longer protect your child?" (207).

The three main sources of danger are defined in the second chapter by recounting the deaths of the three main characters' fathers. The first source is nature, especially the wild forest. The father of the heroine, Wanthong, dies from a forest fever contracted on a trading expedition. The second is human wickedness—Khun Chang's father is killed by a professional bandit gang. The third is authority—Khun Phaen's father is executed by the king.

---

3. For a fuller treatment of this theme, see Chris Baker and Pasuk Phongpaichit, "Protection and Power in Siam: From *Khun Chang Khun Phaen* to the Buddha Amulet," *Southeast Asian Studies* 2, 2 (2013): 215–42.

Finding protection from the third source of danger, authority, is the organizing principle of the social structure known as *sakdina*, at least when seen from below—the main characters' perspective in *Khun Chang Khun Phaen*. Men donate some or all of their labor to a patron in return for protection from various forms of authority. In the classic form of *sakdina*, men become dependents (*phrai* or *that*) in the service of a *khun nang* noble. Khun Phaen's father is an effective patron in the provincial town of Suphanburi because he has an official post as a soldier and recognition from the king. As a result, local officials "shook their heads [and] knew never to cross him" (8). After the father is killed, his servants lament that "nobody dared bully us, because everyone feared Khun Krai. But now they'll all come and push us around" (35). But this classic form of patronage is not the only one. The same principles apply in many other circumstances. After being branded as an outlaw, Khun Phaen places himself under the patronage of a provincial governor who plans to employ him as a guard. The chief of a bandit lair gives shelter to fugitives who in turn must work as robbers. An abbot urges Khun Phaen to stay in the monkhood because the robe is protection against the dangers of conscription.

The model for the role of protector is a parent's custodianship of children, and especially the male in the combined role of father, husband, and householder. Good parents protect their children from all dangers, even the menace of sun, wind, and insects. Husbands shelter their wives like the spreading branches of a bo tree ("Oh, little bo tree shelter of your darling wife . . ." 748).

The king: Formal authority

King Phanwasa of Ayutthaya and Khun Phaen are both presented as figures of power, but with power resting on very different bases. The king's power is legitimated by the political theory, infused by Buddhism, prevailing in late Ayutthaya. We shall call this "formal power" or "authority." Khun Phaen's power is based on education in the use of techniques and devices and we will call it "mastery."

The "beautiful apparition": Power based on supreme merit

The king is generally introduced with a formal invocation similar to those in other literary works of the time:

> Now to tell of the king emperor, ruler of Ayutthaya, the great heaven, who resided in a glittering crystal palace where throngs of palace ladies, / all just of age, radiant, fair, and beautiful, with figures like those in a painting, serviced the royal footsoles. The king slumbered in the golden palace / until dawn streaked the sky, when he woke from sleep and came to bathe in cool rosewater and was arrayed in splendid raiment. / Grasping a diamond sword in his left hand, he went out to the main audience hall to sit on a glittering crystal throne, surrounded by senior officials and royal poets. (777)

These invocations present the king surrounded by abundance and beauty. This "beautiful apparition" is proof that he has accumulated the supreme stock of merit as a result of good deeds in previous lives and thus qualifies to be king.[4] In this kingly role, he has use of the formal machinery of state power—the wealth accumulated in the treasuries,

---

4. Nidhi Eoseewong has argued that the theory of kingship of late Ayutthaya drew in part on the unquestionable, god-given power of the *devaraja*, but more on the idea derived from the Aggana (Akanya) Sutta that kingship came into existence because man needed protection from dangers and evils—especially those visited by man on man—and thus elevated a person "who was the handsomest, the best favored, the most attractive, the most capable" to become ruler. Later texts rationalized that "the person who is king is believed to have accumulated the most merit. This is indicated by his superior status in life, above all others in the same incarnation. He possesses the royal insignia, the palace, and a lifestyle of conspicuous wealth. The fact that he has the most accumulated merit is proven by his ascent of the throne." Nidhi Eoseewong, *Pen and Sail: Literature and History in Early Bangkok* (Chiang Mai: Silkworm Books, 2005), 323–24.

the services of the nobles to carry out his wishes, and the labor of ordinary people to fight wars and perform various services.

This formal power makes the king supremely effective as a provider of protection. Two of the main items of royal regalia, the sword and multi-tiered umbrellas, are symbols of protection. In the invocations that preface his appearances, the king "protects the mass of the populace and soldiery so they are joyful" (506) and "offers protection to the great and small throughout the world" (402) so well that other territories eagerly seek the same shelter. In court formalities, the king is addressed as "lord protector," "divine protector," and "paramount protector." The young Khun Chang is taken to be presented as a royal page so that he will enjoy royal protection.

Concern over revolt

To deliver protection, the king must preserve public order, which means defending the realm against enemies and quelling conflicts among the citizens. These duties depend in turn on the maintenance of his own authority. Threats to the king's authority and his ability to deliver protection are called "revolt" (*kabot*) and are a constant cause of concern.

In the court sources of mid and late Ayutthaya, "revolt" means a challenge to the authority of the king. It is applied to breakaways by subordinate cities or tributary rulers; dynastic challenges, especially during or after disputed successions to the throne; attempted military coups; and uprisings that may have millenarian aims. The word first appears in the later chronicles to describe a challenge for the throne by an alternative dynastic line around 1540, and appears regularly in the chronicles from the Naresuan era (1590–1605) onward, as such incidents became common, especially in the wake of frequent succession disputes.

In *Khun Chang Khun Phaen*, when a city on the boundary between the spheres of influence of Chiang Mai and Ayutthaya is forced to submit to Chiang Mai, the king of Ayutthaya claims this forced defection amounts to a revolt. After Khun Phaen's army regains the city, its ruler is brought to Ayutthaya for trial. He pleads in his defense,

> My liege, please have mercy! I face a charge with a penalty of death. / I'm not dissembling or concealing matters. I did not revolt against the royal footsoles but acted in fear of danger. If I had not submitted to the Lao, I would be dead. (263)

In the parallel military campaign later in the tale, the King of Chiang Mai is captured and brought to Ayutthaya for trial. Again, although the military circumstances are very different, the matter is judged within the framework of "revolt." Later in the tale, Khun Phaen becomes involved in a mock revolt led by his son pretending to be a Mon adventurer who has come to punish Ayutthaya for immoral rule. The king disdains such an attempt:

> I'm the pillar of the land. Though someone may have powers, he can't compete with me. It's known throughout the city that the guardian deities protect the royal lineage. / How can those who are mere servants of the royal dust crave the world? (1053)

When a religious adept transforms himself into a giant crocodile and creates chaos along the Chao Phraya River, a senior noble assumes the adept was sent as part of a planned revolt: "Who entrusted you to come here? . . . You have bold ideas of treachery and revolt." In his defense, the adept pleads: "As for the king, I had no thought of revolt" (1112). Even a Chiang Mai princess caught using a love philter is accused by the king: "Truly you seem to be in revolt" (1078).

Terrible power

While the tale presents the standard theory of the king as protector through invocations and royal titles, the tale also seems intent on showing that the king's supreme power is also a supreme threat.

In several scenes at royal audience, the king is informed of some problem or misfortune, to which he reacts by directing some form of violence. When Khun Phaen's father misinterprets the king's order during a buffalo hunt, the king orders a summary execution:

> The king was inflamed with rage, as if a black vapor had blown across his heart. He bellowed like a thunderclap . . . / Heigh! Heigh! Bring the executioners here immediately. I cannot keep him. Off with his head! Stick it up on a pole and raise it high! Seize his property and his servants at once! (32)

When the king finds that Khun Phaen has evaded his duty as a trainee in the palace, the king reacts in a similar way (though quickly recants):

> . . . he arrogantly dared to climb out over the walls. He is condemned to execution. Skewer his head on a pole as an example to others! (310)

When Khun Chang fails in a trial by ordeal, the king exclaims:

> Don't leave him to pollute the earth. Cleave open his breast as an example to deter others. / He took Wai off to kill in a forest. Go and impale him in that same forest. (769)

When the Chiang Mai ruler offends the king, his reaction is similar:

> Why allow this king to remain a burden on the earth? Heigh! Phraya Jakri, raise an army immediately . . . / Don't spare this Chiang Mai rabble. Wherever they're found, slash them to dust. Lay waste their city and leave it deserted. Raze its walls and fortifications! (543)

When a Chiang Mai princess is found guilty of using a love philter, the sentence is delivered immediately.

> Ha! Heigh! Phraya Yommarat, take her away and slash her dead.
> Open her chest with an axe for public shame. Make an example
> of her to caution others. (1078)

The king is also shown launching wars or other military actions, and the tale dwells on the human consequences. The recruitment of soldiers is portrayed several times in the tale, always as a brutal process, suggesting how much it was hated and feared: "They beat, bribed, and badgered people into the army. If a man could not be found, they impounded his wife and children" (168). The tale also lingers on the aftermath of war, especially the sorrow visited on the families of slaughtered soldiers, and the human devastation when a city is defeated, its population swept away into slavery, and its wealth dissipated by looting.

Royalist litterateur Prince Phitthayalongkon (Bidyalankarana)[5] noted that in *Khun Chang Khun Phaen*, "The King is a queer and thoughtless autocrat."[6] Boonlua Debyasuvarn, the prominent mid-twentieth century literary critic from the royal Kunchon lineage, said at a debate in August 1974: "As for the ruling class as portrayed in *Khun Chang Khun Phaen*, can anyone who reads it say that it shows *good* rule? I say, we're awfully lucky not to have such a king ourselves!"[7]

In sum, the king is presented according to the prevailing political theory of late Ayutthaya as the possessor of supreme merit and thus also of supreme power, which enables him to protect the populace. But two other aspects of the way the king is presented in the tale bring this theory into question. First, the king is constantly concerned about "revolt," meaning any internal or external challenge to his authority.

---

5. Prince Phitthayalongkon (1876–1945) was as an author, editor, and translator, often writing under the pseudonym "No. Mo. So." He was a son of Prince Wichaichan, the last Front-Palace King (*upparat*) behind the Front Palace Crisis of 1875.

6. Prince Bidyalankarana, "*Sebha* Recitation and the Story of *Khun Chang Khun Phaen*," *Journal of the Thailand Research Society* 33 (1941), 13.

7. Quoted in Susan Fulop Kepner, *A Civilized Woman: M. L. Boonlua Debyasuvarn and the Thai Twentieth Century* (Chiang Mai: Silkworm Books, 2013), 297.

Second, seen from below, the king's absolute power is shown to be a terrible threat to life and property. Although he is also a giver of gifts and favors, particularly to those who bring him victory in war, this aspect receives much less emphasis than his capacity to deprive. All the major characters, and many of the minor ones, lose life, liberty, property, rank, spouse, or kin at the hands of the king.

Khun Phaen: Mastery

Khun Phaen is also a figure of power, but the origins of this power stand in sharp contrast to that of the king. First, his power derives in part from resources found in the periphery, in the wild spaces of forests and hills. Second, his power does not come from the formal hierarchy, but is something that can be learned and acquired by an ordinary man. Third, his power is not legitimated by the Buddhist idea of merit, but is underpinned by another aspect of Buddhism combined with other concepts of ancient and exotic origin.

Khun Phaen is born in the provincial town of Suphanburi and retreats further into the periphery of forest and hill over the early course of the story. His family is minor nobility but is ruined and impoverished because of his father's mistake on royal service. Khun Phaen is later elevated back to the minor nobility, but again reduced to penury and jail on royal command. Even after he is ennobled again by the king, Phaen refers to himself as a *phrai*, and his own mother mocks him: "You may be gentlefolk, but what level? Even now, they still call you 'Ai-Khun'" (1024; *ai* is a prefix used for a subordinate).

Yet Phaen becomes a figure of power from skills that he learns. He enters the monkhood and studies with three abbots,[8] two of whom had been friends and teachers of his father. He passes on this learning to his own son, mostly indirectly through the texts he has collected in his

---

8. For a fuller account of this education, see Baker and Pasuk, "Protection and Power in Siam."

library, and partly through direct instruction. Teachers, texts, temple, and family are the transmission lines for these skills.

Lore

This education primarily consists of military skills, but their application is not narrowly confined to war. Phaen famously uses these devices in his career as a lover, as well as to combat natural forces such as disease and the weather.

His skills include the ability to predict events and manipulate natural forces. Prediction is made through astrological reckoning and the interpretation of omens found in nature. Natural forces are manipulated through the command of spirits, and through the use of verbal formulas, natural substances, and constructed devices (especially yantra—geometrical diagrams filled with powerful symbols, words, and numbers). This manipulation operates through two pairs of forces: *repulsion* (warding off danger, or, in its most complete form, providing invulnerability) and *attraction* (inducing love, sympathy, or good fortune); and *constraint* (preventing an event or action, such as immobilizing an enemy) and *release* (removing constraints, such as undoing locks and chains, or ensuring a smooth delivery at birth).[9]

These skills have roots in three traditions. The first is a belief in spirits of the place and of ancestors, which is found throughout Southeast Asia and, indeed, in much of the world. Second is a belief found in Indic tradition that mastery over oneself conveys mastery over natural processes. Through mental control and ascetic practices, a rishi or yogi attains supernatural abilities. Life stories of the Buddha show how he was schooled in ascetic practice and acquired extraordinary powers—such as flying through the air, multiplying his body, and

---

9. Thep Sarikabut, *Phra khamphi phrawet* [Manuals of lore], six vols. (Bangkok: Utsahakam kan phim, n.d.); and Achan Hon Yanchot (Chayamongkhon Udomsap), *Saiyasat chabap sombun* [The complete *saiyasat*] (Bangkok: Sinlapa bannakan, 1995).

recalling previous lives.[10] In his studies of current-day forest saints and spirit mediums, Stanley Tambiah identified the idea of *itthi-rit,* meaning the mastery over oneself that delivers exceptional mastery over other natural forces.[11]

The third root also has Indic origins, but is more obscure. *Athan* (sometimes *athap* or *athanpawet*) is a Thai transliteration of Atharva Veda, the fourth of the great ancient texts of Hindu tradition.[12] This text contains a catalog of verbal formulas and devices for overcoming threats and difficulties that probably derives from north Indian folk practice some three thousand years ago. The difficulties and devices are similar to practices described in *Khun Chang Khun Phaen,* identified in more recent anthropological studies of Thailand,[13] and found in Thai manuals of supernaturalism. *Athan* can mean protection, especially rites for protection of a palace or city, but is also used to refer to the whole range of verbal formulas, natural substances, and powerful devices. Verbal formulas are variously described as *mon* (mantra), *wet* (Veda), *akhom,* or *khatha,* all words that derive from the

10.   Victor Fic, *The Tantra: Its Origin, Theories, Art and Diffusion to Nepal, Tibet, Mongolia, China, Japan, and Indonesia* (New Delhi: Abhinav, 2003), 42–44.

11.   Stanley J. Tambiah, *Buddhism and the Spirit Cults in North-east Thailand* (Cambridge: Cambridge University Press, 1970), 49–51; and Stanley J. Tambiah, *The Buddhist Saints of the Forest and the Cult of Amulets: A Study in Charisma* (Cambridge: Cambridge University Press, 1984), 45, 315.

12.   Two main recensions of the Atharva Veda have survived. This inventory forms the first of four parts in the Shaunakiya, or northern recension. Dating is difficult and controversial but may be around the eleventh or twelfth century BCE. Some scholars have speculated that this inventory is a record of local belief and practice in north India at the time the Vedas were composed. Others argue that the inventory may have earlier origins, perhaps in Central Asia. William Dwight Witney, *Atharva-Veda Samhita,* 2 vols. (Cambridge: Harvard University Press, 1905); Jarrod L. Whitaker, "Ritual Power, Social Prestige, and Amulets (mani) in the Atharvaveda," in *The Vedas: Texts, Language, and Ritual,* ed. Arlo Griffiths and Jan E. M. Houlson (Groningen: Egbert Forsten, 2004); and Axel Michaels, *Hinduism: Past and Present* (Princeton: Princeton University Press, 2004).

13.   About verbal formulas and devices for overcoming threats and difficulties, see, especially, Robert B. Textor, "An Inventory of Non-Buddhist Supernatural Objects in a Central Thai Village" (PhD diss., Cornell University, 1960).

Hindu–Buddhist tradition of scriptures. Compound versions of these same terms (such as *khatha-akhom*) are used to describe the practice as a whole. Alternatively, the practice is described as *wicha* or *withaya*, the Pali–Sanskrit term for learning or knowledge—lore.

In Thai tradition, these three elements—spirits, mastery, and the formulas and devices of *athan*—are closely intertwined. For example, in his manufacture of a powerful sword, Khun Phaen first collects various metals that are invested with special qualities (such as having decorated the roof of a palace or served as the fastening on a coffin). These are then cast and forged following the procedures in a manual, including rites to transfer the mastery of the craftsmen into the weapon; and, finally, the spirits are convoked to instill extra power into the weapon.

In *Khun Chang Khun Phaen*, an adept such as Khun Phaen is *khon di*, a "good person," and the practice as a whole is *thang nai*, the "inner ways," a phrase that nicely captures the depth of the knowledge, its arcane origins, and its reliance on the innate talent of the practitioner.

In sum, Khun Phaen's power derives from mastery over himself and mastery of textual knowledge, which lend him mastery over the spirits and obscure forces in the natural world. With these abilities, Khun Phaen is not only an accomplished soldier, but is able to extend protection to others. He provides protection to his wife when they are in danger, to his troops in battle, and to his horse. Beyond the battlefield, he offers protection in other ways. He protects the kingdom of Ayutthaya from the threat of Chiang Mai. He protects the people of Chomthong from the threat of being pillaged and swept from their homes as war prisoners. He provides money for one wife to buy herself out of slavery, and uses his skill with mantra to rescue another from illness. He spares people from the hated loss of freedom under corvée by declining the king's offer to raise a massive army, and even protects his rival Khun Chang from execution. Within the bottom-up theory of the politics of everyday life, in which protection is the key concept, Khun Phaen is thus portrayed as a figure of considerable power.

Mastery and authority

How do these two forms of power coexist, and how do they relate to one another in the political landscape? This question is developed through the tale.

Authority undermined

In the prelude to the tale (the first two chapters), the authority of the king is plainly shown when he has Khun Phaen's father summarily executed. But in two military expeditions to the north, the ability of the king to impose his authority over vassals is shown as being utterly dependent on the mastery of Khun Phaen and people like him.

When Chiang Mai defies Ayutthaya, the king resolves to send an army north and asks for a volunteer to lead it. Not a single noble in the court volunteers. The nobles are portrayed as flaccid, and the king as powerless to command them. He is obliged to turn to the lineage of Khun Phaen's father, because of their known mastery. Khun Phaen, who at the time is aged around fifteen, is sent north at the head of the army.

In the replay[14] of this scene later in the tale, the limitation of formal authority is more clearly portrayed. When the king asks for a volunteer and none steps forward, he rants at his own nobles:

> You're good only at cheating your own men out of money by using your clever tongues. I don't have to support you with allowances. Your property and rank are a burden on the realm ... / ... Perhaps some slaves from some department or other will volunteer, and I can get rid of the lot of you at once to make room for appointing them in your stead. (544, 547)

Again the king is obliged to turn to the lineage of Khun Phaen. His son, Phlai Ngam, also aged around fourteen or fifteen, volunteers

---

14. Because the "inquel" about Khun Phaen's son is similar in plot to his father's story, several scenes are replayed.

and asks the king to free his father Khun Phaen to accompany him. The scene continues to mock formal power. The king proposes to conscript a massive army, but Khun Phaen declines on the grounds that conscription will be "troublesome" for the people. Instead he asks for the release of thirty-five fellow prisoners who are skilled in lore, thus asserting the superiority of mastery over authority and its system of mobilizing manpower. At a roll call, the thirty-five relate their crimes, presenting themselves as threats to Buddhism, tax collection, merchant wealth, and the administrative frame—in short the underpinnings of the social order:

"Next!"

"Ai-Thong from Chong Khwak, husband of I-Mak. I killed a Lao called Thao Sen, crept in to steal an alms bowl and shoulder cloth from a novice, thumped an old monk, and had a wrestle with the abbot."

"Next!"

"Ai-Chang Dam, from Ban Tham. I burgled a tax collector and took all his money and property—good stuff and no small amount, including jewels."

"Ai-Phao, husband of I-Phan from Ban Na-kluea. I poisoned Luang Choduek[15] and cleaned out his house."

"Ai-Koet Kradukdam, husband of I-Khamdang, convicted of burgling the Department of Elephants with mahout Man, and robbing a forest Lawa. I'm invulnerable with a single testicle and twisted scrotum." (552)

The text stresses the liminality of this army in other ways. Phaen is destitute. His hair is so long he can sit on it, and passersby mistake him for a madman. The ex-convict volunteers have nothing but sacking as clothes. On the march, they smash themselves with alcohol, *kanja*,

---

15. "Luang Choduek" is the official title of the head of the Chinese community in the capital, usually a very rich and influential person.

opium, and *krathom* (a leaf chewed as an intoxicant). In an older text of this passage, they start looting even before they have left the confines of the capital, and continue to seize food, property, and women on the northward journey and return.

In both military expeditions, Khun Phaen triumphs, the king is overcome with relief, and both Khun Phaen and his troops are richly rewarded. The protection of the kingdom is shown to be dependent on the skills of Khun Phaen and his liminal-criminal colleagues.

The king attempts to limit the consequences of this dependence. After both victories, the king sends Khun Phaen away from the capital to guard a remote border. An old Thai saying runs, "After harvest, kill the bull; after war, kill the army chief."[16]

Confronting wealth and authority

In the main thread of the story, Khun Phaen and Khun Chang vie for the love of Wanthong. Khun Chang uses his wealth to suborn Wanthong's mother, and manipulates his court connections to get assistance from the king. He serves the king as both a collector of taxes and keeper of the royal elephants in the strategic town of Suphanburi, and was presented at court in childhood. He first uses his access to the royal audience to have Khun Phaen sent north at the head of the army, then spreads a rumor that Phaen has been killed, and marries Wanthong before Khun Phaen returns. Later he appears at court and tries to frame Khun Phaen for revolt:

> "Then he [Phaen] shouted at me provocatively, saying it was not a good idea to kill me; if he released me, I would go to Ayutthaya and tell everything; / then, were the king to come out, he would engage the king in an elephant duel, win a famous victory, and

---

16.   The origin of the saying is probably *Rachathirat*; see Nidhi Eoseewong, "Set suek kha khun phon" [After war, kill the army chief], *Matichon Sutsapda* 33, no. 1721 (August 9–15, 2013): 30.

seize the city as ruler. These were his vile words. / He has built a royal lodge in the forest and a camp fortified with spikes. Very mischievously, he has constructed a toilet.[17] Before long, he will become a threat to the city." (393–94)

The king doubts the charge, but sends a force to bring Khun Phaen for trial. On finding Khun Phaen in the forest, one of the leaders of this force provokes Phaen with accusations of revolt: "Your lineage is nothing. Defying royal orders is a grave matter. You're full of ambition for kingship" (405).

Equipping with lore

In the face of Khun Chang's deployment of his wealth and royal connections, Khun Phaen feels at a disadvantage. He asks, "How can I protect myself?" (316), and resolves to equip himself to fight the powerful forces arrayed against him. This task takes him into the wild periphery.

> He left at dawn for the upland forests. / In search of what he needed, he delved into every nook and cranny, passing through / villages of Karen, Kha, Lawa, and Mon, and sleeping along passes through the mountains. (317)

He forges a sword "according to the great manual on weaponry" (317), instilled with supernatural power; acquires a personal spirit made from the fetus of a child who died with his mother in childbirth; and buys a horse sired on a "water horse."

Up to this point, Khun Phaen's mastery of lore has played only a small role in the story, but now that role dramatically increases. Moreover, his lore implicitly challenges aspects of royalty. The ingredients for

---

17. At this time, a constructed toilet was one of the privileges of royalty. See "Phra aiyakan aya luang" [Criminal law code], section 115, in *Kotmai tra sam duang* [Three Seals Law] (Bangkok: Khurusapha, 1955), vol. 4, 85.

forging his sword include metals from the summit of a royal palace, and ore from two mines used for making royal regalia weaponry. He names the sword *Fa fuen*, thunder before rain (translated as Skystorm), the name of a weapon among the regalia presented at the coronation of Khun Borom, the great hero king of Thai-Lao legend.[18] Later, Khun Phaen tells his son:

> This Skystorm is superb. Tens and hundreds of thousands of other swords are not as good. Even the king's regal sword is not equal to mine. (575)

With this equipment, he becomes more openly defiant. When his own personal spirit cautions him, "Hold off! Cool down. Don't kill him, Father. Don't you fear the power of the Lord of Life?" Khun Phaen snaps back, "No! I don't fear his power" (345–46). Starting in this stage of the tale, the text often introduces Khun Phaen with a mini-invocation similar though less elaborate than those that regularly introduce the king. These invocations celebrate Khun Phaen "whose mastery was unmatched," or "whose powers were famous everywhere."

The stage is set for a clash between mastery and authority. Khun Phaen abducts Wanthong from Khun Chang's house, and defeats the royal army sent after him, killing two noble officers. Now a wanted outlaw, he and Wanthong flee further into the wild periphery of forests and mountains where they live off lotus roots. When Wanthong becomes pregnant, they place themselves under the care of the governor of Phichit, who has a reputation for harboring those in trouble.

---

18. Souneth Phothisane, "The Nidān Khun Borom: Annotated Translation and Analysis" (PhD dissertation, University of Queensland, 1966), 126. Sujit Wongthes argues that *Fa fuen*, literally "restored by the god," indicates a sacred weapon presented by Thaen, the creator god of Tai tradition. See "Dap 'fa fuen' khong khun phaen chuea diao kap phi banpachon kasat mueang nan nai tamnan" (Khun Phaen's *Fa Fuen* Sword, Same Name as the Ancestral Spirits of the Nan King in Legend), *Matichon Sutsapda* 33, no. 1724 (August 30, 2013), 77.

Play within a play

There are two scenes outside the main thread of the plot in which Khun Phaen confronts a king other than King Phanwasa of Ayutthaya, and triumphs both times. These scenes seem to function like the "play within a play" in Shakespearean drama, predicting or mirroring events in the main plot.

In the first of the scenes, during his search for protective equipment, Khun Phaen visits a bandit lair in the western hills. Although the chief is not a "king," he appears very similar to one. Khun Phaen notes that he seems like "the lord of some country." A guard tells him that the chief "has put many passersby to death already." His residence is "furnished as well as any princely palace" with "throngs of young Lao and Thai girl servants, all just of age and good-looking. The sitting halls were spread with soft mats, pillows, and carpets, and strewn with items of gold, silver, nak, and nielloware" (1176). Khun Phaen enters the chief's service, but they come into conflict ending in a physical struggle, and Khun Phaen's superior lore triumphs.

In the second of these scenes, during the campaign against Chiang Mai, Khun Phaen and his son use lore to enter the Chiang Mai palace with the aim of capturing the king, but first take a tour, violating the sacred space of the palace interior, and inspecting the various "forbidden" women—from queen to consorts to lady attendants. Finally, they approach the sleeping king and use superior lore to drive away the king's protective spirits. Waking up and discovering himself defenseless, the king surrenders himself, his realm, and his family into Khun Phaen's hands.

Mastery and authority

In the texts of *Khun Chang Khun Phaen* assembled in the palace in the mid-nineteenth century and used in the earliest printed editions,[19] there are four places that raise the question of whether mastery can defy authority.

19. See above, note 4.

The monks who teach lore to members of Khun Phaen's lineage are convinced that their pupils can defy the monarch. The teacher of Khun Phaen's father asks Khun Phaen in bewilderment why his father let himself be executed by the king: "I'm still disappointed that he died without putting up a fight. He must have lost his knowledge" (122). Phaen explains that his father had taken the oath of allegiance and would not go back on his word, and hence renounced his mastery and allowed himself to be killed.

Similarly, after release from jail, Khun Phaen visits his old teacher, who is bewildered as to why his pupil languished in jail for a dozen years. "What was up? Didn't you have faith in your knowledge? Or was it fun lying in the jail?" (558). Khun Phaen replies, "I was not lacking in power," but again explains he had taken an oath that he would not escape and refused to break his word.

When Khun Phaen and Wanthong are outlaws in the forest, and Wanthong becomes pregnant, Khun Phaen decides to turn himself in. He reasons, "If I give myself up, rather than being captured in the forest, the punishment should be light. Besides, I can create obstruction with the power of my knowledge" (426). When brought before the king, "Khun Phaen intoned a mantra he had decided on in advance, and blew it with faith in its lore. The king's mood relaxed, and he turned his face towards them" (436). The king promptly absolves Phaen of the serious charge of murdering two senior nobles.

Similarly, when Phaen's son Wai goes to seek pardon for his mother, he equips himself with many devices and "recited prayers to his powerful teachers for the king's anger to recede." The king feels "love and concern for him on account of the power of the lore" (812–13), and promptly issues a pardon (though it turns out to be too late).[20]

---

20. The message arrives too late to forestall the execution and Khun Phaen makes only a half-hearted attempt to thwart it. Phra Wai angrily accuses his father, "You have stunning mantras, powerful enough to immobilize people in droves. Why didn't you blow one to stun this executioner and stop him? She died because you didn't help her. Or have you lost your powers?" (826). Khun Phaen explains to his son that her death was predestined in astrology and thus impossible to prevent.

In the two instances when Khun Phaen uses lore on the king, it is effective. In the two instances when he or his father refrain from using lore to defend themselves, Phaen can rationalize the decision by reference to personal loyalties.

Denouement: Revolt and sacrifice

Khun Phaen and Wanthong leave Phichit and return to Ayutthaya to surrender to the king. In the old version of the tale, their return was quickly followed by the climactic scene of confrontation.

The rivalry between Khun Phaen and Khun Chang has caused two pitched battles, the death of two senior nobles, a court case, ordeal by water, and other mayhem. In short, it has disrupted the social peace that it is the king's duty to preserve, and thus represents a challenge to his authority, a revolt. He summons all the parties to the audience hall, where the king sits in judgment over the whole dispute. The charges that the king brings do not concern the wrongs that Khun Chang, Khun Phaen, and Wanthong may have done to one another, but the ways their actions are undermining or impugning royal authority.

On hearing of Khun Chang's efforts to prise Wanthong away from Khun Phaen, the king calls Khun Chang a robber (*chon*), alluding to the Law on Theft, which reserves its highest punishments for acts that disturb public order. He continues, "It turns out I'm not the Lord of Life. You think I'm just a lord in a mask play with no authority." He adds that Khun Chang "deserves to be knocked unconscious right here, thrashed countless times, and have a ripe coconut stuffed in his mouth" (798). This punishment comes from clause 1 of the Code of Crimes against Government, about infringing on the prerogatives of the monarch.[21]

---

21. *Kotmai tra sam duang*, 4:5–6.

The king turns to Khun Phaen's son (now called Phra Wai) and again explodes against both the disruption of public order and the impugning of royal authority:

> Phra Wai has acted arrogantly. It seems the country has no master. / People don't pay attention to the law but do whatever they like. If they slash and kill one another, it'll be a danger to the populace. That angers me. / . . . There are courts and codes of law. Or perhaps you think I can't make a judgment. (798)

With the phrase "a danger to the populace," the king alludes to the Law on Conflict,[22] which deals extensively with threats to public order, and he proposes that Wai be punished appropriately with both fines and the lash.

By logic, the king would now confront Khun Phaen in the same way, and the issue of their competing power would rise to the surface. Instead, the king turns to Wanthong, accuses her of being the root cause of the conflict, and insists she choose between the two men. Wanthong is terrified. She mumbles that the two men have different meaning for her life, and she tacitly refuses to make a decision. The king's anger comes down on her head:

> You cannot say which one you love! Your heart wants both of them, so you can switch back and forth, having a reserve deeper than the deepest sea ... / Heigh! Phraya Yommarat, go and execute her immediately! Cleave open her chest with an axe without mercy. Don't let her blood touch my land. / Collect it on banana leaves for feeding to dogs. If it touches the ground, the evil will linger. Execute her for all men and women to see! (801)

---

22. "Phra aiyakan laksana wiwat ti da kan" [Law on conflict], *Kotmai tra sam duang*, 3:184 (especially the preamble).

This condemnation and sentencing have nothing to do with the laws on marriage. The penalties prescribed for adultery and bigamy were fines, caning, and public shaming (being paraded around town with hibiscus flowers), not capital punishment.[23] Throughout the tale, neither Khun Phaen, Khun Chang, nor other characters criticize Wanthong for bigamy. Only Wanthong chastises herself for being "two-minded," and then in fear of social reprobation, not criminal retribution. The telling flourish in the king's speech is the order "Don't let her blood touch my land." In the Ayutthaya laws, the only place where this instruction appears is Clause 1 of the Law on Revolt.[24] This is a sentence for revolt, not for a woman's failing to choose between two men.

Although the judgment appears to be about Wanthong's behavior, the issue at stake is the king's authority. In simple terms, Wanthong is in revolt because she has defied his order to make a decision between the two men. More broadly, as the buildup to this climax has shown, the king is concerned about royal authority confronted by a family equipped with mastery. Wanthong becomes a sacrificial victim whose death evades any resolution of the issue of authority against mastery. This finale can be evaluated in many different ways. Viewed from the king's perspective, it can be rationalized as a practical solution: he needs the services of Khun Phaen and his son as soldiers, and the services of Khun Chang as a collector of taxes and keeper of elephants,

---

23. Under the law, the cuckolded husband had the right to execute his errant wife, but only after first exercising his right to execute the adulterer. See "Phra ayakan laksana phua mia" [Law on marriage], clauses 8 and 9, *Kotmai tra sam duang*, 2:210–11.

24. To paraphrase, the law reads: anyone who attempts to dethrone the monarch, or who attempts to do damage to the monarch with weapons or poison, or who refuses to submit tribute as a governor, or who encourages enemies to attack, or who gives information to enemies, is liable to punishment of death and seizure of property for a. the entire clan; b. seven generations of the clan; or c. the whole clan, ensuring no successors; with the executions to linger over seven days "without letting the blood or corpse fall on the realm but be put on a raft and floated with the current 240,000 *yochana* to the next country" [Law on revolt, clause 1], *Kotmai tra sam duang*, 4:124.

while Wanthong is expendable. In terms of the plot, the sacrifice of Wanthong provides a dramatic and enigmatic ending that has probably been a key factor in the story's lasting popularity. In terms of the tale as a manual, a repository of lessons about power, the sacrifice leaves the issue unresolved because, of course, it cannot be resolved. As David Chandler concluded about some nineteenth-century Cambodian tales, "In a sense, the texts 'answer' questions that no one dared to ask, but in the end, what do they *explain*? No more, and of course no less, than songs at the edge of the forest, as night comes on, the time *entre chien et loup*."[25] As a depository of meanings, values, and lessons, the tale maps the territory and lays out the issues but does not provide answers to unanswerable questions.

Besides, in truth, the mastery represented by Khun Phaen and the authority of the king are not irredeemably opposed but delicately balanced.[26] The king relies upon the likes of Khun Phaen and his ancestors to fight his wars. At the same time, Khun Phaen and others who share his lineage accept honors and titles from the king because of their obvious social benefits.

Writing the manual

The discourse on power in *Khun Chang Khun Phaen* is embedded in the plot of the story and hence is probably an old part of the tale rather than a later addition. The story presents King Phanwasa

25. David Chandler, "Songs at the Edge of the Forest: Perceptions of Order in Three Cambodian Texts," in *At the Edge of the Forest: Essays on Cambodia, History, and Narrative in Honor of David Chandler*, ed. Anne Ruth Hansen and Judy Ledgerwood (Ithaca: Cornell Southeast Asia Program Publications, 2008), 45; emphasis in original.

26. Especially in the eighteenth century, kings were attributed with supernatural powers deriving from mastery, and this belief survives in folk tradition down to the present. In *Khun Chang Khun Phaen*, however, the king is never portrayed exercising such powers, only Khun Phaen and other warriors or adepts.

according to the political theory of the era—he is king by virtue of his supreme stock of merit and provides protection to the populace through the machinery of the *sakdina* state. But, the tale also questions this theory in several ways. First, viewed from below, the exercise of kingly authority can have terrible results. Second, in practice, the king is dependent on other powerful figures, such as Khun Phaen, and regularly faces challenges to his authority ("revolt"). Third, others also have the mastery to offer protection and thus can rival the king's power.

We have no way of knowing how this discourse was "read" in the past by those who heard the story. As with any manual or "virtual manual," many readings are possible. For example, the takeaway might be that the execution of Khun Phaen's father at the start of the tale and his wife at the end proves the supremacy of royal authority and shows that claims of mastery are relatively impotent. But equally, the message could be that royal authority is terrible, hollow, and fragile. A third reading might be that formal authority is no more or less powerful than other authority, but, because it is embedded in institutions, is dangerous to defy.

The key point is not how it was interpreted, but the very fact that it was "written." This discourse on power is found in a work derived from oral tradition and believed to have been popular entertainment for commoners in late Ayutthaya. By contrast, almost all other surviving Thai sources prior to the mid-nineteenth century, including chronicles, laws, oral histories, and heroic and romantic literature, originated from the court and reflect its views. Accounts by visiting foreigners also largely present information and views gleaned from the court circle. *Khun Chang Khun Phaen* is an important exception.

Revolt and defiance

The era of late Ayutthaya was peppered with revolts. Many erupted at the time of royal succession. From 1610 onward, all but one of the twelve successions involved battles that varied in degrees of severity. The dynasty was ejected and replaced in 1629, 1688, 1767, and 1782. With the exception of the Burmese sack in 1767, the pretender came from senior nobility, but these events were far from simple palace revolutions. Nobles and their armed retainers divided into rival camps. In 1688 and 1782 (and possibly on other occasions for which historical information is scant), the monkhood became involved, and armed bands and mobs came in from the provinces. The initial putsch was often followed by aftershocks and counter attempts for several years. Provinces broke away—particularly strategic centers such as Khorat and Nakhon Si Thammarat. The purges that restored order could be massive and brutal. Besides events related to the succession, there were other revolts. Mobs marched on the city, led by figures that might be dynastic pretenders or local men of prowess. And foreign forces interfered, too: Japanese in the 1610s, Patani forces in the 1660s, Macassars in the 1680s, and Chinese merchants in the 1730s all attempted to stage a coup in the capital. Thus, it is not surprising that the most prominent work of popular literature of this era should contain a discussion of power in the plot and be able to be read as a guide, a manual.

As many modern anthropologists have discussed, claims of invulnerability are a form of defiance. As Andrew Turton notes, at an individual level, belief in invulnerability involves a "lessening of fear and deference . . . Even more fundamentally assertive and challenging to notions of fixed social hierarchies is the underlying assumption of the perfectibility, or at least the potential for self development, of any who would learn or practice."[27] Turton and Shigeharu Tanabe note that invulnerability is linked to "distinctly peasant ideas of legitimacy" and to a "theme of boldness, of overcoming fear and disparagement— crucial if fear is seen as an ideological mediation between coercion and consent."[28] Turton also argues that a reputation for invulnerability is

27. Andrew Turton, "Invulnerability and Local Knowledge," in *Thai Constructions of Knowledge*, ed. Manas Chitkasem and Andrew Turton (London: School of Oriental and African Studies, 1991), 172 (with some editing of the original punctuation).

28. Andrew Turton and Shigeharu Tanabe, "Introduction," in *History and Peasant Consciousness in South East Asia*, ed. Turton and Tanabe (Osaka: National Museum of Ethnology, 1984), 4, 7.

"virtually a requirement of leadership" at the local level, and suggests that beliefs in invulnerability count among the local "traditions of hope," ideas about the past that can serve as the basis for "hopeful and courageous social mobilization against all odds."[29] Cohen, Turton, and Reynolds have all noted the subversive, "counter-hegemonic" way that *kshatriya*, the Indic term for "warrior" and the origin of a Thai word for "king" (*kasat*), has been appropriated in an alternative transliteration to mean expertise in invulnerability itself (*chatri*).[30]

One well-known development of this theme of defiance, subversion, and hope is the tradition of "men of merit," *phumibun* or *phu wiset*, who led several millenarian revolts, particularly in the late-nineteenth century, but also before and since.[31] There are several similarities between the *phumibun* and Khun Phaen. Both claim the power of invulnerability and the ability to transfer it to others. Both draw on the tradition of self-mastery. Both use *athan* devices, such as yantra and enchanted water or oil. But there are also at least two important differences.

First, *phumibun* observed the Buddhist precepts and practiced Buddhist forms of meditation to acquire exceptional merit (*bun*) that was their qualification to lead. Though Khun Phaen is educated by abbots inside Buddhist *wat*, there is virtually no reference in his life story to Buddhist precepts, texts, or symbols in his education. In rites to summon his powers, he convokes a long list of spirits and Indic deities in which the Buddha may appear as just one among many. While the term *bun* appears in *Khun Chang Khun Phaen* in many conventional phrases, Khun Phaen is never described as possessing exceptional *bun*. In the invocation-like phrases that announce his appearance in the text, he is famed for his powers (*sakda, rit*), not his

29. Turton, "Invulnerability and Local Knowledge," 170, 176.

30. Ibid., 158–59; Paul T. Cohen, "From Moral Regeneration to Confrontation: Two Paths to Equality in the Political Rhetoric of a Northern Peasant Leader," *Mankind* 17, 2 (1987); Reynolds, "Thai Manual Knowledge: Theory and Practice," 234.

31. Charles F. Keyes, "Millennialism, Theravada Buddhism, and Thai Society," *Journal of Asian Studies* 36, 2 (1977): 283–302.

merit (*bun*).

Second, the *phumibun* is essentially a messenger who brings news that the millennium is nigh, that the Future Buddha is about to appear and usher in a just social order. The *phumibun* promises no less than a shift from one era to another and thus demands an extraordinary leap of belief among his followers. But the promise represented by Khun Phaen is less dramatic, more accessible. He is merely an alternative agent of protection, the service that everyone wants.

The tale of *Khun Chang Khun Phaen* goes beyond the technical manuals of invulnerability and supernaturalism by creating the figure of Khun Phaen, an embodiment of these skills, and a potential model for a historical actor.

Revising the manual

Today this political aspect of the tale seems to be ignored. Sombat Chanthornwong's subtle and thoughtful discussions of the political aspects of classical Thai literature conspicuously omitted *Khun Chang Khun Phaen*.[32] Cholthira Satyawadhna analyzed *Khun Chang Khun Phaen* from the viewpoint of masculinity and violence and Boonlua Debyasuvarn concluded that *Khun Chang Khun Phaen* demonstrates that "Thai society is a society without principle," but neither examined the issue of power.[33]

The political aspect of the tale has been obscured in part by the way that *Khun Chang Khun Phaen* has changed over time. Big tales that loom large in popular culture do not remain constant, but are themselves subject to political forces. This can be clearly seen from the history of Robin Hood, a medieval English tale that shares many

32. Sombat Chanthornwong, *Bot wichan wa duai wannakam kan mueang lae prawatisat* [Essays on literature, politics, and history] (Bangkok: Kopfai, 1997).
33. See their essays in this volume.

affinities with *Khun Chang Khun Phaen*, and that has sources for reconstructing its history over several centuries.

The changing meanings of Robin Hood

In Stephen Knight's historical analysis of the Robin Hood legend,[34] there is no clear identification of an actual man named Robin Hood. In the earliest sources, mostly law court records from the thirteenth and fourteenth centuries, the name is used as an epithet for criminals and outlaws. By the fifteenth century, ballads appeared all over England in which Robin Hood is a rebel against the church and the nobility. He robs and he refuses to serve the king. He lives in the forest and wears a green costume that recalls a wild, anti-civilization spirit-figure from Anglo-Saxon legends. From the late-fifteenth century, playlets about Robin Hood were performed at local festivals, especially the May festival. In some of these events, the Robin Hood character was identified with the May King or Summer Lord, a lord of misrule with deep roots in anti-establishment popular culture. In this era, Robin Hood was "the hero who stands for an alternative and natural force of lordship, one who has the will and the power not only to elude but also to resist and if necessary destroy the agents of the world of legalism, of finance, and of regulation."[35] In the sixteenth century, authorities suppressed these performances, and a total ban was enacted in 1592.

In the seventeenth century, there was a deliberate attempt to bring this rebellious tradition under control by rewriting the script. Dramas began to appear in which Robin Hood was given a noble background, and his exploits became less threatening to the social order. He becomes an earl fallen on hard times. He no longer fights against the church and the power structure, but against individual corrupt officials. He no longer defies the king, but appeals to the king

34. Stephen T. Knight, *Robin Hood: A Complete Study of the English Outlaw* (Oxford, UK: Basil Blackwell, 1994); and Stephen T. Knight, *Robin Hood: A Mythic Biography* (Ithaca: Cornell University Press, 2003).
35. Knight, *Robin Hood: A Complete Study*, 81.

to help suppress his corrupt enemy and restore his rightful position. By the eighteenth century, Robin Hood had also become a nationalistic figure, representing values of charity, bravery, and moral uprightness that were supposed to form the national character. By the twentieth century, this version had evolved largely into a tale for children.

Revising *Khun Chang Khun Phaen*

This summary shows how the political meanings of a popular literary work can change radically over time. Precisely because the story is popular, its meanings are contested and manipulated. In the case of *Khun Chang Khun Phaen*'s evolution, the paper trail is more fragmentary and less historically deep than that for Robin Hood's transformation, yet there is enough evidence from the later phases of its history to suggest it underwent similar modification.

A collection of *Khun Chang Khun Phaen* manuscripts telling the whole story was assembled in the Bangkok palace in the mid-nineteenth century. Between then and the publication of Prince Damrong's standard edition in 1917–18, *Khun Chang Khun Phaen* underwent several changes. For example, of the four instances cited above that show that Khun Phaen or his teachers believe his powers exceeded those of the king, three were changed so that such an assertion is unclear.[36] Other editing was similarly subtle. For example, in the early text, Khun Phaen's father is introduced as *khon di*, a good person, a term for someone with expertise in lore. In the standard version, this was changed to *phu phakdi*, a loyal fellow, which is a substantial change of meaning achieved by adding one syllable.

In the mid-nineteenth century texts, Khun Phaen kills only

---

36.   In the first instance, Khun Phaen's explanation that his father did not use his lore because he had taken an oath was omitted. In the third, Khun Phaen's assertion, "I can create obstruction with the power of my knowledge," was changed to, "I think there'll be ways to ask for a pardon." In the fourth, the line stating the king was "feeling love and concern for Phra Wai on account of the power of lore" was changed to say that the king "felt merciful." See Baker and Pasuk, *Khun Chang Khun Phaen*, 122, 426, 436, 812–13, where the changes are detailed in the footnotes.

as a soldier on the battlefield. By the time of the 1917–18 standard edition, he brutally murders a wife, threatens to kill another, kills two innocent peasants, and tries to kill his own son. His heroic character is substantially diminished by these changes.

Similar changes can be detected in revisions made by the court in the Second Reign, though the sources are meager. In versions preserved in popular drama and believed to represent the old story, Khun Phaen is clearly the hero and Khun Chang the villain in the rivalry over Wanthong. But in the version that emerged from the Second Reign salon, Khun Phaen has become a cruder and clumsier character who is partly responsible for his own difficulties.[37]

Earlier revisions can be detected, though dimly. The "inquel" about Khun Phaen's son, which was probably added in the late Ayutthaya era, obscures the political meanings of the plot by inserting fifteen years in the story and fifteen chapters between Khun Phaen's "revolt" and Wanthong's execution. Looking further back for revisions is impossible because there are no sources,[38] but the momentum and direction of change is clear.

Overlooking the political aspect of *Khun Chang Khun Phaen* is also a function of changes in the way the tale is consumed and taught. Since the early nineteenth century, the emphasis has shifted away from the plot to the performance, from content to style. Recitation became more stylized, increasingly emphasizing sound rather than meaning, reaching an extreme in the "beggar" style, in which a single line is drawn out for several minutes of ululation, obscuring all meaning. At court, music was added to the performance, and gradually became

---

37. Sukanya Pathrachai, "'Khun chang plaeng san' ton thi hai pai chak sepha khun chang khun phaen chabap ho samut" ['Khun Chang changes the letter': A passage missing from the library edition of *Khun Chang Khun Phaen*), *Phasa lae wannakhadi thai* [Thai language and literature] 8, 1 (1991): 29–37.

38. Sujit Wongthes suggests that the story goes right back to a hero legend of great antiquity. See "Khap sepha lae khun chang khun phaen mi ton tao thi suphannaphumi" [Reciting *sepha* and *Khun Chang Khun Phaen* originate from Suwannaphum], *Matichon Sutsapda* 33, no. 1721 (August 9–15, 2013): 77.

more important than the text. In the preface to his edition in 1917, Prince Damrong explained that the editorial committee "has the aim of preserving poetic works that are good examples of Thai language, rather than trying to preserve the story of *Khun Chang Khun Phaen*."[39] In keeping with this aim, today's schoolchildren are taught extracts, mostly from the Second Reign revision, as examples of fine poetry and moral values. University literature courses also concentrate on the versification. In academic studies and university theses on the poem, only that of Cholthira examines the plot while others focus on characterization, social background, and ethical values.[40]

Today, Kukrit Pramoj's summary and exposition of the tale, originally serialized in his newspaper *Siam Rath* in 1988, and still in print as a book, is probably read by more people than the original text, not least because it is a highly readable work by an accomplished writer.[41] Kukrit sums up the meaning of the work as follows.

39.   Baker and Pasuk, *The Tale of Khun Chang Khun Phaen*, 1362; translated from Prince Damrong Rajanubhab, "Tamnan sepha" [History of *sepha*], preface to *Khun Chang Khun Phaen* (Bangkok: Khurusapha, 2003 [1917]), 28.

40.   On characterization, two examples are: Saowalak Anantasan, *Wannakam ek khong thai (khun chang khun phaen)* [Major Thai literature: *Khun Chang Khun Phaen*] (Bangkok: Ramkhamhaeng University, 1980), and Suvanna Kriengkraipetch, "Characters in Thai Literary Works: 'Us' and 'the Others,'" in *Thai Literary Traditions*, ed. Manas Chitakasem (Bangkok: Chulalongkorn University Press, 1995). Studies of social background include Arada Kiranant, "Kan chai saiyasat nai sepha rueang khun chang khun phaen" [Use of supernaturalism in *Khun Chang Khun Phaen*], *Warasan phasa wannakhadi thai* 2, 2 (1985); and Woranan Aksonphong, "Kan sueksa sangkhom lae watthanatham thai nai samai rattanakosin ton ton chak rueang khun chang khun phaen" [Study of society and culture of early Bangkok from *Khun Chang Khun Phaen*] (MA thesis, Chulalongkorn University, 1972). Studies of ethical values include Phramaha Suradech Surasakko (Intarasak), "Itthiphon khong phra phuttha sasana to wannakhadi Thai: Sueksa chapho korani sepha rueang khun chang khun phaen" [Influence of Buddhism on Thai literature: A case study of *Khun Chang Khun Phaen*] (MA thesis, Mahachulalongkorn University, 1965).

41.   Kukrit Pramoj, *Khun chang khun phaen: Chabap an mai* [*Khun Chang Khun Phaen*, a new reading] (Bangkok: Dokya, 2000 [1989]).

The loyalty of the characters in *Khun Chang Khun Phaen* can be used as a model for officials and people in general. It is an ultimate form of loyalty without question. Even severe royal punishment does not make the loyalty of any of the characters diminish. They continue to remain loyal. Moreover, several of the characters have command of lore and supernatural powers, including keeping protective spirits. But when they must face royal punishment, their skills—whether from mantra or various amulets or spirits— totally lose their force, and provide no protection against the royal will.[42]

Kukrit instructs readers to find a lesson in *Khun Chang Khun Phaen* that is starkly different from our discussion of mastery and authority. As Saichon Satyanurak has recently shown,[43] Kukrit feared that the monarchy had lost much of its formal political power and was intent on remaking Thai kingship as a focus of moral and cultural power. It is fascinating that Kukrit and Prince Damrong, two key figures in shaping the modern Thai monarchy, should also have had key roles in the modern evolution of *Khun Chang Khun Phaen*. As Reynolds concluded on the role of manuals in general,

Manuals in themselves are not orthodox or authoritarian. They are polysemic, amoral, apolitical. If a teacher, or institution, or powerful or socially influential individual insists on using manual knowledge in a particular way, then the knowledge in the manual is bent for certain purposes.[44]

---

42. Kukrit, *Khun chang khun phaen*, 21.

43. Saichon Satyanurak, *Kukrit kap praditkam "khwampenthai"* [Kukrit and the crafting of "Thai-ness"], 2 vols. (Bangkok: Sinlapa Watthanatham, 2007).

44. Reynolds, "Thai Manual Knowledge," 241.

CONTRIBUTORS

M.L. Boonlua Debyasuvarn (1911–82) was the thirty-second child of a senior noble from a core royal lineage (Kunchon). After both her parents died, she was sent to Catholic convents, first in Bangkok and then Penang. After the 1932 revolution, she joined the first class of Chulalongkorn University to admit women. On graduating, she entered public service and became a teacher of literature and a university administrator. In 1948, she received a scholarship to study for an MA at the University of Minnesota. At the age of 49, she married a man she met through the university alumni. In 1970, she retired early. In the next five years, she wrote five novels and several essays on literature. Among the novels, *Thutiyawiset* is a thinly disguised portrayal of Field Marshal Phibun Songkhram and his wife, while *Suratnari* is a fantasy set in a Southeast Asian country run by women.

Cholthira Satyawadhna took a BA and MA from the Faculty of Arts, Chulalongkorn University, and played a prominent role in the debates on literature and politics in the 1973–76 era. After the Thammasat massacre in 1976, she took refuge with the CPT insurgents in Nan Province. In 1980, she went to the Australian National University in Canberra where she completed a PhD in anthropology on the Lua of Nan under the supervision of Gehan Wijeyewardene. On return to Thailand she pursued a career as a university teacher, writer on ethnology, history, and literature, and activist, especially on issues of human and local rights. She has been a fellow at the Radcliffe Institute for Advanced Study at Harvard University and was awarded a special professorship at Université du Littorale, Academie de Lille, France. In 2009–12 she was dean of the School of Liberal Arts at Walailak University, Nakhon Si Thammarat.

Warunee Osatharom was born and schooled in Suphanburi, the cradle of the *Khun Chang Khun Phaen* tale. She took a BA and MA in history from the Faculty of Arts, Chulalongkorn University, and worked at the National Archives before joining the Institute of Thai Studies (Thai Khadi Sueksa) in Thammasat University, where she remained until her retirement in 2013. She concentrated initially on the history of education in Thailand, before compiling a history of Suphanburi (1989) and subsequently writing widely on issues concerning community, local history, culture, women, and tourism.

David Atherton is Assistant Professor of Japanese Literature at the University of Colorado Boulder. He has a BA in Chinese literature from Harvard University, an MA in classical Thai literature from the University of Wisconsin-Madison, and a PhD from Columbia University. The title of his dissertation is "Valences of Vengeance: The Moral Imagination of Early Modern Japanese Vendetta Fiction." Although now teaching mainly on Japanese literature and publishing principally on the popular literature of early modern Japan (seventeenth through nineteenth centuries), he retains an active interest in the study of premodern Thai and other Southeast Asian literature and culture.

Chris Baker has a PhD in Indian history from Cambridge University, where he taught Asian history and politics before moving to Thailand in 1980. After a career in business, he has worked independently as a historian, commentator, and translator, mostly in partnership with Pasuk Phongpaichit. He is currently honorary editor of the *Journal of the Siam Society.*

Pasuk Phongpaichit is a professor at the Faculty of Economics, Chulalongkorn University. She has a BA and MA from Monash University, Australia, and a PhD from the University of Cambridge. She has worked as an expert with the International Labour Organisation, as a research fellow at the Institute of Southeast Asian Studies in Singapore, and as a visiting professor at Johns Hopkins University, University of Kyoto, Griffiths University Brisbane, University of Washington, and the University of Tokyo. She has written widely in both Thai and English on the political economy of Thailand, as well as collaborating with Chris Baker to author books on Thailand's history, literature, and current affairs.